Sleeping
Under The Stars

Erotic Memoirs

of a

Decade in Porn

Written By
Geoffrey Karen Dior
aka Rick Van

Produced in conjunction with Jill Nagle Literary Services

www.jillnagle.com

Bedside Press

Bedside Press

P.O. Box 461481
Los Angeles, CA 90046.

Printed in the United States of America
First Printing 2001

ISBN 0-9706956-0-8

This book is dedicated to the Porn Brat Pack:
Me, Joey Stefano, Chi Chi LaRue,
Sharon Kane, Tony Davis and yes, even Gender.
We thought we were fabulous and invincible.
At least we were half right.

THANKS

There are so many people that I want to thank, first, of course, thank you to all of the sexy porn stars that were kind enough to have sex with me and make this book possible, and to the fans that buy our movies and fulfill our fantasies of making your fantasies come true. Second, I thank Mark Austin. who saved this book three times without even knowing it. You have brought out of me feelings of love and wonder and delight and passion - that I thought I was too jaded to ever feel again. No one in this book compares to you. Also, my parents and my brother Terry. Thanks to David Purcell; if it weren't for you I wouldn't have gotten laid so much! The person who was my girlfriend during most of the writing of this book, Jill Nagle, for making me believe that real people really do write books and telling me that my stories were interesting; Gloria Ball, my high school English teacher—bet you didn't expect me to write this, huh? Randy and Diana Majors, my church youth leaders who kept me from committing suicide or killing my parents during high school; My personal assistants and staff past and present—Patryk Strait, Jo Anne Maite, Eddie Cacho, Sara DeBour, Kirk Cruz, Freddie Durrie, Steve Greenberg, Clint Steinhauser, Kurt Wickboldt, Allan Gassman, Candy Ass and Erica Brotman.

Much thanks also to Mickey Skee for telling me to write, and for telling me my writing was good. Thanks to Doug Oliver and Adam Gay Video Directory; I forgot a few names and had to look them up! Thanks to Chi Chi and Gender for getting me into this whole business. Thanks to Jerry Mayfield, Morgan Sommer and Tim Lutz for helping me with computer crises. Also thanks to Paul Pelletieri for believing in me, and doing so many other things, we'll always miss you. Many thanks to Stuart Altschuler, Louise Hay, Marianne Williamson, Peter and Dana Delong, Nancy Albertson, Bob Mandel, Rhonda LeVand, Leonard Orr, Dr. Haleakala Hew Len and Sondra Ray for all your inspiration and teaching me for so many years.

Also thanks to all the O Boys, Babaji Zeiger, Gloria Heilman, Carla Thorsten, Greg Thomas, Marshall (O Boy), Sabin, Bob East, Odyssey, Video 10, Chuck Holmes, Falcon, Gordon Schroeder, Greg Ryan, Jim Facet, Dain Noel, Michael Eachart, Richard Soria, Michael Alvarado, Robert Sanford, Carol Queen, Annie Sprinkle, Kate Bornstein, Jeff Ebner, Ron Hamill, Kevin Glover, Joe Iannone, Jacob Hale, Freddie Bercovitz, Frank Boyle, Fred Goss, Eric Scott, Don Weeks, Angie Eakins, Kevin McDaniel, John Mastrangelo, Mark Farndale, Dan Angel, Anaru, Tony West

(Silva), Jeff Hanen (my Eskimo), Tom Mainez, Jay Long, David Holt, Bradley Picklesheimer, Michael Christian, Montana, Andy Devine, Timothy Roderick, Peter Dixon, Tracey Koerner, Terry Sue, Tony Sue, Will Mead, Brad Dickey, Corey Nixon, Burt Defonte, Boy Mike, Bill Davidson, Joey Stefano (Nicky), Stacey Q, Nina Hagen, Boy George, Lucy Lawless, Kirstie Alley, Kathy Najimy, and Sharon Kane. You all helped me grow at different times. And of course, all thanks to my guru Babaji. Om Namaha Shivaya!

CONTENTS

FOREWORD

When I discovered Geoffrey Karen Dior in a seedy little West Hollywood bar in 1988, he was a sweet, innocent, young boy from the midwest. I changed all that. I turned him into a porn star, almost instantly. A much bigger star than even I ever expected. But he deserves a lot of the credit. I didn't make him the non-stop sex pig that he is. That seemed to come naturally. I have honestly never seen his huge dick when it wasn't hard, and many times he saved my scenes by being the stunt dick for others who couldn't rise to the occasion.

I've always teased Dior about his many boyfriends and we all joke that to date him is a sure way to become a porn star yourself. He has been linked with most of the biggest names in the industry, but many of the stories in this book were previously unknown, even to me. Geoffrey has always seemed to make the headlines every time he gets a hard-on, but he obviously has been much busier than any of us realized. None of the bizarre sexual exploits really come as a surprise to me or probably anyone who knows him. He's always been right in the middle of it all, always taking someone home with him from every awards show, porn industry party, and from reading this book, probably even from every trip to the grocery store.

With all of his accolades, performances, records, degrees, his amazing crossover into television, film and commercial roles, and countless awards within the porn industry, one thing stands out beyond all of it. We all love him. He is the beloved darling of the porn industry, and no matter how big of a star he becomes in other areas he has never turned his back on the industry who gave him his start or his friends that have been there throughout the whole wild ride. How many other ministers with a Ph.D. will stand with their heads held high and gleefully tell you about how they got gang fucked the night before? Or discuss being a porn star on *Entertainment Tonight*?

Geoffrey brings an enormous level of class and elegance to this industry and to everything he touches. As I said a few years ago when we gave him a celebrity roast, he doesn't have a mean bone in his body. That's a rare thing here in Hollywood, where most people smile at you while stabbing you in the back.

No one knows where he will go from here, but you can count on two things: He'll do whatever it is in a way that no one ever has before, and you will read about it in magazines, newspapers, and books for years to come.

Chi Chi LaRue

INTRODUCTION

This book is mostly about porn stars that I have known, dated and/or had sex with on or off screen, although I have included some stories about people I was not sexually involved with. While the press has covered some of my relationships with mainstream celebrities, this book is not about them. I have saved those for my next book, which is tentatively titled *From Porn to Prime Time*.

First, a few explanatory notes. My name is now Geoffrey Karen Dior, or just Geoffrey Dior. I don't know the name I was born with, as I was adopted. My adoptive parents named me Jeffrey Gene Gann, which I changed to Geoff Gann while in college. When I started doing drag, I picked the name Anaïs, but soon changed to Karen Dior. This was also the name I used in porn videos I did in drag. In movies in which I appeared as a guy (out of drag) I first used the name Ricky Van, which soon became Rick Van. A few years ago, I combined my names into Geoffrey Karen Dior to help eliminate confusion, among other reasons.

From time to time throughout the book, I note whether or not new acquaintances "know who I am." Among gay men—especially porn fans and industry members—I am famous to some degree. This means that, among other things, many men who recognize me want to have sex with me *only* because of my fame. They are called starfuckers. I don't trust the overtures of fans or people who "know who I am." I have been hurt many times in these scenarios. In general, I feel more comfortable meeting people who do *not* recognize me. I want to know that they are interested in me, not my fame, power or money.

My friends often accuse me of turning people into porn stars: meet me, date me, do a porn film. I don't talk anyone into it, I swear. It just seems to happen. They usually bring it up, and if they are sexy, then why not put them in a porn film? It seems, very often, simply to be fate.

Since many of the stories in this book are about things already recorded on film, I know the subjects won't mind me writing about them. I tried to contact everyone that I wrote about who didn't do a film with me, but if I missed you, oops!

If it seems like I am trying to avoid mentioning a particular name, guess what: I am. I name porn stars, but out of respect for their privacy, I usually don't use without permission non-porn names, or names of those not in the porn industry.

I use both "he" and "she" when referring to Chi Chi LaRue, as well as his real name, Larry. I do this because sometimes I think of him/her as a "she," and sometimes as a "he." This can change, often in seconds, so I try to be true to that feeling in these pages.

These stories are arranged in roughly chronological order, which I often had to make phone calls or pull old files to reconstruct. I make no claims to exact representations of time periods. Also, some people overlapped. My relationships have mostly been open, so while I was seeing or living with someone, I was also fooling around with others on the side.

After my brief biography that covers my life before porn, the book is divided into sections containing chapters about my experiences with individuals. You can read it straight through or use the index in the back to look up your favorite porn stars first.

As I was writing this book, I realized how lucky I have been. I've never really felt the way many people do about work. For over ten years now, I have been paid to have sex with hot guys (and sometimes girls) or to direct them in having sex. Who could complain about that?

When I started writing these memoirs, I had no idea just how many porn stars I have dated or fucked. As I kept writing, the list grew and grew! I guess I've kept busy. People ask me if I am going to leave the porn business now that I have achieved mainstream success on TV, in commercials, in movies, and as a recording artist. I can't predict too far into the future, but as much as I love singing and acting, I also love watching hot guys fuck. I don't see myself completely leaving the porn industry anytime soon.

I also want to say that unless otherwise specified, the sex was safer sex, even if I don't always mention the condoms. Almost every scene I ever did in a video was with condoms. By the time I entered the porn industry, condoms for fucking were becoming standard in gay videos, although of course the straight industry refused to follow our lead until ten years later.

There were a few times that were not safe, and I was tempted to skip those, just as I was tempted to never mention my former drug problem, but I decided long ago that I wanted to tell the truth. I am HIV-positive now because I did drugs and had sex without condoms sometimes, and I don't want this to happen to anyone else. My intention is not to eroticize the drug use or the unsafe sex, but to tell the whole story. Apart from those issues, this book is meant to titillate and entertain you. I hope you enjoy reading it as much as I enjoyed living it!

As I mention elsewhere, I have not included everyone in this book that I might have. Several people not mentioned are female porn stars. I included two of them for various reasons, and excluded others for still other reasons, including the fact that some of them might not want to be associated with a "gay porn star," for justified fear of losing work in the straight industry. It's funny—homophobic straight guys say they want gay men to turn straight, to just try it with a woman—but not one of "theirs!"

A few male porn stars I was involved with were left out for various reasons, as well. One I know people will ask about is my fairly recent partner, Babaji (who shares the same name as my guru). We have broken up but are still friends. I describe our relationship in my next book, which tells a lot more of the story of my life. Though we had fantastic sex, it didn't feel right to put him in this book. The end of that relationship is still too close; the wounds too fresh. Also, I find it hard to limit any discussion of him to just the sex. He has been so much more to me.

I am sure there will be a part two to this book - since just in the time that has passed since i finished writing it, until the time it actually went to press, I have had over a dozen new encounters with some of the newest "stars" in the buisiness, including several in bathrooms at parties following the 2001 GayVN awards show and even a few that happened on a bed in the middle of Chi Chi LaRue's after-show party. The porn industry and the people in it continue to be very kind to me.

Oh, and one more thing: If anyone is jealous of me because of all these guys I've fucked, you should know that any of them who have been in the porn industry as long as I have, could probably write their own book, which would have just as many juicy stories. We are a horny, friendly bunch and we all tend to get around a lot. If you are envious, then just get into shape and come on out to L.A. and start doing videos with us. We'd be glad to have you, both on screen and off!

IN THE BEGINNING

I was born February 14, 1967 in St. Louis, Missouri. My parents adopted me when I was eight days old. I always knew I was adopted, even before I knew where babies came from, so it didn't mean anything good or bad to me—it just was. I grew up in Ozark, Missouri, a little farm town in the region called The Ozarks or The Ozark Mountains, despite that there aren't any real mountains there, just big hills. Until I moved away and came back to visit, I didn't realize just how beautiful that land is. Fields and trees; rivers, lakes and waterfalls; all without smog, traffic jams, or mobs of people. Before I moved to Los Angeles at 21, I had never stood in a grocery store line behind more than two people. The big city was a completely different world.

My adoptive father was a Republican State Representative, and a construction worker. That may sound like an odd combination, but he was (and is) smart and sexy. Big, muscular and tan. For the first several years of my life, he had a crew cut.

Dad was a school teacher for one year before he became a State Representative. He set out to change things, instead of just complaining the way a lot of people do. I always admired that about him. My mother was an elementary school teacher. My parents were Southern Baptist, and very devout. My father was a deacon in the church, and both of my parents were Sunday School teachers.

Growing up, I enjoyed many typical 'boy' things. I loved climbing trees and hiking through the woods. I loved riding my motorcycle, and as soon as I got a car, I drove it much too fast just like all the other boys. I also liked the other boys in a way that (as far as I knew) was different from how the other boys felt. I played doctor with a couple of the little girls in my neighborhood, and also with a couple of the boys. I liked both. A lot.

In junior high, I noticed more acutely that I was interested in the boys as well as the girls, but I had no idea what that meant. I didn't think about it until much later, but it may have begun with admiration of my father, who was and is still to this day very handsome. He was also diabetic. Some of my earliest childhood memories were of eating breakfast in the kitchen every morning and watching my half naked dad, a very beautiful, masculine man, giving himself an insulin injection in his ass. A big ol' homoerotic fantasy right there in my kitchen to start each day. You'll notice that as you read this book, I talk about the guys' asses a lot. It's on my list of my favorite things, even before raindrops on roses and whiskers on kittens. No wonder.

I also remember that when I was younger, my dad would do pushups with me riding on his back. Perhaps a completely straight little boy wouldn't have felt the same way I did, but Wow! I loved it! I still love riding a big, muscular, construction worker. Another one of those favorite things.

During a recent visit home, I looked at old pictures of my parents and I gasped. I had forgotten that they were both absolutely stunning. My mother was unbelievably gorgeous; she looked like a movie star. My father was beautiful, boyish and manly at the same time with full lips that I had never noticed before.

Sometime during elementary school I accidentally discovered jacking off when I was washing my dick in the bathtub. I noticed that it felt really good when I rubbed it, so I just kept washing it and washing it. I eventually discovered that it felt even better if I stuck my finger up my ass while I was jacking off. I didn't have any dildos or even know what they were, but I reasoned that if my finger felt good then other things would feel good shoved up my ass too. I used hairbrush handles, mousse bottles, and anything else I could find that would fit. I was surprised at the size of some of the things that would fit. I'm sometimes still surprised at the size of some of the things that I manage to fit up my ass. I guess that practice early on has paid off.

When I was in junior high, my best friend Kevin and I ended up playing strip poker. We were both really nervous and excited. When at last we found ourselves naked with our dicks rock hard, we decided that the person who lost the next hand had to suck the other one's dick.

I lost on purpose.

That moment when I wrapped my lips around a cock for the first time was probably the most exciting of my entire life. Suddenly, my boring life was worth living! My mind was exploding and so was my body—I felt electricity running through every part of me. We played a few more hands, managing to take turns losing. I didn't know which was more exciting: Having another guy's dick in my mouth or having another guy's mouth on my dick. Actually, to this day I still can't decide.

We ended up playing our game a few more times, at his house in his bedroom, and at my house in mine, late at night with my parents asleep in the other room. Once we "camped out," that is, slept outside in the shed with the boat, lawn mower, tools, and all my dad's other butch stuff. This time when Kevin was sucking my dick I started to come. It was amazing. I shot all over the place, and then was very embarrassed. He told me not to be. It turned out that he had done this before.

I didn't have another sexual experience until just after high school. Kevin and I reunited, but this time with another boy, as well. We were all at church camp. During those days I had a girlfriend, but at nights, we three boys who were sharing a room would fool around. We would give each other massages, nude of course, and I would always keep going until I was massaging my friends' assholes, sticking my fingers in, rubbing their hard dicks, until we all came. We never spoke about it until a couple of years ago. We had lost touch when I moved to L.A. Kevin had been following me in the press for years and he wrote to me in care of a magazine that had done an article about me. He is a dancer now and still looks the same (very handsome) except that now he has grown into a man. He has the cutest ass and I desperately wish that I had fucked him back when I had the chance. He is a big fan of porn and is considering doing a video, so soon maybe you too can see the reason I started sucking cock.

In high school I wasn't popular at all. I thought I was ugly and boring. Now I look back at pictures and can see that I was very cute, and remember that I was anything but boring. Interestingly enough, when I went away to summer camps out of town, I always had girlfriends and was very popular. I was actually engaged to my girlfriend during my senior year of high school, but we didn't have sex, because, as she told me, "God didn't want us to, until we were married." I would have anyway if she would have agreed. I would have asked God to forgive me later. I was horny, and for God's sake, I was eighteen! I finally broke up with my girlfriend to date another girl from another school. Thank God I didn't get married then!

When I went away to college, I started dating a girl named Lori, and fucked for the first time in my life. Almost immediately though, my intense religious upbringing kicked in. The guilt from having sex overwhelmed me, and we stopped fucking. Not before we almost had a three-way with my best friend Jerry, though. Looking back, I had wanted him since we met, although I didn't really know it. Somehow we all ended up in his bed watching the movie *Summer Lovers*, about two girls and a guy on vacation in Greece who form a menage à trois relationship. After the video, we all started fooling around a little. I was kissing Lori, and then so was Jerry. Then I reached over and grabbed his dick. It was hard. I was completely turned on yet terrified. Terrified that Lori would call me a fag. Terrified that my friend would call me a fag. Terrified that lightning would strike from the sky. We didn't go much further that day, although I know we all wanted to.

Around this same time, I was fooling around with my other best friend. He was the son of the preacher at my church. His family had sort of adopted me since I was in a new town away from my family for the first time. I even called his mom "Mom." He was a jock, butch and strapping with a beautiful ass and thick thighs. I would massage him by rubbing his shoulders. Then he would take off his pants and underwear and I would rub his legs and slowly work my way up to his ass. Then I would rub his ass forever, slowly getting closer and closer to his asshole. Eventually I would be squirting baby oil directly on his asshole and rubbing his asshole up and down and all around, just barely sneaking my finger the tiniest bit inside, but not too far. His dick would be hard, sticking down between his legs tempting me to suck on it, but I never did more than "accidentally" brush it with my hands. It never went any further than that. I was afraid to do more, although now I realize I probably could have slipped my dick up his ass and he would have loved it. After all, you don't let a guy play with your asshole for hours if you don't like it.

The next semester I transferred to a different school. I was going to go to seminary and become a preacher, but the day before classes were to start I decided to go to a different school to major in music and dance. My parents were not thrilled.

I moved in with three guys who were sharing a two-bedroom apartment in Springfield, Missouri, closer to my parents. I shared a room with Joie. We each had our own beds on either side of the room with about three feet in between them. We talked a lot and became friends and by the third night we ended up having sex. It was only oral sex, but this time it felt different than ever before. We kissed and held each other and sucked each other off. Then we talked and stayed up for hours. Joie informed me that the other two guys, Cliff and Brad, were lovers. And now so were we. It was so exciting. Joie and I never fucked; we only ever had oral sex, but finally I had a lover!

Joie and I (and the other guys) lived together for a year, but again, my religious indoctrination created so much guilt that I stopped having sex with Joie after a couple of months. We were still boyfriends, we just didn't have sex. After a year I couldn't take the guilt anymore. I had to get out. I moved out while Joie was away visiting his parents for Christmas. It was perhaps the worst thing I've ever done to someone. I didn't mean to hurt him, but I did, deeply. For at least a year he left notes on my car, saying that he still loved me. It was horrible. I wish I could find him today and tell him how much I loved him. At that time I didn't know how to deal with my feelings and I didn't know how to say so.

Right around the time I moved out, I had two friends who were girls. Even though I was having my guilt issues, I thought that I was gay and as far as they knew, I was. One night I was over at their house. Dana was in the living room with her boyfriend making out. Cindy and I were in the bedroom making fun of them. We were making loud moaning sounds and pretending to have sex. The next thing I knew we actually *were* having sex. When it was over Cindy looked at me in amazement and said, "I thought you were gay." "I thought I was too," I said. I felt a wild mix of emotions. I had really thought I was gay but I really liked what I had just done. I was confused. We started dating (and fucking), but eventually broke up because I was still interested in guys too, and she couldn't handle it.

One night while we were still together, I was at her house with a new friend, Gary. Gary and I had just met, and I wanted him desperately —so desperately that the sexual tension filled the room. I think everyone was aware of my feelings. Gary and I left to get some ice, and we never returned that night. We went out to my car and started making out. This was the only guy at this point that I had ever kissed other than Joie. The passion I felt was more intense than ever before. This was what I had always wanted, but not allowed myself to acknowledge. I wanted to be held by a man. I wanted to be kissed by a man. I wanted to feel a man's cock up my ass. We were making out furiously and decided to go back to my apartment. We got into bed and he said that he wanted to fuck me. I told him I had never been fucked and I didn't know if I could be. He put on a condom and slowly started pushing his dick into me. It hurt, but at the same time it felt great. Finally it was all the way in. He started fucking me and I started moaning and groaning. Probably closer to screaming, really. I'm sure the neighbors heard me. To this day I'm really loud when I get fucked. I can't seem to help it.

I was dizzy and in heaven. I had never felt anything like it before. Then he wanted me to fuck him. I had never done that with a guy either, but I was game. I put on a condom and my dick went into him much easier than his had gone into me. He had obviously done this before. I started fucking him. It was amazing. I had never felt anything like this before. A guy under me, holding me while I fucked his ass. I loved it, and I'm sure I always will. I wasn't sure which I had liked more, fucking, or getting fucked, but I knew I loved having sex with a man.

That was it. I started fooling around with guys more, and taking fewer classes at college. I had to leave some time for sex! There were a few girls along the way, but I was mostly with guys. It just seemed to happen that way. Guys were much more available.

There was one girl, Connie, who moved in with me for a while. She was punk and had wildly colored hair and a pierced nose. We had sex a couple of times, but she thought I was gay and wasn't really interested. I actually was in love with her, but thought she wasn't interested in me. We eventually parted ways. Connie moved away and I missed her a lot.

Just after Connie, I met Angie, who became my best friend. Within a week she had moved in with me and we went everywhere together. We would dress all in black and wear pale, pasty white makeup with black eyeliner and paint our lips black (it *was* the 80's) and go out to the clubs. We almost got arrested once for drinking wine on top of a mausoleum in a cemetery in the middle of the night. We were a little out of control, but probably not any more than most college students.

In 1989, an ex-boyfriend of mine named Jamie moved to L.A. Angie and I decided that for Spring break, we would go to L.A. for a vacation and stay with Jamie. The moment I stepped off the plane I knew this was where I wanted to be. The weather was great and there were men everywhere. Gay men, men who wanted me.

Every time I went out to a bar, I went home with someone, or fucked them in the parking lot or bathroom, or elsewhere. Once I met a guy at a club called Studio One, and we walked around the corner to a restaurant. He got under the table and gave me a blowjob. I loved this town! Angie told me later that everyone in the restaurant knew what was going on because there was a mirror on the wall and everyone could see the guy under the table in the mirror. Oops!

Angie and I decided to move to L.A. as soon as the semester was over. She changed her mind later, but I finished the semester, finished cosmetology school (which I was attending at the same time), packed up my car and drove out to L.A. While on vacation in L.A. that fall, I had also met Marshall, who would later become Marshall O Boy. He was one of the guys I had gone home with. I called Marshall and told him I was coming. He had invited me to stay with him until I found a place of my own. After a couple of weeks, I did.

I was pretty lonely the first year I was here. I didn't know anyone and I wasn't very good yet at meeting people—except for sex, thank God for sex!

I worked for about six months doing celebrities' hair in a salon in Beverly Hills. Soon that career changed and I had a new one, one that I never would have dreamed of. I went to a party with a friend of mine for a drag queen, named Chi Chi LaRue. Chi Chi asked me to do a video, and before you could say "Beverly Hillbilly," I was the newest porn star in town. Instantly, I was hanging out with the porn crowd: Joey Stefano, Chi Chi LaRue, Sharon Kane, and Tony Davis, as well as people like Boy George, Grace Jones, Jeffrey Sanker and Jimmy James. We were the "gay A-List" that everyone wanted at their parties. I was recognized around town and treated like royalty. It got really wild, really fast.

Soon after I started doing videos, I started getting other modeling jobs, both print and runway. I also got a couple of good television roles, *The Commish* and the TV movie *The Price She Paid,* with Loni Anderson, although my mainstream acting career didn't take off really until a few years later.

Three or four years after I started appearing in videos, I began directing them. At the AVN ceremonies (the Oscars of porn), I've won awards every year since I started directing. In 1995, they inducted me into their Hall of Fame, and I'm now the most nominated actor/director/producer in AVN history, in categories from Performer of the Year, to Best Director, to dubious honors like Best Groaner.

I had been a singer all my life, and was even an opera singer for a while in college. In L.A. I started singing again, first with my band The Johnny Depp Clones, in clubs and with our single, *All American Boy,* and later our album, *Better Late Than Never.* I sang for a while with my ex-girlfriend Sharon Kane, then I started doing concerts with both the "Mother of Punk," Nina Hagen and *Two of Hearts* diva, Stacey Q. Stacey sings with me on my song *Little Red Riding Hood,* on the *Porn to Rock* compilation C.D., and on a couple of other songs on my new album *S E X.* Sharon and Prince protégé, Elisa Fiorillo, also sing backup vocals on that album.

In the past few years, I have been writing a lot for various magazines, as well as scripts, songs and now, books. I did many other things along the way, studied many spiritual paths, went to India to my guru's ashram, studied with the Kahunas in Hawai'i, finished my Ph.D., became an ordained minister, traveled all over the world, and all sorts of other things. I will go into the details of all of this in another book; this book is about porn stars and sex.

As I began to write this book, I realized there were more guys that I had been involved with than I thought. *A lot more.* As I wrote and I remembered certain times and people, I had to stop typing to jack off a lot. There are some I haven't included in this book on purpose, and I know there are some I just can't remember. I was in over 100 videos in the past ten years and I don't remember every one of the videos or everyone I fucked. And of course, I'm still going, so maybe there will be a part two someday. I'm definitely doing my best to gather material!

The Pre-Porn Days

Most of these
encounters
happened before
or right around
the time I started
appearing in
videos.
I seemed
destined to end
up in the porn
industry by
association.

JEFF STRYKER

Jeff was in the first porn video I ever saw. I think it was 1986. I certainly never imagined then that one day almost ten years later Jeff and I and one other person (Ryan Idol), would be the only three gay porn stars, in the Adult Video Hall of Fame. (Now there are a few more, but for a while it was just us three, along with many stars of straight porn)

I was attending college in Missouri, and a friend showed me the video. I was fascinated. I didn't particularly think that he was my favorite in the video (I preferred Michael Gere and Tony Bravo). Jeff seemed to have a bit of a cranky attitude. (Later when I actually met him and saw how incredibly short he was, I understood how that might have contributed to that chip on his broad shoulder.) Anyway, I was fascinated by porn. I had grown up in a very conservative Southern Baptist home where I wasn't allowed to watch *Mork and Mindy* because a man and a woman were living together who weren't married. Porn was the most forbidden of the forbidden, and it was delicious. I kept expecting lightning to strike me from the sky every time I watched the tape, and God, did I scramble to pull up my pants and turn the TV to *The Brady Bunch* that one time when my roommate came home and almost caught me!

A couple of months after I saw those first two videos, I was on a weekend vacation from college to Kansas City. Jeff happened to be at the club that I visited. He was there to make a personal appearance and to sign autographs. I didn't get an autograph, but I did meet him. He seemed pleasant enough, but he looked like he wished he could just go home and go to bed. He was talking over the microphone to the crowd—leering and saying things like "I want you all to suck my big, hard cock!" I could tell he just wanted to take his poor cock back to his hotel room and let it rest for a while. He still looked cute though, with his baby face, man's body, and a big bulge in his painted-on jeans. His dark brooding eyes looked much nicer in person than on video. I had to admit that he had more sex appeal than I had noticed before. I was fascinated with the way he was just standing on the stage throwing out those random dirty lines like he was quoting Shakespeare. All the guys in the bar had their eyes riveted right on him. Was this not incredibly silly to anyone other than me?

Years later when I saw Jeff again, he was in a fight. It was in the lobby of a hotel in Vegas during one of the awards shows. He and some guy from the straight side of the industry apparently had a little too much testosterone and alcohol that day and got into a fight about something that no one could recall when it was all over. They were punching and kicking and knocking people over. Very glamorous and impressive. It, of course, endeared the entire porn industry to that hotel, as well.

Eventually though, Jeff and I did end up hanging out a couple of times backstage at the awards shows. He was friends with a lot of my friends: Gino Colbert, Mickey Skee, and Jordan Sable. Jeff would always close the door to his dressing room so that no one could tell he was smoking pot—as if no one could smell it.

Once, he was getting ready to go out on stage with his dick showing (there was always a rule at every porn awards show: no complete nudity, no dicks, but Jeff broke the rule every year by walking out on the stage with a hard-on). He asked me to help him to get hard. Now, he may not be my very favorite, but I'm not stupid, and certainly not *that* picky.

Let's just say that that year I was partially responsible for the rule being broken. Even though his dick looks much bigger because he is so short, it still is pretty big. Especially when it gets hard. Although we've met many times, I doubt if Jeff even knows my name. He seems to live in his own world.

TONY BRAVO

Tony was also in the first porn video I ever saw: *Powertool*. I jacked off over and over thinking about him. His scene was with Jeff Stryker, but I wasn't interested in Jeff really, just Tony. I didn't think I could possibly want him more until I saw him in *The Other Side of Aspen*. His little tattoo was so cute, and I wanted to fuck him so badly, I could practically taste him.

When I met him in St. Louis, I was taken aback. First, because I was meeting him, my (wet) dream man. Second, because he was so short. I realized that was probably why they paired him with the diminutive Jeff Stryker. I was even more excited to learn this, because I love guys that are shorter than me (I'm 6 feet). Actually, I love most guys and a lot of girls but that is beside the point: being short is one of the things that really does it for me. He told me that he liked guys that were taller than him.

I was excited but I could barely speak. My fantasy was not only talking to me but...coming on to me? I wasn't sure. I met him before I moved to Los Angeles. I was pretty shy back then, and the only other porn star I had met was, strangely enough, Jeff Stryker. I didn't realize at the time how odd it was that the first two porn stars I ever met were the first two I ever saw on video.

"Can we go somewhere?" Tony asked.

Now I was sure he was coming on to me. I wasn't *that* naïve. Close, though.

We went back to the hotel where I was staying in the gay area of Saint Louis. We started kissing before I could get the front door closed. He turned around as he took off his jeans and slowly lowered them over his buns. I pulled him into my room and closed the door before anyone could see the half-naked man in my doorway. He knew I was crazed watching him and he liked it. He pulled down his jeans and stepped out of them. He slowly rubbed his ass cheeks then bent over a little and pulled them apart.

"Is this what you want?" he asked.

"For the past two years," I thought.

"Yes," was all I could manage to get past my dry lips.

I moved up to him and slowly slid my cock into his ass, taking a full minute to get all the way in. He let out the most amazing low moan of pleasure the whole time it slid in. I started fucking him

17

slowly, in and out, taking forever with each stroke. He continued making these sounds, which drove me crazy. Soon he started thrusting back on my cock and telling me to fuck him harder. He pulled off me and lay down on the floor, sticking his ass up in the air.

"Now pound me," he said.

I did. I shoved my dick back in his gorgeous ass and pounded it like a jackhammer. It was fantastic, I was so hot I was dripping sweat down onto him and he was screaming so loud I was sure the neighbors could hear. Finally he came, but he begged me to keep fucking him. I did for about ten more minutes, until I couldn't hold back any more; then I came. He lay under me for a minute without moving, then he turned over and we kissed. A long, deep, wet, passionate kiss.

Suddenly I realized that I hadn't had his beautiful thick cock in my mouth yet. I moved down to it and started sucking it; running my tongue all around his foreskin and then taking his dick all the way down my throat. Before long he gave me a load of cum down my throat too. He moved his lips down to mine, kissing me and tasting his own cum. Almost before I could say good-bye he was gone and I was alone in my hotel room, the door standing open once again. I never saw him again. Except in my fantasies.

I was devastated a few years later when Chi Chi LaRue told me he had died. I never get used to people dying; it just doesn't seem right or natural. It keeps happening, though.

MARSHALL O BOY

Marshall was the first person I met when I came to L.A. in April of 1988. My best friend Angie and I were on vacation for Spring break from college in Missouri. We were staying with my ex-boyfriend Jamie from Missouri who had moved to L.A. Marshall wasn't in the porn industry, then and of course, neither was I. In fact, he was just ending his career doing sound and singing with musical acts such as David Bowie and Led Zeppelin. He still manages bands sometimes, though, and has recently revived his singing career with a new album, *Little Men, Big Ideas* and new band *The Well Hungarians.* He also has a song on the *Porn To Rock* CD, as do I.

I met Marshall in a bar that was at the time called Cheers. He came up and started talking to me and I was tingling all over. I was very turned on. He was sexy and sweet and sincere and nasty and slutty, all at the same time. At this point in my life, I could still count the people I had slept with on one (okay: two) hands. I'm sure I seemed quite naïve. I went home with him that night and we had wonderful, fabulous sex. I have often said that Marshall has the perfect dick to get fucked by. It is big but not *too* big and has a huge mushroom head that slides up and down inside you like the perfect toy. I've never felt anything quite like it. It really is a great cock. He fucked me into ecstasy that night. You must try it some time. He's not stingy with it.

I liked Marshall a lot. The next day, he drove me over Laurel Canyon at rush hour (my first experience with the horrors of L.A. traffic!) back to my friend's house where I was staying. During the ride, I told him that I was seriously considering moving to L.A.

He instantly offered to let me stay with him for as long as I needed. Over the next few months we sent letters and cards back and forth.

I had actually made the decision to move practically as soon as I had stepped off the plane in L.A. Not too long after arriving back in Missouri, I packed up my stuff and drove out to L.A. Well, actually I packed my car full of my stuff and still had lots more left over, so I took half of it to my parents' house, repacked the car, and started the next morning.

When I finally got to L.A., I was a little freaked out. I really *was* fresh off the 'turnip truck'—21 years old in the big city. The tiny studio apartment Marshall had at the time was barely big enough for him, let alone me and all my clothes and other possessions I had packed into my compact car with me. Somehow the romance just wasn't working either. The sex was great, but we were very different people, and I was very nervous about having moved so far from where I had lived my whole life. Marshall was completely understanding, and remained there for me, letting me stay with him as long as I needed, even though we stopped having sex.

Throughout my time in L.A. (most of my adult life, really,) Marshall has remained my most consistent friend. He has always been right there if I asked for anything. Although we are very different, we care about each other a lot. Marshall is the kind of guy that would do just about anything to help anyone. A few years later, the O Boys, a sex party group, began exactly where we had met. The bar now had a different name and it was having an underwear night. Everybody was walking around in their underwear, totally horny, but not doing anything about it. Marshall and I invited a bunch of guys back to his house, and the O Boys were born.

Over the years, there would be small parties and huge ones. I even made two porn documentaries about them that won lots of awards: *The Orgy Boys Parts I* and *II*, and a couple of years later, *O Is For Orgy.* Of course, as it happened with nearly all of my other friends who had a sex drive, Marshall eventually ended up in my videos. He is always very popular with his co-stars.

One year for his birthday, a bunch of us blindfolded him, kidnapped him and "forced" him to suck each of our dicks. The game was for him to figure out who he was really sucking. We do know how to throw a party! I mean what do you really want in your mouth on your birthday, brie and crackers or 10 big dicks? I know my choice. Marshall liked our style, too. The funny thing was the

20

only one he guessed right was me. I didn't know how, but nearly everybody else did (because they had all had sex with me before!) It seems that I have an unusual ridge of tiny bumps around the head of my dick that you don't really see when looking at it, but you can feel when it's in your mouth (remember this the next time you are in a 'tea room'). Anyway, of course the party progressed to an all-out orgy after that.

Marshall has had a boyfriend for several years now, and they have an open relationship. Marshall dates and fucks other guys (and an occasional girl), and so does his boyfriend. We recently decided that it has been far too long since we have had sex, so we are planning it again soon. You gotta always have something to look forward to, that's the key to life!

JOHN HOLMES

John Holmes was another guy that, believe it or not, I didn't recognize when I met him. It was long before I had started doing videos, and I had only seen two or three porn videos in my life. Even if I had seen him in videos, I probably wouldn't have recognized him; somehow in videos he always looks goofy, but in person he was actually pretty cute and sexy.

Then again, I might have known on a subconscious level, since his face and name were quite public. He was in films, not videos, mostly, and when I was growing up they advertised the films with all the other movies in the newspaper. I surely must have seen his picture somewhere growing up, since a couple of years after my encounter with him I realized who he was. Still, I hadn't seen him in a movie, I just saw his picture on a poster outside a porn theater, recognized him as "that guy I sucked off one night," and was told, "that's John Holmes!" by my then-girlfriend, Sharon Kane. She had done a movie with him years ago—he was yet another guy we had in common. There were quite a few!

Looking back on it all now, it ran like a scene out of *Boogie Nights*. I think he was probably high on something, but in 1988 I was pretty innocent in that area and didn't recognize the signs. It's sort of funny, because usually my experience of the porn industry has not been at all like *Boogie Nights*. People aren't doing drugs or drinking shots of scotch on the sets or fucking in the other room while filming is going on (well, sometimes!). More often, it goes something like this: While we are getting set up, Drew Andrews leads us all in singing *The Brady Bunch* theme song or Petula Clark's *Downtown*. We have apples, veggie burgers, and green salad for lunch and the strongest drugs are the cigarettes that only a few go outside to smoke, because most of us quit a long time ago. In the other room, someone is studying for their college final or doing a crossword puzzle. Maybe Sweet Williams is reading the Hindu scriptures, *The Upanishads.*

I met John in an alley after the bars had closed and I was walking to my car. He asked if I wanted to see the biggest dick in the world, and I said, "Sure!" (What am I, stupid?) I didn't expect it to be all that big, but he was a skinny, geeky-looking guy, and they do always seem to have the biggest dicks, so I thought, "What the hell, let's see."

We got into my car and he took out his dick. It was hard and I had to agree with him that it probably was the biggest dick in the world. I think it really was a foot long, and thick too. Suddenly I felt hot and tingly and my breathing got very shallow. I was never a size queen, I don't think, but I had never seen anything like that dick before. It was almost magical.

His cock pulsated, alive and almost breathing, waiting for my lips to wrap around it. He wanted me to suck it and I tried, but I could barely get my mouth around it, let alone go all the way down to the base. I started jacking off while I licked all the way up and down his huge dick, and all around his balls. Eventually, I managed to get more of his dick into my mouth. I started bobbing my head up and down, and swirling my tongue around the head each time when I came up. I was working hard, I realized, but that cock seemed to deserve the hard work that I found myself unable to stop doing. I was possessed with a need to satisfy this monster cock that seemed to have a personality and spirit separate from the guy it was attached to. I guess whatever I was doing was good enough, because pretty soon he started to come. He shot all the way onto the windshield.

As soon as he came, he immediately acted guilty and mumbled something about having to go make some money. He jumped out of the car and was gone, with me still holding my dick in my hands. Suddenly, the interaction felt a little creepy, and I didn't finish jacking off. I just left. I felt somehow dirty, something that I never felt after sex. His energy post-cum creeped me out. I drove home and got in bed, still feeling unsettled.

It wasn't until later, when I was *in* the porn industry, that I realized who he was, and even years later when I saw the documentary about John called *Wadd*, that I understood what was probably going on with him. I think he had issues with his feelings for men,

23

and couldn't deal with them unless he was high. I don't necessarily think he was gay, probably just very sexual, like most of us in the porn industry. There are a lot of guys on the straight side that occasionally place a toe (or something else) across that line for a minute, then pull it back feeling guilty, looking around desperately to see if anyone was watching. You would think that the porn industry would be the one group that would say, "Hey, fuck whomever you want, we don't care!" but they aren't, necessarily. It's too bad.

KRIS LORD

My one encounter with Kris was very brief. I don't know if it was before or after he did his few videos that made him so famous, like Falcon's *Shadows in the Night*. Maybe it was even during one of them, since I met him in San Francisco, where they were probably filmed, and I don't think he lived there. I may never know.

When I saw that particular Falcon video, I was amused because we met in a way similar to a scene in the video, except that it was in broad daylight instead of the shadows of night. I was just walking down the street in San Francisco and passed him. I turned around to look and so did he. I walked back to him. We started talking and quickly decided that we needed to fuck. Neither of us had a place nearby, and we both were feeling adventurous, so we went back into an alley behind a huge dumpster. When he pulled out his cock, I truly couldn't believe it. It had looked big in his pants, but when it was hard it was honestly bigger around than a beer can. Take a look at a beer can. Now try to shove it up your ass. (If you can, call me—definitely call me!).

Anyway, I went down on my knees on the asphalt and started sucking the monster, licking all around it, and down to his balls. They had a slightly funky smell which normally would have turned me off, but with the sleaziness of the whole encounter, it seemed to work for me. The smell of the trash and the oil on the street and now on the knees of my jeans completed the sleazy picture, all of which was perfectly lit by the sun beating down directly overhead.

It is almost always cold in San Francisco, but that day it was hot. Kris pushed my head back farther and I licked the sweat from his ass hole as it ran down the crack of his muscular butt. He pushed out and let me work my tongue farther up his hole, cleaning it out for him. It tasted salty and delicious. He kept pushing down on me to get more of my tongue up his hole, until I was pushed against the street with him sitting on my face. Only in San Francisco do you get guys to sit on your face in the middle of the street in the middle of the day.

Pretty soon Kris pulled me up, spun me around, leaned me over a trash can, spit on his dick and shoved it in me. No warning, no warming me up, just using my hole for his pleasure. I screamed, but he put his hand over my mouth. It was killing me, yet at the same time the whole situation was turning me on so much I loved it. One tear fell from my eye as I reached back between my legs to start jacking off my dick, which was rock hard and banging up against the trash can. My pants were twisted around my ankles and Kris had one of my arms pulled behind my back. I was totally at his mercy.

More often, I am a top, but I was really getting off on being a slut bottom for him in an alley, knowing that we might be caught at any minute. He kept fucking me, pulling his cock all the way out then slamming it back in. Just as my ass was getting used to it, he would change the angle slightly, making it hurt like hell again and making me continue to work hard to take his cock.

When I had reached a thoroughly altered state, he came all over my ass. I felt his cum running down my legs, and suddenly I felt something shoved back up my ass. I realized it was a beer bottle from the trash, and I shot all over my jeans (which I then had to walk home in). He left without saying much more, he just sort of slapped my butt and walked away. I pulled out the beer bottle, pulled up my jeans and tried to get home as discreetly as possible with cum and oil all over my pants.

It wasn't until a while later that I saw him in videos. That dick and the way he uses it is unmistakable. So are his eyes and his thick dark hair. He has by now vanished from porn and no one seems to know where he is. Everyone help us keep an eye out for him in the alleys, okay?

DICK MASTERS

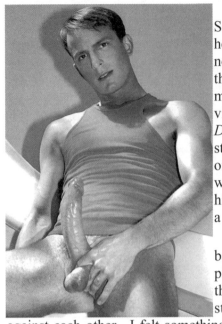

When I met Dick in a bar in San Francisco, I didn't know who he was, in fact, I'm not sure even now if he had done any videos by that time, since it wasn't until much later that I recognized him in videos such as *Manrammer*, and *Deep In Hot Water* . He was standing by himself in the corner of a little bar on Castro street. I went over and started talking to him. He was really shy and it took a while before he would say much.

After a while I invited him back to my hotel, a seedy little place just a few blocks away from the Castro. He came in and we started kissing and rubbing up against each other. I felt something that seemed to be a dick in his pants but I thought 'no, it was much too large to possibly be that.' There are, after all, limits to even porn stars' penises.

When he took off his pants, I nearly fainted. I had never seen a dick so big in all my life. I know I've said that before, but this time it really, truly was a monster. He seemed embarrassed by the size of it.

"I can't help it." he said.

"No, you shouldn't help it, it doesn't need any help!" I said, although I knew there was no way I was ever going to be able to get that 'anaconda' up my ass, and I had really wanted him to fuck me, too. I said, "You should be in porn movies." He laughed, and now I'll never know if it was because he already was or just because he had heard that line so often.

He said he wanted to fuck me, and that he would do it slowly. He said he would stop if I wanted. I was *seriously* nervous, but I decided to give it the old college try. Very slowly, inch by inch and with lots of lube, he worked his humongous cock up my ass. Just when I thought I couldn't take anymore, another inch would slide in. He kept asking me if I wanted him to stop. My head was spinning, and it hurt a lot but I still wanted to keep going.

At last, it was all the way in. I felt a feeling of accomplishment, the same sort of feeling I had when I got my Ph.D. Honestly! I was proud of myself. He held it there for a few minutes for me to get used to the feeling of it, and then slowly, very slowly, started to pull it out. When it was almost all the way out, he slowly slid it back in. Now the feeling was starting to change from pain to bliss. He started fucking me, first very slowly, taking forever to slide out of my canal, then just as long to cram that monster back in; then faster and faster, building speed for about ten minutes. Soon to my astonishment I was begging for it harder, and he obliged. I could hardly believe it, not long before I had thought there was no way I could even get that baseball bat up my ass, let alone ever ask for it to be rammed in.

He fucked me on my back first, holding my knees up by my ears, then he turned me over, with his dick still in me. He just spun me around on it, then he fucked me while I screamed into the pillow. By now he was ramming into me like a freight train, and then ripping his cock all the way out of my ass, churning my bowels and nearly turning me inside out. Sometimes he'd hold it just out of reach of my greedy hole and make me beg him to slam it back in. He wouldn't put it in when I just asked him to fuck me; he would make me beg, "Ram it in my ass hard!" Then he would, all the way to the hilt. He used that huge club like a weapon, pummeling my ass, making tears run down my face, and the whole time I was screaming for more.

He finally pulled out and came on my ass, letting his cum run down into my still gaping hole, then he sucked it out and then went down and licked my balls while I jacked off, until I came. I just lay there stunned and quivering, unable to speak for a few minutes. For someone who was usually a top, I had just been turned into quite the piggy bottom. He kissed me and then jumped up and said he had to leave. I only ever saw him again in videos, but he left me with a wonderful memory, burned deep into my body.

MATT RAMSEY

Matt is now Peter North, a straight porn star who sometimes denies his incarnation as Matt Ramsey. I met him many years ago. We quickly went back to my apartment. I told him that I had seen him in the videos. He seemed a little uncomfortable when I said that and told me that he was bisexual, and I told him that I was too. That was about all the talking we did. He immediately pulled off my pants and started sucking my cock. My head was swimming, he was so good at giving head; one of the best in fact. I was just about to come when he said he wanted my cock in his ass. I certainly couldn't say no to that. I would be more than happy to spear his guts with my dick.

He spit on my dick and sat all the way down on it in one move. It was extraordinary. It wasn't the first time I'd fucked someone dry, but it sure was the easiest I'd ever gotten into anyone with nothing but spit for lube. He immediately started sliding all the way up, and then slamming all the way back down on it. He would sometimes come all the way off of it, then shove it back in, his pink pucker almost begging for my dick during the seconds it was out of him.

I thought he was the sexiest thing I had ever seen. His pecs were flexing and his whole body was glistening with sweat as he furrowed his brow and worked on my cock with his tight ass. His hard cheeks were bouncing against my pubes and he was starting to get louder and louder, working himself into a frenzy.

I grabbed his hips and pulled him down onto me even harder, and he ground his ass around on my cock. His hair was hanging down in his eyes in the most sexy way. I'd never seen him with a hair out of place, almost as if when he did those videos, he had stopped every few minutes to do a touch-up with a blow-dryer. It was a mess now, and that made him look even sexier than before.

He seemed to need desperately to be fucked, and I was certainly glad to fill that need, and to fill up his amazing ass. We were like animals now, fucking as though our lives depended on it. I was lying on the floor looking up at his hole and his cock and his gorgeous body, and was in complete awe of him while he rode me like a cowboy on a wild horse.

Matt started to come, but kept bouncing up and down on my cock for several minutes, seeming to enjoy that part even more than before, until I finally came too. He seemed a little nervous and uncomfortable when we were done. He left quickly and without showering. He mumbled goodbye and something else I couldn't understand, and then practically ran out of my apartment.

After that I only saw him once or twice and I'm not sure if he knew I was the same person. Both times we were in situations where I didn't want to 'out' him, so I may never know if he even recognized me.

A Porn Star is Born

I met most of these people during the early days of my porn career, before I started directing. These stories caught me in some pretty naïve moments, but that would soon change...

JOEY STEFANO

I met Joey, (or Nick Iacona, his real name,) on the same fateful day that I met Sharon Kane and Tony Davis. It was in 1989 at the photo shoot for the box cover for my first video ever, *Sharon And Karen*. Tony had brought Nick to meet Chi Chi LaRue (Larry), because Nick wanted to be in videos. He was absolutely gorgeous. When he walked in, the room fell silent. I think on that very day Larry, Sharon, and I all fell in love with Nick. He was very shy, but reeked of sex. I wanted him desperately, and knew that he was the perfect boyfriend for me. He always seemed to have that immediate effect on everyone. Boy, were we all wrong.

Larry had the photographer take some test shots of him. He was sitting in a director's chair and was so comfortable in front of the camera. His brown eyes and brown hair and beautiful lips just made me want to run over and jump into his lap. I stole one of the Polaroids and went home to jack off looking at it. I still have it. He looked perfect in every picture. He always looked great in every picture, even later when he was so high he didn't know where he was.

The next time I saw Nick was on the set of the movie. It was shot at Paul Pelletieri's studio. It was both Nick's and my first video, and we were both nervous and excited. We didn't have any scenes together, but we both had three-way scenes with Sharon Kane: Nick with Andrew Michaels, and me with Tony Davis. Neither of us had been with a woman for quite a few years, though we both got into it immediately and totally. When Sharon started fucking him with a huge strap-on dildo, he ate up every minute and every inch.

After our scenes, we sat on the steps to Paul's bedroom, and Nick told me that this was his dream, what he had wanted to do his whole life. He was like a kid in a candy store. I had never heard of someone who's life's goal was to be a porn star—at the time, it was sort of an experiment for me. He was so cute in his earnestness as he told me about all the stars he had watched on video.

After that video, Nick and I became friends and started hanging out together. Nick moved into an apartment with Tony, who I was dating and who soon persuaded me to move into the same building. Tony and I soon stopped dating but remained friends. Larry, Sharon, Tony, Nick and I became known as the "porn brat pack." We were always going out together and coming back to Nick and Tony's for late night parties, that usually turned to sex. It was a sort of friendly sex, although it was often fueled by drugs and our new "fame." I remember one time on Nick's bed when he was sucking my dick while Sharon instructed Larry (who was in full drag) on how to eat a pussy. Joey and I watched as Sharon gave her 'pussy 101' class.

"Yes, that feels good; okay up a little bit is the clit."

She showed us all her pussy and explained what everything was and what felt good and what didn't. Tony and a couple of other guys that we had brought back from the bar were on the bed too, and they all looked a little shocked. Looking back, it all seems very surreal.

The first time we all went to Las Vegas together for the AVN awards show, we all ended up in a big orgy in Nick's room. Matt Powers was there with a girl on one bed and Sharon and Nick and I and another guy were on the other bed. Nick was fucking Sharon and I started to fuck him. With all of the fooling around that we had done, I still hadn't fucked him until now. It really was amazing.

I love fucking and as probably most gay men know, Nick had one of the most fuckable asses ever. It was absolutely delicious. Big round white orbs with that hot famous puckered hole in between. Now that I think of it, he probably has the most famous asshole in the world. We didn't know it then of course, and that certainly was not what any of us were thinking about. I was just thinking about getting into him, and I shoved my dick in without even spitting on it.

It slid right in all the way to the base. I felt my balls pressing up against the ring of his hole, and it quivered as it clenched my dick. He always was wet inside, ready to be fucked like he was naturally lubed up. He would see a hot guy and say, "My pussy's getting wet." I think it probably really was.

It felt so good, feeling my dick sliding against the walls of his scorching hot hole. He moaned and cried out with each thrust as Sharon kissed his ears and neck, holding him as we shared him. I was pounding into him while he was fucking Sharon, when my dick slipped out of his ass and what seemed like a gallon of water gushed out of him onto Sharon. It seems that it had stayed up inside him when he had douched. Nick was embarrassed and ran to the bathroom to clean up again, but for some reason the situation struck Sharon and I as hysterical, and we couldn't stop laughing until he came back. We still laugh about it, in fact. It was just one of those very real moments that you don't expect. Matt and his girlfriend probably thought we were nuts and they soon left, but the rest of us continued for half the night.

Soon after Las Vegas, Nick asked me to go to Palm Springs with him. I didn't have enough money to go, so Nick said he would pay for everything. He could be very generous; money didn't mean anything to him. He would think nothing of giving you his last dollar, but he would also think nothing of asking for and taking your last dollar if he wanted it. He could be the most giving person in the world and also the most selfish.

Anyway, we agreed to go on vacation together and off we went to Palm Springs. It was raining on the drive down, and all of a sudden a semi truck lost control and started spiraling all over the highway. I slammed on my brakes and we skidded straight towards the truck. Suddenly the car was stopped (facing the wrong way in the freeway). The truck had stopped too. Somehow no one had been hurt. Little did I know then how Nick's life was about to start spiraling out of control just like the semi, only with a different ending.

We arrived in Palm Springs, checked into the hotel, and for the first time made love alone and not on drugs. It was incredibly hot. Nick always had trouble connecting emotionally with people, but during sex all of his inhibitions were gone. We started kissing and tearing each other's clothes off. I ran my hands up and down his body and he grabbed my dick and squeezed it. I licked his neck and it tasted sweet, and a little like smoked wood. He always had the same strange but wonderful taste—it was one of the things I started loving about him.

He took my dick into his mouth, and my eyes rolled back in my head. I reached down and just barely touched his asshole with my finger and he moaned and pushed himself onto it. I went down and started licking his hole, kissing it, licking all around it and then finally shoving my tongue up inside. Same smoky sweet taste. I could have kept my tongue inside him forever. He loved it too, and pushed out so I could get deeper into him. He was writhing and moaning on the bed in a way I had never seen before.

I turned him around and pulled him to the edge of the bed with his ass hanging off the edge. I leaned over him and I slid my dick into him, and fucked him, and held him, and squeezed him, while we kissed for what seemed like forever. It was the most romantic sex I ever had with him or ever saw him have with anyone else, for that matter. I fucked him slowly, pushing in and pulling out with intention, making sure he felt every inch of me every second as intensely as possible. I pushed all the way in and held my dick there without moving, just pressing against that spot deep inside him. He looked up at me and pulled me down to kiss him again.

We were deeply in love, at least for those moments. Everything was perfect and if we could have just kept fucking forever, the world would have been a perfect place for us both. Time seemed to stand still, and today it remains such a crystalline memory for me, like a slow motion scene in a romantic movie.

I started moving in him again, though, this time getting faster and faster. He was gasping and I was whimpering as we fucked and fucked and fucked. He kept staring into my eyes and started crying when he shot onto his stomach. Then he ate all his cum. He always did that on film because he did it in his real life. He loved cum. I shot my load up his ass into a condom. He pulled it off my dick as soon as I pulled out of his ass and he sucked the cum out of it before I could stop him. It wasn't the safest sex, but it was the sexiest thing I ever saw. I kissed him and he shared our cum with me. It was actually one of the few times we used condoms. We tried, but not hard enough, and we were always getting caught up in the moment.

About ten minutes after we finished, we both were horny again. Nick had brought about 100 hits of *ecstasy* with him, and we did a few and went out to the clubs. I don't remember much after that, except that we ended up with about five people in our room, fucking us both, all night. Finally Nick went to sleep first, I guess he was more used to the drugs. The guys and I went into the bathroom to continue so we wouldn't disturb Nick. I leaned over the bathtub as the guys took turns at my ass. I don't know how they kept going after fucking both of us for hours, but they did until the sun came up. They left and I went and got in the bed with Nick.

We slept for about an hour and then got up and went out by the pool. Nick was singing the song "The Candyman" and feeding me a hit of ecstasy every hour. Actually he was feeding them to everyone lying around us as well. People were sort of in awe of us. Our fame had just begun to take off. People recognized my name, but not my face, while they certainly recognized his face (and the rest of him). We were being treated as sexual royalty, something that was new for both of us at the time. Or then again maybe it was just the ecstasy, I'm not really sure now. We kept bringing people back into the room all afternoon, both separately and together. I don't think we got much sun.

That night, we decided not to go out; we couldn't possibly have more fun than we were having at the hotel, not to mention that we couldn't possibly drive. The hotel room had sliding glass doors that opened out to the pool area, so we started fooling around with the curtains open, the lights on and the door halfway open. Guys would watch us from outside, and some would occasionally be brave enough to come into the room and join us. We were up late again that night, but by around 2:00 in the morning we were falling asleep.

I woke up a little later with a dick up my ass. It was Nick. He just smiled and kept fucking me. I couldn't believe it, I had never seen him be a top, but he sure knew what he was doing. Bottoms always make the best tops. He fucked me face down on the bed, then pulled my hips up so he could get deeper into me. I was on my hands and knees getting fucked by him and he was loving it—ramming into me, abusing my hole like I had always abused his. I was in such bliss, knowing that I was pleasing him in the way he had always lived to please me and so many others. We started coming together. I shot all over the bed, and Nick shot up my ass. Then he went down immediately and sucked his cum out of my ass. It was so nasty and hot I actually started cumming again a second time within about a minute. This time he pulled my dick back, between my legs, into his mouth and sucked my cum down his throat as I shot, and shot. It was running out of the sides of his mouth but he licked it all back, into his mouth, not wanting to waste a drop of it. We curled up together and went back to sleep.

We slept very late the next day and Nick woke me up by sucking my dick. I tried to maneuver around to suck his also, but he wouldn't let me, holding me down and keeping me in his mouth, until I shot my load down his throat. Then he came up and kissed me, so I could taste some of it.

The next day when we went to check out of the hotel, the manager thanked us both profusely, and gave us our room for free. He said we were invited back anytime. No wonder, since between the two of us, we had probably fucked everyone in the hotel.

On the way back from Palm Springs, Nick told me he wanted me to move in with him. He was tired of living with Tony (they weren't getting along) and he wanted to live in a house. I told him I would think about it and within two days he had found a house. It was a duplex actually, but it was huge with three bedrooms, three bathrooms, an enormous kitchen, a separate dining room and even a fireplace in the huge living room. The house was a little tacky, but it made up for the lack of charm by being so fucking big. Again, I didn't have enough money for the down payment for first and last month's rent, so Nick made up the difference. It evened out soon enough, though. There were many months that I would pay the rent for

both of us. Nick could have tons of money one day and none the next. I didn't realize just how much money he was spending on drugs and even on hiring prostitutes. Imagine the prostitute that would show up expecting a middle-aged, balding customer and discover that Joey Stefano had hired him.

At first it was great. Sharon Kane rented the other room from us, but never moved in, so after a couple of months we got another roommate. The house became the 'porn hotel' for the next nine months, with a different porn star moving in or out nearly every month. Nick and I got along great in the beginning. We didn't really think of ourselves as lovers, although we had sex a lot and I think that in a bizarre way we were in love with each other.

Soon, however, problems started developing. One of the things that I didn't figure out until years later was that we were actually quite jealous of each other. I was becoming a big drag porn star as Nick was becoming a big gay porn star. The guys that liked me were always big butch straight-identified guys. Exactly the type that Nick loved but I hated. The guys that liked him were gay identified, exactly what I liked but he didn't.

We each wanted to be the other.

He actually tried on my drag a few times, and even once made a cameo appearance as Josephine Stefano in a play we did at a local club. He was a disturbingly ugly woman.

It was also annoying that while I was going to the gym and eating vegetarian food, he ate nothing but peanut butter and jelly on Wonderbread; he did ecstasy and smoked cigarettes constantly. The more he abused his body, the better he seemed to look. It just didn't seem fair.

Things were starting to get a little difficult in other ways. Nick would say he was going out for a walk. He wouldn't return until hours later, and I always wondered where he was walking that took so long. It wasn't until much later that I discovered our street was heavy with guys cruising for sex. Nick was addicted, and just

39

couldn't ever get enough. He was insatiable. It wasn't a problem when he was with me, and it didn't bother me that he was with other guys, but it did bother me that he was lying about it. I get really freaky when people lie to me. He wasn't outright lying, just not telling the whole truth, but it felt the same.

I didn't realize just how bad things were for him until one night when I found him crying on the front porch. He wouldn't talk about what was wrong, he never would, and I couldn't help him. I just sat and held him as he cried and cried. He had such demons inside and I just couldn't help. I was learning how to heal the hurts of my past, my childhood and adolescent agony, and I wanted him to be able to do the same, but it wasn't happening. We were growing further and further apart. One day we got in a fight and he punched a hole through a wall. We both knew it was over then. He moved away to New York before the end of the month.

I didn't see him much more after that. Once when he was in town and owed Sharon a lot of money, she called me and begged me to put him in one of my videos so that he could pay her and she could pay her rent. I was hesitant. While we had never done a scene together, we had been in many of the same videos, and I knew that he could turn from an angel to Linda Blair in seconds on a shoot; I had seen it happen many times. By now, most directors wouldn't work with him, but as a favor to Sharon I hired him. The video was *Bi Golly*, and it was a fiasco.

When he first showed up, he was great; it was like old times. We hugged and kissed and things started to really heat up. Then it shifted abruptly when the guy he was supposed to work with showed up. Suddenly, he was pure evil. It was as if his head spun right around, and out of nowhere, pea green bile came spewing out.

The guy who showed up was really excited about working with the great Joey Stefano, but Nick was rolling his eyes and acting like he didn't want to be there. I don't know if it was because of me, or because he just didn't like the other guy, but it was so uncomfortable that by the time they were ready to fuck, the guy, of course, lost his hard-on. I took Nick aside and said,

"Look, you have to at least pretend to like this guy, or he's not going to be able to get hard. Do you want me to be a stunt dick and fuck you?"

He said, "No way!" and just glared at me.

I knew not to push that, so I suggested a dildo. He didn't

want to do that either, but I told him we would all be there until they fucked, so he finally agreed. I knew he loved dildos, I used to fuck him with huge ones. He even had one shaped like a fist that I would ram in and out of his ass. Just before he moved away, he gave it away by throwing it out to some fans when he was doing a show at a strip club.

He complained with every stroke, and wouldn't let the guy really fuck him with it. The scene looked horrible in the video. It was very un-erotic. Nick was so hateful that the other guy never did another video after that one.

After that, I decided that I couldn't be around him in any capacity. I loved him, but I just couldn't take his mercurial moods, and watch him in his misery. He called a few times, from New York or Miami, or wherever he was at the time. He always sounded like he was about to cry, and I longed to see him, but I knew that we couldn't get back together. It would be disastrous. Occasionally, it would seem like we were connecting again, and once we even had phone sex. He had a guy with him and he told me about everything, as the guy sucked his dick and then fucked him. It was great to hear him moaning and screaming again as he was getting fucked, but after it was over he got all quiet and depressed again and he wouldn't talk.

The next time I saw him was a few years later at Chi Chi LaRue's birthday party. He looked really good, the tiny amount of baby fat was gone from his face and he looked more handsome than ever. His hair was getting long, near his shoulders. He said that he was totally clean, that he had an AA sponsor, even. I even saw someone offer him some drugs and he said, "No." So I believed him. I was very happy for him. We started making out in a room in the back until someone walked in on us. I thought that *maybe, just maybe*, if he was clean and sober now, things might work. Unfortunately, it was not true.

He came over to my apartment a few days later. The person he was staying with brought him. He only stayed for a few minutes, he didn't talk about much, he just sat with me on the couch. When he went to leave he kissed me, long and slow. He said, "I love you, Geoff."

I don't think I had ever heard him say that before. I couldn't remember, but I don't think so. I stood there stunned as he walked out. He seemed so odd, I wanted to run after him, but I was terrified. My life wasn't such a mess anymore, not like it had been when

I was with him, and I couldn't imagine going back. Still my heart sank as he left. It was the last time I ever saw him. Two days later I got a call. He was dead from a drug overdose. He hadn't been clean, he had just switched his substance of choice—to heroin.

Nick was an amazing person: loving, hateful, caring, selfish, giving, childlike, and childish. I will always love him and miss him. I'm sorry he's gone, but I'm glad he isn't suffering anymore. So many people have focused only on the bad times in what they've written about him since his death, but there was substantial good in his life. He was loving and loved many of us: me, Sharon, Chi Chi, and a few other people. Love always makes a life worth living. There were happy times, and he was the happiest when he was having sex. He would have loved knowing that people still watch his videos and jack off and cum with him.

CHI CHI LARUE

You all turned to this chapter first, RIGHT??? As Chi Chi would say, "You are sick bitches!" Chi Chi is actually very handsome out of drag. His real name is Larry, and that's what I usually call him. He's six-three, big and strapping with that gorgeous Roman nose, and lots of charisma.

I first met Larry in 1988 at a bar that was then called the 4-Star. It was a seedy dive drag bar down in the middle of West Hollywood, now called Mickey's. I didn't know then that he directed porn videos. I was invited to his birthday party and he asked me to be in a video. It all started from there.

Being in video and having someone direct you is a very sexual, intimate situation and Larry directed the first several videos that I was in. When he was directing he was not in drag of course, he was Larry, a big, huge, handsome, Italian man with a raspy, sexy voice telling me to, "Suck his cock! Stick your tongue up his asshole then spit on it!" Larry is 6' 3" (without high heels), and I have no idea how much he weighs. Most people would certainly say he is fat, but his girth isn't a turn-off for me. It apparently isn't for many others, either. He has intense charisma, in or out of drag. Sexy, sexy, sexy! I know that many other models like working for Larry and I am definitely not the only one who has had sex with him/her. Ironically, in his book *Making it Big*: *Sex Stars, Porn Films and Me*, he says that he won't name the porn stars he had had sex with, goes on and on about how wrong it would be to name them and then the only one he does name is me!

What kind of slut does he/she think I am!?

Larry and I have had many adventures together. One time in the spring of 1990, we brought a guy named Jeff home to my apartment. Jeff and I took off all our clothes and got in the jacuzzi with Larry (still in full drag) lying at the edge. We were both sucking Jeff's dick. My most vivid memory of that evening was Larry lying down in his drag outfit in the puddle of water beside the jacuzzi, his wig swirling around and around in the water while we both lapped at this guy's dick.

There were many other occasions when we shared guys' dicks. He had this way of ordering, "Show me your cock!" and right in the middle of the bar the guy would take it out. One time we were at Peanuts, a local drag bar. They had performers out on the dance floor lip-synching. The stage behind them was completely mirrored. I looked up and saw in the mirror Larry giving head under the table to the guy sitting next to us, and I realized that everyone else in the bar could see it too. They were far more interested in that show than in the one on the stage that night. Of course we took that guy home with us later that night.

When I was in Minneapolis for a week on tour with Joey Stefano, Andrew Michaels, and Tony Davis, Larry flew in for the last few days. One night I brought a guy back to my room. We were having sex and suddenly in walked Tony Davis and Larry, both with mischievous looks on their faces. I was sitting on the guy's face and they walked over and started taking turns sucking his dick. Finally the guy said "I'm gonna cum!" I gave Larry a look that said, "If you make him cum before he fucks me, I'm going to rip that wig right off your head!" They stopped before they guy came, and allowed us to continue.

One night Larry (in drag), Sharon Kane, Tony Davis, Joey Stefano and I, along with a couple other porn stars of the moment, had been out on the town. We all went back to Joey and Tony's place and were sitting around on Joey's bed. I remember Sharon explaining to a Larry how to eat a pussy "This feels good, this doesn't..." Then Larry started sucking my dick. I swear to God it was the best blow job of my life. I finally came all over his face, with everyone else watching in amazement. I developed a huge crush on Larry that night. I realized that he was smart and funny and sexy and gave great head. The next day I went over to his house to tell him. When I got there I was really nervous and hemmed and hawed and beat around the bush, saying things like, "Last night was really great! You give really good head..." He seemed incredibly uncomfortable with me being there, so I finally left. As we became very good friends, I told him much later that I had had such a big crush on him and he couldn't believe it. I don't think he sees himself as attractive out of drag, but he is. He gave me head a couple of other times and I am here to tell you, if you ever get the opportunity, don't pass it up!

SHARON KANE

Everyone in the gay porn industry knows that we count Sharon as one of our own, as a gay male porn star. A book of sex stories about guys in the industry just wouldn't be complete without her. You'll notice she is in a lot of the other chapters. She could write her own book that would be just as hot and juicy as this one. It would probably have even more stories.

Sharon probably has had more non-sexual roles in gay videos than anyone else. She has also been in more bisexual videos than any other woman. She has now been in the porn industry for about 25 years. She is a legend. She started back when they made films, real films, with big budgets that took a week or two to shoot rather than the one or two days that are standard now. They were, of course, shown in movie theaters. It was long before video was around. So many times people have come up to her when she was with me.

"You were in the first porn movie I ever saw, back when I was fifteen," they would say. "It was *Pretty Peaches*, and I've been a big fan ever since."

Pretty Peaches was Sharon's first movie, and it is a classic.

Sharon also has probably fucked more gay men than any woman I've ever known—more than a lot of gay men I know too, now that I think of it! They love her. Guys that haven't been with a woman for ten years, guys that have never been with a woman, they all seem to love her, and want to fuck her. Just off the top of my head, I can think of over 30 porn stars who are totally gay-identified that have slept with Sharon. She brings out the bisexual in people. Women too.

We met for a second at Chi Chi LaRue's birthday party in

1989. I didn't remember meeting her, but she remembered me. Chi Chi asked me if I could do a scene with a woman in my first video. I said 'yes', and he decided on Sharon Kane. The video would be called *Sharon and Karen*. I met Sharon and fell in love the day of the box cover shoot. I asked her to go out with me and we went to a party. We were so hot for each other we left the party right away, and barely made it out the door before we were making out furiously. We didn't have sex that night, though.

On the set of the video, we met again, and I was looking forward to our scene. That night we all went out to a club and I brought Sharon's boyfriend, Rick, home with me, with her blessing. Chi Chi nearly killed me the next day on the set. She was at the club with us and saw me leave with Rick.

"Are you insane?" She screamed. " You can't have sex all night before a shoot!"

She ate her words later as I did the scene and was rock hard the whole time. After that I was the only person that she never forbade to have sex before a scene. She would even call me lots of times to be a stunt dick when other guys couldn't get hard. Before that first scene, though, she was understandably nervous.

I wasn't. After doing the solo jack-off scene the day before, I knew this would be easy. I was going to fuck Sharon and Tony Davis, and I was really into both of them. If I could do it alone in front of a camera crew, I could certainly do it with two incredibly sexy people. You will read about that scene in the Tony Davis chapter, unless you're purely a Sharon fan who skipped straight to this chapter. I know there are a lot of you. Well, guess what? You have to read the whole book now, cause she's in many of the chapters and you wouldn't want to miss reading more about her, would you? Don't worry, you won't become a gay man if you read this book.

47

Well, probably not.

Anyway after that movie our on-again off-again relationship was on-again for a while. Over the next few years, we would have fabulous furious sex, alone and with others.

One time when I was living with Joey Stefano, Sharon came over. I had a big dildo lying by my bed. I had used it the night before, with someone else. She saw it and got that flirtatious look on her face. The one that always drove me crazy.

"What were you doing with that?" she asked.

"I was hoping to get someone to shove it up my ass." I answered.

Sharon was happy to oblige.

We were engaged several times, neither of us remembers how many. I gave her a ring the first time. Another time was after I came back from my guru Babaji's ashram in India. Muniraj, a great Hindu saint, had told me that Sharon and I should be married. We got engaged, again. That time it only lasted a week.

The last time was in 1997, just before I filmed *Xena: Warrior Princess*. I had a boyfriend who was not in the porn industry. Sharon and I were singing together, and recording music, trying to get a record deal. We were called "Goddess." Working together recording one night, we just couldn't focus on the music. Once again we ended up in bed, with me fucking her most of the night. Since then we have been just friends; we decided that we really weren't right for each other as a couple, and continuing to have sex was just confusing the whole issue.

Sharon has a really cute, really nice boyfriend now and I'm happy for her. She deserves someone wonderful like that. And we will always be good friends.

TONY DAVIS

I had a scene with Tony Davis in my very first video, *Sharon and Karen*. He showed up for the box cover shoot at Don Mantooth's studio on Sunset Boulevard that fateful day in 1989. The box cover was shot before the video, a month or two before the taping. He was bringing Joey Stefano to meet Chi Chi LaRue. Neither of them was supposed to be on the box or even in the video. I was staring at Tony and he was staring at me. Leering at me, really, in an incredibly sexy way. It was obvious to Chi Chi that we liked each other, so she put him in the video with me. Our scene was a three-way with Sharon Kane.

The scene was supposed to be oral between only the guys, with us both fucking Sharon. It was shot in a bed, one of the few scenes I ever did in a bed. Usually they were on a bale of hay, or on concrete, or swinging from a chandelier, or on top of a refrigerator, anywhere other than a bed. I didn't know how lucky I was to have this special comfort for the scene. Sharon and I were sucking Tony's dick, passing it back and forth between us. I was really turned on, I had already started dating Sharon, and was into her, and Tony totally turned me on.

He started sucking my dick with a vengeance and I loved it. When he gives head, his facial expression always looks like he is doing the nastiest thing in the world. That was one thing I loved about him, no matter what we were doing he looked like he was thinking dirty thoughts. Sharon and I called it "the porn sneer"; a lot of porn stars have it. Just look at pictures of any several of them and you'll see what I mean.

After Tony sucked my rod for a while, I fucked Sharon. Then we all sucked and licked and fingered each other until finally

Chi Chi asked me if I could cum. I really wanted Tony to fuck me, so I said that I could probably cum if I got fucked. Tony smiled wickedly and asked for a condom.

He slid his dick into me gently, then started fucking with a vengeance, the same way he sucks dick. He was pounding me while Sharon was sort of holding me in her lap. It was really turning me on, getting fucked, having a girl plus a whole camera crew watch me be a slut. I loved it! We fucked in a couple of positions then Chi Chi asked me again if I could cum. This time I said yes. I could have earlier, but then I wouldn't have gotten fucked by Tony! Anyway Tony and I both came and the scene was over. I went home that night and couldn't believe I had just done a porn video. I wondered if it would change my life forever. As it turns out, it did.

Tony and I started dating. We would go out dancing to Rage in West Hollywood, or to Apache in the Valley, or to dinner, usually Italian or Mexican food. People recognized him everywhere and looked at me like I was the luckiest guy in the world. I think it turned Tony on, to be recognized. He would sort of flaunt me in front of people, like they couldn't have him because he was with me. He would grab my ass or kiss me or hold my hand whenever people were looking at us. Then we would go home and fuck.

Tony and I had a scene together with Alex Carrington [*see his chapter*] in my first gay video, *The Rodz*. The scene was hot and I got off on sharing Tony with someone, something I hadn't done since that first scene with Sharon. After that the romance didn't last much longer, though. It seemed to have gone as far as it could and quickly turned into more of a friendship, although we occasionally still fucked, usually with other guys.

Tony and Joey Stefano moved in together as roommates soon after we did that first video. A couple of months later I was looking for a place and Tony convinced me to move into their building, Confetti Apartments. There were other porn stars who lived there and between all of us we kept the building pretty jumping with sex. There was a pool and jacuzzi and a sauna on the roof and I could see the jacuzzi from my bedroom window. Often, I would look out and one of the guys would be having sex with someone (or someone's) and I would go out and join them. It was almost like living in a bathhouse.

We often wound up going out to clubs and picking up guys, then going back home to Joey and Tony's apartment for wild sex parties. One time Tony and I brought home a guy and fucked him at the same time. We had been taking turns fucking him, then Tony told him to sit on both our dicks at the same time. It was very, very hot, feeling our dicks rubbing against each other inside this cute guy's ass. The door to Tony's room was open and Joey and the others would come and stand in the doorway and watch us for a few minutes, before going back to their own orgy.

A few years ago Tony met a lover, a very handsome man, and moved away with him; then a couple of years later, they moved back to L.A.. Tony seems more calm and much happier now. The relationship seems good for him, and I'm glad. He is a beautiful man and a sweet guy and deserves a great relationship. I occasionally still see him around town. When I least expect it someone will honk at me, and I'll look up and it will be Tony waving at me from his car.

ALEX CARRINGTON

I met Alex Carrington on the set of the first all-gay video I was in: *The Rodz: Boys in the Band,* in the Spring of 1990. He was in the second scene I did, the one with Tony Davis. I was dating Tony [*see his chapter*] and my first scene the day before had gone well, so I wasn't too nervous. That scene was on a motorcycle and there were extras standing around watching. Since I had made it through that one, this scene should be a piece of cake. At least there wouldn't be twenty extra people standing around staring at us.

Tony and I were living in the same apartment building, so we rode to the set together in his Porsche. I had never met Alex

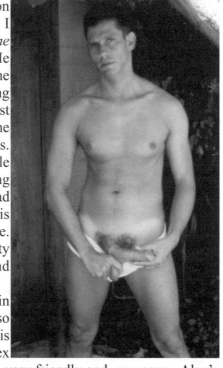

before and I thought that he was very friendly and *very* sexy. Alex's and my scene started with some very bad acting (from both of us) then he pulled me across the desk and started kissing me. I was totally turned on. He was a great kisser. By the time his clothes came off and I saw his huge dick, I was glad I had told Chi Chi that I only wanted to be a top. Alex's dick is certainly one of the wonders of the world, and now I'm sure it wouldn't be a problem, but at that time I don't know that I could have handled it .

The one moment that stands out most in my mind was when Alex was on his back on the desk sucking my dick with me sort of kneeling over him. It's become frozen in my mind like a movie that I re-play whenever I want. The feelings are as vivid now as they were then. He was extraordinary. I don't remember much else except that the scene ended up being scorching hot with both me and Alex fucking Tony. We were all really into it. Tony, of course, always loves getting fucked, and I loved watching another guy fuck him as much as I liked doing it myself.

A week later, Chi Chi had a big party and I went in drag in a dress I made simply from wrapping cellophane around my body. I saw Alex at the party and went up to him and said, "Hi. Do you know who I am?" He didn't. "We had sex last week," I said. He looked very surprised. "Are you sure?" He still thought I was a real woman. When I told him who I was, he didn't believe it at first. Then he decided that the whole thing was great and we danced all night.

I didn't see Alex again until several years later—he had retired for a year, then come back into the industry, performing in some videos for me and other people. I directed him in *Doggy Style* (his scene with Cole Reece sizzles!) and *Behind His Back*. His acting in *Doggy Style* was great, much better than that first video we did together. He is still as sexy as ever and every time he sees me, he recites to whomever is around the story of the night at Chi Chi's party and how surprised he was to find out it was me.

TED COX

I met Ted on the set of the first gay video I was in, *The Rodz: Boys in the Band,* in January of 1990. It was the second video I was in, but the first one was bisexual, not all gay. After I was done filming, Ted asked me if I wanted to come over to his house that night. I said "Sure." He was living with Johnny Johnson, a porn agent, whom I didn't know at the time, although now of course I do, and he's still around.

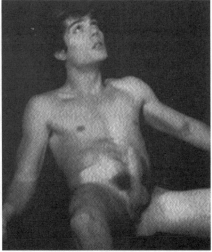

Ted's other roommate was Sparky O'Toole. Ted introduced me to Sparky and told me that Sparky was a big porn star that had nearly retired by then. I had never seen any of his videos, but he didn't seem to mind. He just said, "Hi," made a bit of small talk, and went off to his room. He seemed a little shy.

Ted and I went behind the house and got in the jacuzzi in the back for a while. I was so excited, naked in the jacuzzi. It was pretty risqué for me; I had never been in a jacuzzi nude before. I thought Ted was so cute, and I couldn't believe that I was hanging out with a porn star and that now I was one, too, or at least on my way. I remember the smell of the plants around the jacuzzi mixed with the smell of chlorine, even now. Everything about that moment is forever embedded in my mind; the moon, the stars, the smells, the feel of the warm water, and Ted looking shy and so cute.

After a while we went in to find Sparky. We all sort of started making out. Sparky and Ted pulled out my dick and started sucking it. I helped them take off their clothes and we got into a daisy chain. As I choked on the cock down my throat, I realized that this was just the second video I had been in, and just like the first time, here I was having sex after the video was over. I decided I could really like this gig.

I was sucking Sparky's dick and Ted was sucking mine and

Sparky was sucking Ted's. Soon Sparky wanted to get fucked and I was ready. He stuck his ass up in the air and I stuck my cock right in. Sparky moaned a little and pushed back on my cock so it was all the way up his hot, famous, little porn-star ass. I pulled almost all the way out and grabbed his hips as I speared back into his hole. Ted stroked his cock, watching us. I started fucking Sparky harder and harder, and all of a sudden he came. Ted told me to keep fucking him, so I did as Sparky's moans got louder and louder. Finally, Ted came over and stuck his dick in my mouth and I slipped out of Sparky's hole, finally ceasing my use and abuse of it. He sighed and smiled, then said he was tired and left Ted and me alone.

Ted said that he didn't usually get fucked, but that he wanted me to fuck him. He was really tight, and I do believe that he hadn't done it much. It was hard to get my dick up his ass, but I finally did. He was practically crying as he told me to shove my dick up his asshole. I started fucking him and he was grimacing. He was crying "It hurts," quietly. I asked if he wanted me to stop and he said 'no.' It seemed like he really wanted to please me, but that he wasn't getting any pleasure out of the whole thing, so I stopped. By then it was getting pretty late, and I decided I should leave. We jacked off together before I left, but it was a little odd. I didn't see Ted again until the Robin Byrd Benefit on Fire Island and the orgy at her house there afterwards. [*see the Aaron Scott chapter*]

ANDREW MICHAELS

Andrew was one of the cutest guys I had ever seen, and I was delighted that I was going to be doing a scene with him in *Karen's Bi-Line*. It was the early Spring of 1990 and it was just my second or third video, so I was still really excited and nervous beforehand. Andrew was supposedly straight (perhaps bi?). Usually I would have had a problem doing a scene with a guy who said he was straight, but he didn't say it; the make-up artist told me. Sometimes guys feel the need to insist a hundred times that they are straight while they are sucking your dick, and that can be annoying, but Andrew never really mentioned it. As long as he was acting like he wanted to be there

left, with Aaron Scott

with me, I didn't care what he thought he was. It was a bisexual video after all. In fact, Andrew also had a scene with Joey Stefano in that video. Their scene is really cute, they're in a bathtub with suds all over them. It was just before Joey and I decided to move in together and I was a little jealous. Now I think I just wanted to be in the tub between them!

We filmed the movie in Sabin's house. He was the publisher of the no-longer-in-print *GV Guide*. Our scene was in a room full of dolls, including ones from *The Six Million Dollar Man, Charlie's Angels*, and every other doll you could think of. It was bizarre. At one point in the scene we were kissing and Andrew started laughing. I asked him why and he told me that it was because he usually didn't like kissing at all but suddenly he realized he was kissing a guy and liking it. He was so sweet and so cute and so positively yummy, I almost couldn't stand it.

Once we got onto the bed, I began sucking his dick. He

moaned and writhed around like a kitten. My mouth was too full to make much noise, but believe me, I was moaning on the inside. Andrew's dick was delicious. I couldn't believe I was getting paid to suck the gorgeous dick of such a cute boy! What a job.

Every once in a while, I would look over at Chi Chi LaRue. Whenever he was directing a scene I was in, I would sneak looks at him. It was sort of like we were in on a sex secret together. I could tell that, in his mind, he was right there with me sucking that same dick. I'm certainly that way now, when I'm directing.

In any case, after sucking Andrew's dick, we got into a sixty-nine position. I just have to say that Andrew gives really good head for a "straight" boy. I was disappointed that there was no fucking in the scene, but sucking each other off was great. We both came at the same time. Then he kissed me again!

I didn't have to stay disappointed about us not fucking for long. A few months after that movie we went on a summer tour along with Tony Davis and Joey Stefano. The show consisted of the guys stripping, interspersed with me singing songs. This was when Joey and I were living together. Everyone met at our house, all four of us, and when the cab came, we realized that there was not enough room for all of us and our luggage. By the time we got a second cab and got to the airport, we had missed our plane. We had to call our manager and get on the next one. After that I became sort of a den mother, trying to watch out for the guys and get us to our gigs on time. We still missed about half of our flights on that whole tour.

For a week, we were in Minneapolis, at a bar called The Gay 90's. One night, Andrew got drunk enough to punch someone in the bar while he was stripping, and on another night, he got drunk enough (not very drunk really, just a couple of drinks) to insist on coming back to my room with me. We ran back to my room and got into the shower together.

We started kissing (he's such a great kisser) and washing each other all over under the hot water. It was incredibly sensual. We got out of the shower after the entire bathroom was steamed up, and he wrote my name in the fog on the mirror. It was sweet, and it made me remember the looks he had been giving me during the whole trip. It all started to make sense now. He always managed to sit next to me on the planes, and at restaurants. He was so shy that he had to have a couple of drinks to make a move. I was glad that he did.

He grabbed my hand and pulled me to the bed. He is so amazingly gentle and sensual. We immediately had each other's dicks in our mouths, and then I was licking his asshole. It was so pink and sweet and hairless and beautiful. I shoved my tongue as far up it as I could, licking his hole like a cat lapping up milk. The way he was whimpering would make anyone cream. I looked over and saw his face in the mirror. I had forgotten that the look on his face, when he is having sex, was so incredible.

Finally, he wanted to fuck me. Finally! After months of waiting since that video. He got on top of me and kissed me as he slid his dick in my ass and started fucking me. It was marvelous, his cock was perfect, not too big, and not too small. Definitely just right. I could have gone on for hours, he was so sweet, so sexy, so gentle and loving. I wanted it to last forever, but it didn't. Far too soon he announced, "I'm going to cum." I started jacking off my dick and came while he was fucking me, then he kept fucking me as he came, filling the condom in my ass. We kissed for a while then fell asleep holding each other.

Joey found us together the next morning and was teasing us but I think he was a little jealous. He always acted sort of weird whenever I was with anyone else, even though we had an open relationship and he fooled around with other guys far more than I did. Andrew and I might have gotten together again, but I think he could tell that there was something up between me and Joey, so he was careful not to cross the boundary of friendship with our relationship from then on.

Soon after the tour, Chi Chi LaRue told me the story of getting a phone call from Andrew's father, who was a sheriff. Apparently Andrew lived with his parents, and had a child who lived elsewhere. One day, Andrew's aunt saw his face on a box cover in a video store and told his parents. His father walked into Andrew's room, threw the video on the bed and just looked at him. Andrew started crying and said "They made me do it!" (Obviously, this wasn't true since he did about twenty videos with different directors.) Andrew's father called Chi Chi in a rage, but Chi Chi explained that she didn't make him do anything, that he was an adult etc., etc. Finally he calmed down, but now Chi Chi was pretty freaked out. Andrew did a few more videos after that, and then seemed to vanish. I haven't seen him for years, and no one seems to know where to find him. I and all of his other fans want him to come back!

LEO FORD

Leo is one of the most well-known porn stars of all time, appearing in many classics, including: *Leo & Lance*, *Spokes*, and *Class Reunion*. Anyone who knows their porn history knows who he is.

I met him by chance at a friend's house soon after I had started doing videos. I recognized him, and my friend just introduced me as "Geoff," and said that I had just started doing videos as "Rick Van." Leo and I hit it off. He told me that he had a lover (whom I met years later after Leo had died in a motorcycle accident), but that they had an open relationship. I didn't know if he was particularly interested in me, or, like so many porn stars, was just horny all the time (I suspect it was the latter.) I definitely felt a comfort, and a friendliness about him that drew me in. My friend conveniently had to go out for a couple of hours. Leo and I decided to stay and 'talk.'

As soon as he was gone, Leo began kissing me. Passionately. I've never been kissed in quite the same way. His tongue searched my mouth and his hands roamed my whole body. He felt a lot gentler than he looked in videos, at least for a while, then he ripped the buttons of my pants open and started sucking my dick. Again, it was amazing. He sucked dick like he loved it more than anything in life. I was completely getting into him sucking me, but I wanted his dick too, and I still hadn't even seen it.

I knelt down and took it out of his pants. It was huge— massive, even. I sucked it as best I could and actually did a pretty good job of swallowing most of it. He started getting a little rougher and more nasty like he was in the videos, but there was still a light playfulness about everything. He scraped the back of my throat with his cock as it went down it, in and out, making it sore, but still feeling oh-so-good.

There was a strange little toy on the floor, sort of a sculpture with a knob sticking up on the top. It was just perfect for an asshole, almost shaped like a pacifier, but bigger and longer.

"Sit on it," Leo said, and I scooted back and rocked back on it as he kept fucking my throat with his horse cock. I felt so trashy and nasty as I sat on the sculpture, bouncing up and down on it with my slutty hole as I sucked Leo's dick, kneeling on the hardwood floor. "What kind of a person shoves art up his ass while down on his knees sucking the dick of someone he just met?" I thought. "A filthy sex pig," I realized, and I loved it all the more as I thought about it.

All of a sudden he turned around and told me to fuck him. "Just shove it in" he said, "I can take it." I shoved my cock all the way in to the base and he sighed as I held it there for a minute. His hole was already wet inside, so it seemed like he cheated. "Shove it in," is nastier if a cock is shoved in totally dry, but I guess having your hole all lubed up and ready all the time already makes up several nastiness points. I started fucking him slowly but he was saying, "Harder, faster!" So I fucked him harder and faster, grabbing his blond hair and pulling him back onto my dick. I shoved his face down so he was now sucking the pacifier sculpture, sucking the taste of my asshole off it.

Suddenly he pulled off my dick and spun me around and slid his dick in me. I don't know how he did it so fast without it hurting but, he did, and it didn't. He immediately started pounding my ass. We were standing up, but then he pulled out and laid me down on the couch facing him and slid his cock back up my ass. He was looking into my eyes and it was the most intimate feeling I'd ever felt with someone that I'd just met. It was also incredibly, intensely, erotic. We were still looking into each other's eyes as we both started to come. He shot all over my stomach, chest and face, more cum than I have ever seen. I was drenched in white, sticky goo.

We were just pulling our pants back up when our friend returned. I pulled my shirt on quickly, forgetting about the cum all over me, and was then wearing a shirt soaking with cum. My friend knew what had happened, I'm sure, but he didn't say anything. We all spent the rest of the evening just hanging out. By the time I left, my shirt had gotten a little hard and crunchy.

I never saw Leo again, and felt very sad about that. His casual, natural attitude about sex during that one encounter really helped me deal with some issues that I had been going through at the time. Even though it took a while before I was truly done with them, I think he helped me a lot. He had an acceptance for his sexuality that now might be a bit more common, but then was rare. I was very upset to hear of his tragic death in a motorcycle accident soon after I had met him. He was an amazing person; I feel very honored to have known him. It felt like the world really lost something special when he left.

LON FLEXX

When I met Lon in 1990, I was struck by his dark good looks. Swarthy almost, but in a more clean cut way, if that is possible. And that thick, dark hair! We soon became friends and lovers. The first time we kissed, he seemed really nervous. I thought, "Isn't that sweet, I'm making him nervous. I must be really sexy." Ha! When I reached up to caress his head, I discovered that he was wearing a hairpiece. That was why he was so nervous. And why his hair was so thick. It wasn't real! I told him it didn't bother me, and it didn't. He was sweet and sexy and gorgeous and right there kissing me. What else could matter?

His kisses were deep and probing, like he really meant them. He started kissing my neck and my ear and I went wild. The one way to really drive me crazy and make me powerless over you is to kiss my neck and nibble on my ear. I turn to butter. I melted all over him. Too soon he left that area and started making his way down my chest with his kisses. He started biting and sucking on my cock through my shorts. It was very hot, although I remember laughing at one point because it seemed so much like a porn script: I could almost hear Chi Chi's voice, "Okay, now suck his dick through his underwear until it's all wet and we can see it..." That was exactly what he did though, and I continued to boil over with passion. He was taking his time, he knew exactly what he was doing, and it worked.

At last, he took my dick out. He looked at it, then up at me, and then started to lick the sides of it, watching my face. My body was writhing uncontrollably now, trying to get more of my dick into his mouth, that wonderful, warm, wet, mouth. Finally he took the whole thing in. I gasped and grabbed the back of his head (Oops! The hairpiece!), quickly moving my hands down to his shoulders as he gave me one of the best blow jobs of my life. I didn't think I ever wanted it to end, but then he did the most very perfect thing. He came back up to bite my neck again, this time much harder. I couldn't believe the electricity and emotions running through my body. He leaned over and whispered in my ear "Do you want to fuck me?" I looked in his eyes as I said, "YES!!!" to let him know that I wanted it more than anything on earth.

He lay down on his back and lifted his legs straight up. I started licking and kissing his asshole and then came up to kiss his lips as I slid my dick into him. It fit perfectly. Like everything else about our encounter, it was magical. I looked into his eyes as I fucked him slowly, then built up to faster and faster. We finally both came at the same time, with my dick still inside him and our eyes still locked. We held each other like that, and kissed for a long time.

We got together a few times after that, and a couple of times Lon fucked me. It was just as satisfying every time. We didn't have any sort of commitment or official arrangement or even call it a relationship, so I wasn't surprised when one day I realized I hadn't seen him for a long time. A few years later I heard that he had died. Another one. It's not fair, to lose so many people so young and so fast. But we all know that. At least every one who ever met Lon will remember him, as, I am sure, will many of his fans.

MATT POWERS

I met Matt Powers within my first year of doing porn. It was early 1990, and I was out at the club Studio One with what local gay media had dubbed the "porn brat pack:" Joey Stefano, Chi Chi LaRue, Sharon Kane and Tony Davis. Matt was there signing autographs for one of his videos that had just been released. He was very interested in me and flirted quite obviously with me. When the bar closed, he asked if he could come with us; we were all going back to Joey and Tony's to hang out. This was when we all lived in Confetti Apartments and I lived just two floors up from them.

Matt came back with all of us, and everyone wanted to have sex with him. He seemed interested in only me though. The others were starting to take off their clothes and fool around. Matt asked me if we could go up to my apartment and be alone. It seemed like a good idea to me. We got to my apartment and he was instantly all over me. He had been a little bit restrained around the other people, but now that we were alone, the restraint was gone! I took him to my bed and said,

"Why don't you take off your clothes while I take a shower?" I was sweaty from dancing all night. He wasn't, since he had been sitting, signing autographs. When I came back, he was naked and his huge dick was rock hard. He asked if I had any dildos.

At this point in my life, I had never used a dildo on myself or anyone else, but I did have a bunch that I had gotten from one of the porn companies, all still wrapped up. I wasn't all that interested in the dildos *per se*, but I was interested in *him*, so I got them out. He grabbed my dick and started sucking. Heaven! Then we got into a sixty-nine position. Now I had his huge dick down my throat while he was vigorously sucking mine. All of a sudden he rolled over and pulled his knees up to his chest with his ass in my face and asked me to fuck him. I fucked him for probably an hour. At one point we were both drenched with sweat and went and took a shower together.

When we went back to the bed, he picked a dildo and asked me to stick it up his ass. I did, a little tentatively at first, then suddenly I totally got into watching this big thing sliding in and out of his ass. He had the most gorgeous hole and the lips would grip the dildo; when I would pull it all the way out of his asshole, it would stay open. It was so hot! This was a whole new thing for me, playing with someone's ass other than just fucking it with my dick, or sticking my fingers in. I loved it.

He kept asking for bigger and bigger dildos, and told me to shove them in hard. Finally, I stuck a huge double-headed dildo up his ass. He told me to push it all the way in, so I did. I watched his hole swallow it up, and it disappeared as he gasped. It must have been two feet long.

"Okay...out," he said.

I couldn't. I tried to reach inside and grab it and I just couldn't get it. It just seemed to go further up inside him. I started to panic and he looked like he was about to also. Finally, I calmed down and told him to push it out. Sure enough, his asshole started peeking open and the head of the dildo came out. I grabbed it and pulled it out. He looked at the length of it and said in amazement

"Was all of that really in me?"

"Yes, and it almost stayed there!" I said.

He lifted his legs up in the air and said,

"My ass still needs more. Stick your fingers in me."

I had never really done that before either, but I loved it too. First I put one, two, then three fingers up his ass, sliding them in and out. I put the fourth finger in and he said,

"Give me your whole hand."

I didn't really understand. I had never heard of fisting and wouldn't have thought it was possible, except that I had just seen him taking huge dildos up his ass, so I thought, "Well, he can probably take it, if anybody can." He told me how to put all my fingers together and I did and slid my hand up his ass. Once I was totally inside, he said, "Now make a fist and just move it slowly."

I started doing it. I was amazed at the fact that my entire hand was *inside* this guy. It really turned me on. I started moving my fist faster and faster until I was fucking him with it. All of a sudden he stared shooting, all the way up onto his own face. Some of his cum landed on his lips and he licked it off. I slipped my hand back out of his ass and jacked off and came on him, too.

After about ten minutes, he was ready to go again. We kept playing all night long, with him fucking me, too. At one point, we used a double-headed dildo and bounced our butts together with it inside of us. He was one hot, wild, man.

Finally, long after the sun had come up, he said he needed to go and asked if I would drive him home. I did, but as we drove up to his house, I freaked out a little. It was the house of Bill Sheffler, who was the manager and basically made all the decisions at that time at Catalina.

"Um, is Bill your boyfriend?" I asked.

"Well, not exactly, we have uh, an arrangement."

"Oh," I said, horrified, "Well, maybe you'd better not tell Bill who you were with."

He said he wouldn't, but mysteriously, Catalina didn't hire me to be in one of their videos again for a long time. Chi Chi ragged on me for a year about that:

"I can't believe you fucked Bill Sheffler's boyfriend!"

"I didn't know!" was all I could say. It was true.

I didn't see Matt again until the awards show the next year in Las Vegas. He signed a picture to me that said, "Here's to a night that never ended." Later that night he came back to Joey's and Sharon's and my room with a girl for a sex party. I'll never forget Matt. He was the man that taught me to love sticking my fist, dildos, and anything else I can, up a guy's ass.

Thank you, Matt!

KEVIN WILLIAMS

I met Kevin one summer when I was cruising around in my car very late at night in an area where guys meet, down by Melrose Avenue. Our eyes locked. I stopped my car and he got in without a word. It was hot out, and I could smell honeysuckle and sex in the air. Other cars prowled around us like Jaws stalking his lunch, through the shadowy jungle of cars, houses, trees, and bodies barely visible in the dark night.

Because of his blond hair and those unmistakable eyes, I realized who he was as a car drove by like a moving spotlight hitting him for a second or two. I didn't say anything. I didn't know if he recognized me, and I didn't care. Fame wasn't the drug I wanted that night. Sex was. We went back to my place.

Before I knew it, he was on his hands and knees with his ass in the air. His first words to me were, "Fuck me." I was more than happy to. I watched him wiggle that ass around for a minute, then I shoved my cock inside and started pounding immediately. If anyone had done this to me I would have screamed, but he just moaned, "Yeah!" It turned me on that he loved getting fucked so much. He seemed to need it, like his ass was hungry. I fed it. His knees must have been raw because I fucked him furiously all over the floor before we finally made it up onto the bed, slowly crawling up as I kept my dick lodged all the way up his wet hole.

Once we were actually on the bed we covered most of the positions I was familiar with and a couple of new ones. He seemed to know all sorts of new ways to get fucked, usually with his face somehow buried in a pillow or under the covers. The hottest was with him sitting on my dick, bouncing up and down on it. He would pull all the way off it then slam his ass back down on it again, almost like his body was floating over mine, sweat dripping from his blond hair and clinging to his eyelashes. His eyes were glazed over and he looked almost like he was in a trance. And that ass! He had the most gorgeous ass! A couple of times, he spun all the way around on my dick. Well, he didn't actually *spin*; he turned himself, quite gracefully, not awkward as you might expect. No one had ever done that to me before. He was obviously very skilled. I kept fucking him, amazed.

He came twice while I was fucking him, but he wanted me to keep going each time. I love fucking a guy after he cums, just like I love getting fucked after I cum—it's more intense, and I've always been a big fan of the intense. I kept fucking him half the night until the sheets were wet from our sweat. I finally was so exhausted that I had to stop. I just couldn't come for some reason. I assured him that it wasn't him and that I had thoroughly enjoyed our many hours together. He smiled and kissed me and was gone before I knew what had hit me.

I didn't see him again until years later when I met him at one of the gay video awards shows. He didn't seem to recognize me and I didn't remind him of our previous encounter. I wonder if he ever figured out that it was me, or if there was always a new guy every night for him.

I know reading this book it probably seems like there is every night for me, but there really isn't. This book spans ten years. If there had been a new guy each night, this book would have over three thousand chapters!

AARON SCOTT

I was living with Joey Stefano in the summer of 1990 when I met Aaron Scott, on the set of the video *Painted* which was directed by Chi Chi LaRue. I wrote and starred in the film, and it was made in Joey's and my place. The first day I had a scene with Storm (who has his own chapter). Storm and I were so into each other that he came back over that night after the shooting was done.

The next day Aaron Scott walked in for his scene with Andrew Michaels. I saw Aaron, his tan, his long golden hair, and was in love, or at least lust. I watched the scene on the monitor with Chi Chi, drooling over every moment of those cute boys. After shooting that day, he, Andrew, Tony Davis and I went out to the bars in West Hollywood. We had a great time that night, high on our fame, (and probably a hit of ecstasy), we danced until the bars closed, enjoying the stares from people who recognized us. I still have a picture of all of us from that night.

I was actually just hitting a very obnoxious phase in my life. My fame was just starting to sink in and people were recognizing me. Suddenly I didn't have to wait in line at clubs, my drinks were free, and people wanted to be seen with me. My attitude, was "Don't you know who I am!?" until Sharon Kane pointed it out: "Geoff, you know how sometimes Joey acts really obnoxious? You're starting to act that way too."

I got it. I instantly was humbled and realized I was no better than any one else, and that I was becoming a big brat. Thank God Sharon stopped that monster in its tracks or it could still be devouring everything in its path today, like Dragzilla, crushing the city with her huge high heels. Sharon actually called me a baby *Tyrannosaurus rex*. She didn't mean it as a compliment!

Anyway, we were out having fun and that night Aaron came

home with me and we spent our only night alone together. I was thrilled—I felt like I had made it. I had been dancing for hours with gorgeous porn stars, gay royalty practically, and now I was in bed with Aaron, the man of my dreams. Well, the man of my dreams that particular day at least. We started kissing and the passion built fast, or rather started coming out fast. It had been building all day. We started undressing each other and couldn't get our clothes off fast enough. Shirts ripped and buttons went flying. It all looked very dramatic and porn movie-like until my sleeve caught on my wrist and we had to stop for a couple of seconds to get my shirt off my arm before continuing.

Finally, our flesh was touching with nothing between us. Aaron started licking down my chest to my rock-hard throbbing dick. He started sucking it and I didn't know what to do: close my eyes, let them roll back in my head, or try to keep them focused on his beautiful ass in the mirrored doors of my closet. I decided to watch. I was just learning that porn stars *never* turn out the lights. Absolutely never. And they always seem to have mirrors around their beds. His sucking was wonderful. The hair on my arms and legs stood up with goose bumps. I watched his ass wiggling around. I wanted that ass so badly, but I wanted his dick too.

We swung around into a sixty-nine and I had to give up the view in the mirror for a nice fat cock in my mouth. Not a bad trade, definitely worth it. We sucked each other with a fervor, like teenagers doing it for the first time—very naturally skilled teenagers. He was taking my dick all the way down his throat so I tried to do the same for him. He started licking past my balls to my asshole and I went crazy, and was so incapacitated, it threw my sucking off for a while. I soon went back to it and also reached back and stuck a finger up his ass. Now he was the one going crazy. He bounced down on my finger a couple of times, then he jumped up on his hands and knees with his ass in my face.

"Fuck me, please fuck me," he begged.

He didn't need to ask twice. I had my dick up his ass before he got all the words out, and then he was wailing and moaning and making sounds that made me even more insane with lust. I started fucking him slowly, taking forever to push my dick in and then just holding it, pressing into him, when it was up to the hilt. Then I started drawing it back out just as slowly until he was just holding the head of it in his sphincter. I teased him by pulling back a little and he swayed back too, so that it wouldn't come out, then I moved he swayed back too, so that it wouldn't come out, then I moved quickly, just enough to pull it all the way out. He begged me to put it back in.

"Please! Ram it in me!" he pleaded.

I looked at his pink, open hole, then I rammed it all the way back in. I started fucking him hard. Aaron screamed.

"Yes, yes!" he cried as his hands searched the bed for something to grab on to.

I hear the door squeak and looked over and Joey was in the doorway watching us and jacking off. We were lovers often, but we each had our own bedrooms. It was rare for him to watch and not join in but he just stayed in the doorway jacking off until he came. He had just done something very similar the night before when I was with Storm. I don't think Aaron ever realized that he was there.

After hours of romping around the bed, we finally both came and fell asleep next to each other, exhausted from the long day of shooting and night of dancing and sex. We got up at about two the next afternoon and went to breakfast at Authentic Cafe on Beverly, which is still one of my favorite restaurants in L.A.

Later Aaron and Sharon Kane got into some sort of relationship (they even called her mother and told her that they were getting married, although they didn't do it), and just about that time Robin Byrd invited all of us out to Fire Island to do an AIDS benefit at a bar called The Ice Palace. We all flew out to New York and spent the night with Jim Bentley. Sharon and Jim fucked that night, which really annoyed Aaron. He left and didn't come back until the morning, just when we had to leave to catch the ferry. He wouldn't ever tell us where he had been, but he made it clear to Sharon that he got laid too.

We caught the ferry to Fire Island and did the show. After the show we went back to the house Robin had rented for all of us to stay in. Robin, Aaron, Vladimir Correra, Ted Cox, and I had a big orgy in the middle of the living room with Robin's boyfriend filming us. I don't know what ever happened to that tape! In the next few days it seemed that everyone got around to sleeping with everyone else in between going to the beach and going out to the tiny Fire Island bars at night. The important things to do seemed to be sun, drinking, and sex, but probably not in that order. By the time we left I thought we were worn out, but really we had only begun.

We went back into NYC to do Robin's cable TV show, *The Robin Byrd Show*. Aaron, Sharon and I were staying in a hotel room together for a week. We were all insane, going out every night and coming back and having sex all over the room. We took quite a few baths together, although I don't remember whether or how we all fit into one tub. Some nights one or more of us wouldn't come home until the next day. Then we would tell the other two about the adventure from the night before.

One night Aaron did a live sex show in a club. He got fucked by a guy on a pool table while Sharon and I and the rest of the people in the bar watched. The drag queens in New York, Lady Bunny, Linda Simpson, and the rest thought we were wild. It's pretty hard to shock a New York drag queen, but I guess we did. Everyone always seemed so baffled by our bisexuality. It's not really all that rare!

Finally, we all came back to L.A., frazzled and spent, but all in one (well, three) pieces. Aaron eventually moved away from L.A.. I still hear from him every few years. We talk about the old days and how crazy we all were. It's a miracle we all made it.

STORM

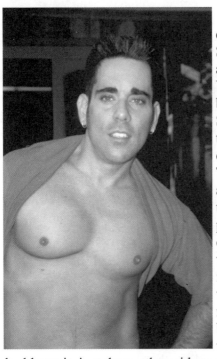

I first met Storm at the box cover shoot for *Painted* in the Spring of 1990. The shoot was at a photographer's studio down on Venice Boulevard in L.A. I was to be on the front of the box, and Storm and another guy were on the back. I was wrapped in cellophane, wearing nothing else. They were wrapped in cellophane also, their crotches pressed together, with their shoulders pulled back, looking out at the camera. Storm was very sexy, and when we were all naked changing in the dressing/makeup room, he was looking at me, up and down my body. I was turned on beyond belief. I was nervous, too. This was only my fourth box cover. I had been in just three other videos at that point, although by the time we shot the video itself a couple of months later, I had been in a few more.

The video had been postponed because Chi Chi never wrote the script. Finally, she asked me to write it. I did, then was a little annoyed (okay, really pissed) that she didn't give me credit for writing it—especially later when it was nominated for several awards. I learned to make my agreements with her very clear after that. They paid me about $5,000 for that video though, which was a lot in those days. It's still a lot more than most guys get paid for a video, ten years later. I guess I couldn't complain too much.

Storm had a beautiful body, hard and muscular, but not overdone. His ass was perfect, and his big dick hanging down between his thick sinewy thighs jumped a little when I casually glanced down at it. I tried to be nonchalant, but he knew what I was thinking. He was thinking the same thing. When the photo shoot was over and we were leaving, he grabbed my ass and said, "I'll see you at the shoot!" I could hardly wait.

I wasn't originally going to be in a scene with him. It was a bisexual video. I was to be in a scene with Sharon Kane again, and with another guy. Storm was supposed to be in a different scene. Chi Chi changed her mind about the concept of the video later when she asked me to write the script. She had seen us and noticed the thick sexual tension in the dressing room, so she told me to write myself a scene with him. I was happy and horny for two months waiting for the shoot. Thanks to Matt Powers, I had recently discovered how much I like fucking guys with dildos, so I wrote a dildo into the scene, too.

In the video I play an artist whose girlfriend, played by Sharon, leaves him. I freak out and am comforted by my friend, played by Storm. Supposedly, my character had never been with a guy before (yeah who believed that?) and Storm's character seduces me. It was really hot, one of the scenes that I can still watch today and get turned on, although I was so young and skinny and chicken then that it's like watching another person. I looked about 16. I was, of course, still six feet tall, but I only weighed about 145 pounds compared to my 180 pounds today. We filmed the video in the house on Sierra Bonita, where I was living with Joey Stefano.

Storm started sucking my dick, and I loved it. He is an excellent cocksucker. I could have gone on forever just getting sucked. Then he pushed me down on his dick. I resisted (just for the video, no way would I resist in real life) and finally started sucking it. It was big and hard and felt perfect in my mouth, with just a hint of a salty taste and smell. I love that smell of a fresh, clean dick. You just can't wash the smell away. Thank God, because it is one of the finer things in life.

We were both getting really crazy and turned on and holding each other's gaze. Even though we were being filmed, and watched by the crew, I felt like we were sharing something private. I knew that after the video was over and Chi Chi and the crew were gone, I would be seeing more of Storm. I started playing with his ass, shoving my fingers in; first one, then two and finally, three, finger-fucking him hard. Then I put my cock in his ass; the ass I had just loosened up and taken control of. I started fucking him, pounding into him so that he would know I wanted more later, and know that I was fucking him for real, not just for a video. Finally I pulled my cock out of his hot quivering hole, and shoved the dildo up. I started ramming it in and pulling it all the way out to look at his gaping asshole that begged for me to shove it back in again. In and out harder and harder, I raped his hole with that big dildo until we both came. Afterwards, he kissed me, and whispered, "I'm not done."

I knew that already.

Later that night, after the filming, he came back over and we spent several hours in my bed reliving the scene from the video and throwing in a few extra dildos. He left at about two in the morning. As soon as he left, Joey came in and wanted to know all the details. He knew some already, he had been listening outside the door, getting turned on for about an hour. He turned around and showed me that he had a huge butt-plug stuck up his ass. I pulled it out and shoved my dick in, and we continued where Storm and I left off for another hour before finally going to sleep. I rarely saw Storm after that, although he still seems to be in the business. He pops up in a video now and then, and of course I always remember him fondly.

AL PARKER

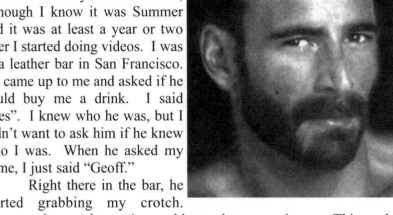

Al Parker is a classic porn star from the golden age of porn and will always be remembered. I met him years ago, before he did his last few videos, I believe. I'm not sure exactly when it was, although I know it was Summer and it was at least a year or two after I started doing videos. I was at a leather bar in San Francisco. He came up to me and asked if he could buy me a drink. I said "Yes". I knew who he was, but I didn't want to ask him if he knew who I was. When he asked my name, I just said "Geoff."

Right there in the bar, he started grabbing my crotch. Anyone who cared to notice could see what was going on. This made me both nervous and turned on at the same time. He shoved his hand down inside the back of my pants and shoved a dry finger up my ass. I couldn't believe it. I was so turned on, so hot for him, and standing in a crowded bar with him finger-fucking my ass was driving me wild. It seemed so nasty and I loved it. He stuck two fingers in my hole and leaned over and whispered in my ear,

"You're a filthy slut boy, letting me stick my fingers up your ass." Oh Daddy! I melted into him even more, shoving myself back on his fingers so he would know for sure how much of a filthy slut boy I was. If he had wanted to fuck me right there, I think I would have done it, lube or not, but instead he wanted me to leave with him. As we left he guided me out of the bar and up the street with his fingers still up my ass like he owned it. Even though it was Summer, I shivered, perhaps from the chill in the air, perhaps the thrill of the situation. Maybe a little of both.

When we got back to his place, he took out some penis pumps and started pumping up his dick. It got really huge but looked a little like a Mr. Potato Head. He showed me how to use a pump on my dick. It was interesting and novel, but didn't really turn me on that much. He told me he wanted my ass again. That turned me on! I gladly rolled onto my back so that he could get to my hole. He spread some Crisco on it and then slid in one finger, then two, then three, slowly playing with it, coaxing it to relax and open up more and more. By the time he put in four fingers I was really concentrating on my breathing. It felt incredible, and so intense that my mind wasn't able to think, just feel the electric jolts running through my body. He asked if I wanted more and I couldn't speak, so I just nodded.

Slowly, very slowly, he worked his entire huge hand up my butt. I felt like I was stretched to the limit, almost beyond the limit, but he kept going so obviously I wasn't past my limit. As he started moving his hand back and forth in me I started moaning, long and loud. I had never heard that sound come out of me before. He worked my ass until I was screaming for him. I worried about his neighbors, then realized that they were probably used to sounds like these coming from his apartment. He slowly pulled his hand out and I felt very empty, and desperately needed to be filled again. This time it was Mr. Potato Head. His dick may have looked a little odd but it felt great. After having his hand in me, his dick, big as it was, went right in with no problem. He started fucking me hard and calling me his little slut pussy boy. I loved it. He was pounding my ass as hard as he could and slapping my chest and I still wanted more. He was on top of me holding my legs in the air and his sweat was dripping down on me, onto my lips where I could taste it. I couldn't believe how much I loved it. He told me to open my mouth and he spit in it. As soon as he did that, I came. He kept fucking me after I came and I was still in heaven. The feeling was getting more and more intense. I never wanted him to stop, but after about fifteen minutes he finally pulled his dick out and sprayed his load all over my face. Then he leaned over and licked it off and fell down on top of me, holding me. I was shaking. We held each other for a long time, it was very sweet and tender, a nice completion to the rough intensity we had just experienced.

I saw him a few more times, when I was in San Francisco, but not nearly enough. Then several years went by before I made it up to SF again. Al had died during that time. I and thousands of others will always miss and remember him.

STEVE FOX

Steve was truly one of the most beautiful models ever in porn. With his blond hair and beautiful blue eyes and perfect tan he was a living Malibu Ken doll, only anatomically complete. I met him when I was on tour years ago in Atlanta; I think it was Summer, either in 1990 or 1991. He knew who I was from my videos, and I had seen him in a couple of Falcon videos, my favorite being *Compulsion*, when he got huge dildos shoved up his ass. I told him I wanted to do that to him. He agreed, but wanted to make sure I knew he was bisexual. "Okay, Ken, so am I, who cares?" I thought. What I said was, "Great, so am I, let's go." We raced back to my hotel room.

When we got to my room, I wanted to take a shower; I was still sweaty from the show I had just done. Steve wanted to take a shower with me, which sounded great. We got in the shower together and started washing each other and kissing very passionately. Looking into his beautiful face with water streaming over it and kissing him was like kissing an angel. A wet angel. Pretty soon though, the angel turned into a mischievous devil.

Steve turned around, put his hands up on the blue tile of the shower wall, arched his back, and said, "Stick a finger up my ass." I did. It was velvety smooth and water was streaming down over his ass and my hand. He reached back to spread it for me with his face pressed against the tile. My dick was rock hard, watching the water run over his perfect white bubble butt while I finger-fucked him.

Soon, he was asking for more and more fingers, and I eventually had four ramming in and out of him. He said, "I need something bigger."

We got out of the shower and got out the dildos I just happened to have with me. He picked the biggest one, which was huge and said, "Stick this up my ass, I really need it." I really needed it up his ass, too, and soon I was fucking him hard with that huge dildo. He was bouncing up and down on it, coming all the way off so I could see his sweet hole, then slamming himself back down, the whole time talking to me telling me how much he had needed this, how good the dildo felt in his ass. The ceiling fan was squeaking and the bed was squeaking but it didn't matter, all I could hear was him begging me to fuck him harder, please, harder. It was amazing to witness.

"I want you in me!" he finally cried, so I put on a condom and started fucking him. It felt great in his ass. He was so tight, I would never have known that he had just been fucked by a huge dildo if I hadn't done it. He had incredible control of his ass. I had never met anyone like that before, except Joey Stefano.

I fucked him on his knees first, then on his back. I fucked him across the bed until his head was hanging off the edge and then I fucked him right off the bed! We just couldn't stop, so we continued on the floor instead of getting back on the bed. The bedspread had come off with us, so at least there was some cushion under us other than the light blue carpet that perfectly matched his gorgeous eyes. He came at last with me on top of him, kissing him as I fucked him. As soon as he finished, I started to come, too, and I shot my load into the condom, up his perfect bubble butt.

I squirmed on top of him for a while, just then really noticing that we were on the floor. Finally, he gave me a long passionate kiss and said, "I've got to go." We took another quick shower together (hmmm...was Barbie waiting at home?) He got dressed, asked if it was okay to take an apple from the fruit basket on the table, and left. I never saw him again, except in videos. He was a very sweet guy and I was really upset to hear that he died a couple of years ago. There will never be another blond with such a beautiful face, such blue eyes, such a great personality and such a perfect, perfect ass.

CHRIS BURNS

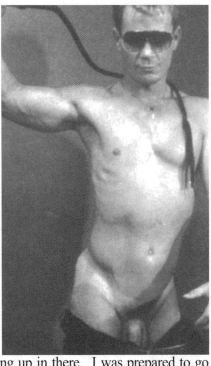

Chris Burns is a legend, especially if you are into fisting, which of course, I am. I was delighted to meet him. Joey Stefano had talked about him for a long time; Chris was sort of an idol to him. Joey could get a lot up his ass, but even he wasn't as big of a bottom as Chris. Or so I had heard.

Chris was always delighted to meet someone who wanted to stick a fist up his butt. I actually got together with him and another friend of Joey's—a guy that wasn't in porn, but sure could have been. We started out sucking and kissing, normal foreplay type stuff, but soon we both turned our attention to Chris's legendary butthole. He could make it do all sorts of things. We were fascinated watching him push it out and even open it at will.

Soon I had to stick something up in there. I was prepared to go slowly, but he sucked my entire hand up immediately, like a huge vacuum. Then he told my friend to put his hand up there too. He did and it was unbelievable. The stories were obviously true.

We both had our fists up his ass, practically holding hands inside him. He told us to start fucking, so we did, first together, then opposite each other, one pulling all the way out and then going back in as the other pulled out. He kept wanting it harder and harder. He told me to stick my dick in, and my friend grabbed it and started jacking me off. It was the most amazing experience, being jacked off inside someone's ass.

I really wanted to fuck him now and so did my friend. He told us to do it at the same time. I got on top of Chris and my friend was underneath him and we both started fucking for all we were worth. Chris was saying things like, "Yeah fuck my pussy ass, do you like that loose, sloppy hole?" I did. We all came in short order.

I saw Chris a few times after that, and we had some similar adventures together, one involving a bet and a softball. I lost the bet. And the softball. He was amazing.

SCOTT O'HARA

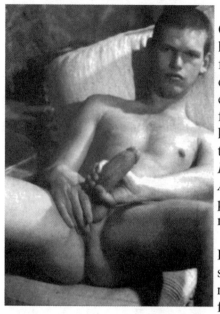

I didn't really know who Scott O'Hara was, or realize that I had had sex with him until after I found out he had died. When the obituaries were appearing everywhere and some of my friends were talking about knowing him, I put it all together: the videos, like *In Your Wildest Dreams* and *The Other Side of Aspen II*, the journal *Steam* that he published, and suddenly I realized that I had been with him.

I was in San Diego at Black's Beach. It was a hot, gorgeous summer day. I was sunbathing nude, but I wasn't really looking for sex. I hardly ever cruise parks or tearooms or anything like that. It's just not the way I usually have sex. Except for when I'm with a lover, the casual sex I have is almost always by chance, like it was that day. That's not to say I'm not usually ready, even though I'm not exactly looking. I was a Boy Scout. They taught us to always be prepared!

So...there was this really sexy guy (Scott) lying on the beach not too far away from me. I noticed that he was watching me. He started stroking his dick and soon it was hard. Big and hard. I noticed that my dick was hard, too. I was a little nervous because we were so out in the open and there were other people there, although no one else was really close. I started stroking my dick, too, as I watched him. He spread his legs and turned so that I could see his asshole. As he looked into my eyes, he stuck two fingers in his mouth then stuck them up his ass. I couldn't believe that he was doing all this in public, but there he was, finger-fucking himself and stroking his dick in the afternoon sun at Black's Beach.

He got up and walked over into the bushes, his huge cock bobbing up and down, then he motioned me to follow him. I looked around nervously and went after him. I walked through the bushes

81

and there he was, down on his knees, so I stuck my dick in his mouth. As he sucked my dick, I grabbed his dirty blond hair and fucked his face. He was taking my dick all the way down his throat, and I grabbed his head and held it there. He loved it. He was a total dick-pig, and I loved that.

Then I had to have his huge cock. It was my turn to be the dick-pig. I started sucking it and licking up and down it. He grabbed the back of my head and fucked my face the way I had fucked his. Then he turned around, spread his ass with his hands and said, "Eat my ass." I stuck my tongue up his ass and fucked him with it for about fifteen minutes, shoving it in and out and swirling it all around. The taste of his asshole was making my dick drip pre-cum all over. I couldn't get enough of his ass, and he couldn't get enough of my tongue.

Finally he said, "Fuck me." I stuck my dick in his wet asshole and started fucking. He wanted it harder and harder and I gave him just what he wanted, with both of us still standing up and with him still reaching back and spreading his ass. Suddenly, I noticed someone walking by not too far away. I shoved him down on his knees and kept going. I was fucking him like the slut that he was and he was loving every second of it. When I said I was about to come he spun around and started sucking on my dick. I tried to pull out of his mouth but he wouldn't let me, he wanted to swallow all of it, and he did. It was so intense that I was shaking after I came. I probably would have fallen over if we were still standing.

He kissed me and let me taste some of my own cum, and then he was gone. I didn't know who he was and he didn't know who I was, but once again, the world turned out to be small. Now I know.

GINO COLBERT

Gino has been in videos as well as directing them since well before I was in the business. He also still appears in them sometimes. Anyone who has seen him in a video knows why. He is totally hot and is an absolute sex pig. He has this way of leering at you that you just have to love (at least I do) because it makes you feel like you are the sexiest man alive. He always looks like he is thinking nasty thoughts and he probably is.

I first met him in New York on a hot night in 1990 when I was stripping at one of the gay strip clubs, The Showpalace. They had the regular guys that worked there that did the jack off shows and they had a porn star headliner each week. You would do five fifteen minute shows a day for one week. I noticed him when I was doing my show, but just thought he was some hot guy that had come to see me. After the show, he introduced himself to me and flirted with me pretty heavily, but for some reason I didn't think he was truly interested; I just thought he was being polite. He walked me back to my hotel room through the hot, smelly streets of the theater district in that city that was still overwhelming to me. He made small talk about the business. Maybe he could tell that I was a little scared being there, with my small-town naïveté, and everything happening so fast with my porn career, and he wanted to be a friend, to offer a shoulder to lean on. We did become friends, and occasionally saw each other both in New York and L.A.

One hot summer night I ran into Gino in L.A., out at a club. It was soon after I had moved in with Joey Stefano, but Joey was out of town, so I was out by myself. It was closing time, and I was becoming more sure of myself than when I had first met Gino. Back then I needed a friend, but that night I needed something else.

"So what are you doing now?" I asked Gino.

"Going home with you," he answered, much to my surprise and delight.

I hadn't really believed that he was interested in me in that way, but we ended up bringing another guy with us and we all fucked each other's brains out for hours. He is just as wild and nasty in real life as he is in videos. When he was sucking my cock it felt so great I wanted to close my eyes, but he looked so hot that I just couldn't. The other guy and I took turns fucking Gino. It was totally animal and primal and raw. We finally both came on his face. He gulped down all the cum from both of us, wiping it all over his lips, then flipped me over and stuck his dick up my ass. I wasn't expecting this, but instantly decided that it was a good thing. He fucked me, then threw the other guy down and fucked him, then came back to me again. Eventually he came and I came again. It was amazingly hot.

A couple of weeks later, someone (I think Ed Daru) hired me to be in a video and asked who I wanted to work with. I called Gino and asked if he wanted to do it. He said, "Sure." In the video the oral part went great but when it came time for the fucking, he just couldn't seem to get hard enough to fuck me. I didn't take it personally. Occasionally these things happen even to the best of us. In fact, I know it happened when Gino did a scene with Joey Stefano. I was still living with Joey at the time, and when I got home from the shoot I told him what happened and he told me about his scene with Gino. It was one of Joey's first scenes and it sort of threw him off when Gino couldn't get hard. I think the director (who was straight) was sort of bugging Gino. At least that's what he said. We decided that I would fuck him instead, and the rest of the scene went off without a hitch. We both came and went home. It was a lot of fun, whether I fucked him or he fucked me; what did it matter as long as we were fucking?

After that, but before I started directing, Gino hired me many, many times to be in *his* videos. He had perfect timing; he would always call right when I really needed the money for rent. I would be worrying about it and then the phone would ring, right on cue! His sets were always relaxed and the scenes invariably went quickly and smoothly. He was one of the few directors who took genuine interest in the well-being of his models, and always wanted to make sure that everyone was okay on the set.

Gino was also one of the few people who encouraged me to start directing, suggesting it to me before I had even thought of it. His confidence that I would be a great director helped me a lot, and I started directing soon afterward. He has helped a lot of actors to start directing, which is not something most other directors do, for fear of more competition. I don't see him a lot, but whenever I do he still leers at me in his inimitable, nasty way, and I still get butterflies. Wouldn't you?

LEE JENNINGS

In 1990, soon after I started appearing in videos, and long before I started directing, I was having dinner with Chi Chi, Joey Stefano and Tony Davis at Numbers, a restaurant and hustler bar and in L.A. Numbers had been around since the old days. The entrance was in the back parking lot, not in front on the street. Years ago, all the bars used to be like that, so that "innocent" people didn't wander in by mistake and discover a gay bar.

I had been working for only Chi Chi up until then, but I wanted to do more videos and work for more people. I didn't know if s/he would help me or if she would be upset. It wasn't that I didn't want to work for her anymore, I loved it. I just wanted to do more. As I later worked for nearly every other director, I must say that Chi Chi was and is my favorite. She always made me feel very sexy, and her sets were always fun. She got me work for almost every company that did gay videos.

As I nibbled my mushroom tortellini, I casually mentioned that I would like to do more videos and I realized that she couldn't put me in *every* video she did forever. She was really supportive, not at all upset. I was learning that Chi Chi really did care about the models, and not just about herself, as people might think. The standard stereotype of people in the porn business was just not the way things were.

I had a mini-tape recorder with me, the kind reporters (well good ones anyway) use when they are interviewing people. I carried it around all the time to help me remember things. I would just talk into it and use it as my notepad if I had an idea or something during the day that I wanted to remember. I didn't know yet that I had ADD, Attention Deficit Disorder. A few years later it was diagnosed. One of the tricks they teach people was to carry around a tape recorder or to write everything down. Anyway, I didn't know exactly why it really worked for me, but it did.

Of course Chi Chi couldn't let an opportunity to tease me go by, or an opportunity for even a glimmer of glory and glamour. She took the tape recorder from me and very dramatically cleared her throat and spoke into it. She said, "Call Lee Jennings, at Eros Casting." The way she did it was absolutely hysterical and we all cracked up. You would have thought she was announcing the Best Actor winner at the Oscars.

Lee was a porn star from videos like *Friendly Obsession* and *Private Workout*, who now, it turned out, was also working as an agent. Chi Chi said he could connect me with other directors and companies. I called him and made an appointment. I went to meet him and he wanted to take some pictures. I asked him to help me get hard and he was immediately on his knees sucking my dick.

After he took the pictures he asked me if I would like to get together with him again, to finish what we started. I said "Sure." He came over to my house and we started making out on the bed. In short order, I was fucking him; I couldn't hold back very long. I fucked him all over the bed and I remember specifically a position with him leaning back, knees practically beside his ears with his butt up in the air. I stood over him and pointed my dick down and plunged it into him. You see positions like that on porn films but you don't think people ever do them in real life. Well, we do once we've learned how much fun they are!

He was a total dick pig, he couldn't get enough and loved it more the harder I fucked him. Soon I was pulling my dick all the way out of his ass spitting down into his hole then shoving my dick back in. Sweat was running down my body and dripping onto him as I plunged in and out, ravaging his ass that he was holding up there so carefully for me. His eyes were wild, his teeth clenched.

"Harder, fuck me harder," he gasped, between plunges.

I rammed down into him harder. I felt a head rush, which signaled that I was close. At last, I pulled my dick out and shot all over his face and chest and into his mouth. He shot his load down into his mouth too, sucking all his cum down. I went down and kissed him, getting a mouthful of cum as well. Our faces smeared with sweat and semen, we stumbled out to the shower, laughing, as we passed Sharon Kane, with whom I was living at the time. Sharon and I had a very open relationship. She always wanted to know all the details of who I had screwed. I knew that as soon as Lee left, I would be having coffee with Sharon, reliving the whole hot scene again.

Lee and I got together several more times and it was always really hot. Sometimes I would go to his house, and sometimes he would come over to mine. I loved fucking his ass, and he loved getting fucked. He got me a lot of jobs, too. Hmmm...do you suppose there was a connection?

DALLAS TAYLOR

Dallas started in the business about the same time that I did, so it was practically inevitable that we would eventually do a scene together. It turned out to be for director Mark Fredrick's in a video whose name I can't recall; I just remember it was in the studio behind the house Mark had at the time in North Hollywood.

It was such an odd place, because although he only filmed gay porn, there were pictures all over of topless girls. In particular, I remember pictures of Samantha Fox. Mark had a reputation for talking straight guys into doing gay porn. I guess the girlie photos all over his studio were part of his method.

One of Mark's claims to fame was that he had "discovered" **left, with Frank Sterling**
Rex Chandler, by first talking him into doing nude photo shoots, then porn, then gay porn. Rex said he hated Mark for that, that Mark had promised him millions of dollars which, of course, never came.

Mark liked to begin filming by shooting the fucking scenes first, before the sucking or anything else, to make sure that the models were actually going to be hard for the fucking. Otherwise he would cancel the scene. This might be a good plan, the only problem was that many models, (like me) like to build up to fucking. You know, start with kissing and foreplay and let the excitement grow and progress. Many porn stars are simply mechanical, going through the motions of sex, but I almost always had a great time and had "real" sex. I mean, sex in front of the camera is never going to be as good—at least for me—as sex without a camera, without worrying about how I look, switching positions whenever I feel like it, rather than when a director wants me to, but I almost always truly enjoy myself. I don't need to fake an emotional or erotic state.

In this case, it felt very artificial to just stick my dick up Dallas' ass without any prelude. We did the scene and it probably looked okay on film but it was not an entirely enjoyable experience for me. I thought Dallas was hot, but it was just too weird.

We never did have any other scenes together, although he has been in many of my videos and I have fucked him as a stunt dick a couple of times. Those times were better than the first. He does have a hot ass, and I do love fucking it. Someday, I hope to do so without a camera!

CAL JAMMER

In 1990 Joey Stefano talked about Cal Jammer nonstop. He was obsessed. Chi Chi told me that Cal was a straight porn star. We started making a joke of it, since Joey would talk about him at inopportune times. Chi Chi and I had a routine that went something like this: Me: "I just found out my parents died and I'm trying to quit valium cold turkey, and my house burned down!" Chi Chi (playing the part of Joey): "Yeah, but I wanna fuck Cal Jammer!" The point we were making was overdramatized of course, but when Joey was in a Cal Jammer mood, he didn't hear much of anything else. One day Sharon said quietly,

"I'm going to set up Joey with Cal Jammer."

"What do you mean—" I asked, "isn't he straight?"

"Not entirely," she said.

Great, I thought. Now we'll never hear the end of it! Actually, as soon as Joey went to see him, he rarely mentioned it again. One day Joey told me that Cal had a big boner for me. He had seen pictures of me and he wanted to do me in drag. I told Joey I wasn't really into having sex in drag. Even though it was something that fascinated Joey, I had never been in drag when we fucked. I just couldn't. He said that Cal didn't care if I was in drag or not, he was into guys too, and thought I was hot. So off we went to go see Cal.

He was very sexy for a straight guy, or whatever he was. Soon, we were all naked and Cal was fucking me, then Joey, then me again, then Joey again. He would ram his big dick into my ass, pump a few times, then pull it out and stuff it up Joey's ass. Then he would come back to me. Joey was on top of me, kissing me, as Cal reamed both our asses. Joey was more into him than I was, but I was turned on that he was so turned on, and both of us getting fucked by the same guy felt really wild. I couldn't tell when Cal was going to shove his dick back up my ass. It took my breath away each time, and Joey loved watching me getting fucked. He didn't see that very often—usually I topped Joey.

Joey and I got on our knees and took turns sucking Cal's dick until he came, shooting all over our faces. We kissed and passed his cum back and forth in our mouths then swallowed it. I didn't see Cal again, but I think Joey did one more time. A couple of years later Cal shot himself. It was very upsetting; we never knew why. I always wondered if it was because he was gay or more likely bisexual, and couldn't deal with it.

MR. ED (EDDIE, TREVOR)

For the past fifteen years, Eddie has been known to many people in the porn industry as a makeup artist. He has also done some nude layouts in a few magazines and has been in a few videos of mine such as *For His Own Good*, and *The Dildo Voyeur*, using the names Eddie and Trevor. As a makeup artist, he always uses the name Mr. Ed.

I met Eddie in 1990 when I was living with Joey Stefano. Sharon Kane introduced us at a club called Sit and Spin. She had told me about him and was sort of setting us up. He was very handsome—he had beautiful long hair, and didn't look like every other West Hollywood clone. I asked him if he wanted to go on a date with me and he said, "Yes."

We went to a nightclub, then out for Indian food at a restaurant on La Brea. When we got back to my house, we were immediately all over each other. We made it to my bedroom, but not quite to the bed. We started kissing and pulling each other's clothes off and I fucked him on the floor. We just couldn't wait the extra two seconds it would have taken us to cross the room to the bed.

Eddie has a gorgeous body and a very big dick, but he's mostly a bottom. I certainly didn't mind. As I started fucking him, he began moaning loudly, something I learned he always does the whole time he is being fucked. He was soon screaming for me to pound his ass harder, so I did. I never would have thought he would be so wild when I first met him; he seemed so shy! He was definitely not shy now, as he screamed while I rammed my cock into his hole and pulled his hair. He started to come while I was fucking him. He shot all over his chest with that huge cock. I kept fucking him and he got louder and louder. I couldn't hold back anymore. I shot my load into his and fell over into the pool of cum on his stomach.

Lying next to him, I told him how he had surprised me. Eddie looked over at a picture I had beside my bed. He asked, "Who is that cute guy?" It was Allan Gassman, whom I had dated for about two days and then we became friends. Years later, Allan became my publicist for about two years. I gave Eddie this history, briefly, and Eddie asked if I would introduce him. Now that I think back on it, that was pretty bold, asking to be introduced to a guy I had dated while my cum was still all over him! Eddie and I went out (and fucked) a couple more times, and then just sort of became friends. A couple of weeks later, Eddie and I were at a club and Allan was there and as promised, I introduced them. They started dating, and then moved in together for about four years.

Years later, after he and Allan had broken up, Eddie called me to borrow something, a suit jacket I think. I was feeling horny and said, "I'll trade it to you for a blowjob." He was sort of shocked but said, "Okay!" He came over and we had wild, mad, romping sex all over the bed. It was friendly sex—that's the only way I can describe it. We didn't tell anyone (like Allan, for example) because we didn't want the rumor mill to start up. We also enjoyed sharing a secret and laughing about it without explaining to people why we were laughing. It was just a one time thing. At least we thought so. We fooled around a little at sex parties after that.

Years later, Eddie worked for me as one of my personal assistants. He was fabulous. I went away to Hawai'i one time and came back to find that he and one of my other assistants, Jo Anne, had completely reorganized my office, with new shelves and cabinets and everything you can imagine. I know it doesn't sound that exciting, but it was, terribly! Finally everything had a place, and I could find it! I don't know what I would have done without him.

Eddie isn't working for me anymore, except sometimes to do makeup on the set, but we are still really good friends so I guess it's okay to have sex with him again, isn't it?

ROD PHILLIPS

I had seen Rod in old classic Falcon videos like *Spokes*. When I was living with Joey Stefano in 1990, he was obsessed with Rod, and somehow, finally managed to track him down. He came over and we decided to have a three-way—very generous of Joey to share with me, don't you think?

After just a few minutes, Rod pulled out his huge cock and Joey and I looked at each other like it was an ice cream cone we were about to share. Joey got down on his knees and started sucking on it first, then passed it over to me. We both licked up and down the sides of it, then he sucked on it while I licked Rod's balls and stuck my tongue up his asshole. Then we got into a daisy chain, each with a dick in our mouths. I had Rod's massive cock down my throat while Joey sucked on mine and Rod sucked on his. This kept us all happy for quite a while.

Then Rod said he wanted to fuck both of us. I got on top of Joey, sort of piggy-back, so that Rod could get to both of our asses. He had to ease his cock into me slowly, but then I got used to it. All of a sudden he pulled it out and rammed it into Joey. Joey loved it. Rod kept on like this, going back and forth between the two of us, fucking each one for a few strokes, then pulling out and slamming his dick back into the other one.

After a while Joey started begging us to both fuck him. I expected his hole to be totally stretched out and loose from Rod's huge dick, but it wasn't. I slid my dick into him and he clamped his ass down around it. I started fucking his ass while Rod fucked his face, then we switched places, with my dick in his mouth and Rod's up his ass. We switched back and forth a few times then Rod told Joey to sit on both our dicks at once.

I had never done this before, but the idea alone almost made me come. Rod and I lay down on our backs with our heads away from each other and our dicks together. Joey first lowered himself onto one then came up off it and slid down on the other. At last, he slowly sat all the way down on both of our dicks at the same time. He started riding up and down on them and the feeling was incredible; being inside his ass and feeling Rod's dick rubbing against mine. All of a sudden, without missing a beat, Joey smiled, pointed to the window, and said "Look!"

It was night and we were on the floor of our living room that was huge and almost totally barren except for Joey's black fake leather couch, and matching fake leather chair. We didn't even have any pictures on the walls. We had giant windows, no curtains, and we were fucking facing Sierra Bonita street, where guys cruised all the time.

Three guys peered in the window at us, jacking off, and they were all really cute. There were two white guys, one blond and one brunette, and a Latin guy that I swear looked like a construction worker. It was like half the Village People. We all got so into the fact that these guys were watching us that we really started putting on a show (not that we weren't already). Soon we all started to come at the same time. Joey shot all over my chest, and Rod and I came up his ass all together. The guys in the window all shot all over the glass and then vanished. Joey didn't want us to take our dicks out, so Rod and I just lay there still inside him for a few minutes until we each finally slipped out with a plop. We all started laughing at the thought that the guys had probably been watching us for a long time before we noticed. We wondered if anyone else had walked past the house and Joey and I vowed to be more careful about sex in the living room in the future (although we weren't).

Joey started sort of seeing Rod after that. I would occasionally see the two of them as they were heading to Joey's room, but I knew Joey really liked Rod so I stayed out of the way. He really cared about him a lot, more than I ever personally saw him care about anyone else in that way, except for me. He was totally freaked out and depressed when Rod died. He tried to hide it but he couldn't. I know he loved him.

MATT GUNTHER

When I met Matt Gunther, I didn't know who he was and he didn't know who I was. It was early on in my porn career when I was living with Joey Stefano in 1990. We sort of met in a dark alley one night. I was wearing jeans and boots, looking as butch as I could manage. I had been lurking in the bars, looking for sex—something I've long since stopped doing, mostly because, like that night, it doesn't seem to work for me. It was late, the bars had just closed, and I was walking to my car, which was parked by the West Hollywood Park. I walked very slowly, still on the prowl. Matt just walked up and said,

"I need to get fucked, you wanna do it?" He grabbed my dick through my jeans and it started to get hard immediately. I could tell that he was going to be a lot of fun and was just what I had been hunting for. I grabbed his ass and he leaned up against the wall sticking his ass out. I stuck my hand down his pants and my finger up his ass. It was already all lubed up. He ground his ass back on my finger. We walked to my car with my finger still up his hole.

He got in my car and was sucking my dick almost immediately as I was driving home. I hadn't been drinking, but I almost wrecked the car twice. Then a police car pulled up next to us at a light on the corner of Santa Monica and La Cienega. I nearly freaked out, but after the light changed they drove away. They didn't notice Matt, still sucking on my hard cock.

We pulled the car behind the house, parked, and he got out. He got down on his knees and said "Piss on me." I looked around, praying that no neighbors were awake looking out of their windows. I had never done this before, but here was a hot guy groveling at my feet begging me to piss on him. I had to get my hard dick to go down a little before I could do it. I sprayed all over his chest and then he wrapped his mouth around my dick and drank the last of it. As he gulped down my piss and it ran out of the sides of his mouth, my dick got completely hard again. Then we went inside.

Since he seemed to be into it, we got into a bit of a master/slave thing. I slapped him around and ordered him to suck my cock. Then I told him to turn around and show me his ass. I made him spread his hole by sticking his fingers into it and stretching it open for me, then made him beg me to fuck him before I would. I asked him if he really wanted it, bad enough to let me slam into his hole and rape it. He growled, "Yes." I made him shove the edge of the sheet up his ass first, just the corner, to dry up any lube before I shoved my cock in. I was really into it all by now and I wanted to hurt him. I wanted him to always remember the moment my dick went in his ass, and I made it mine.

When I finally slammed my dick into him hard, he screamed so loud I thought Joey might wake up, but he didn't; he could sleep through anything. Matt kept begging me to fuck him harder and call him my "pussy boy". I fucked him in every position we could think of, then he said, "I want your fist up my ass."

I had only fisted someone once before, at that time, Matt Powers, but I had loved it. I pulled my cock out and lubed up my hand. I put in first one finger, then two. I made him beg for each finger before I would give it to him. He finally reached around and grabbed my hand and pulled it into his ass. I started moving my hand inside him slowly, and soon I was inside him up to my elbow.

"Punch fuck me," he said. I started fist fucking him really hard, sometimes pulling all the way out, then shoving my hand back in. He was like a wild animal. We looked into each others eyes and started to come. We both shot all over him. I pulled my hand out. He jumped up, put on his clothes and practically ran out of the house without so much as a "thank you". I realized I didn't know his name and he didn't know mine. All he had called me was "Sir."

A couple of weeks later, Chi Chi LaRue rented our house to shoot a video. I had left for the morning, but when I came back, I walked into a scene-in-progress. As I sat down quietly beside Chi Chi, I realized that the guy getting fucked was the guy that had come home with me two weeks ago. During a break in the scene, Chi Chi introduced us.

"Matt, this is Karen Dior." A look of horror came over his face. He said hello, but his look was pleading with me not to tell any one that he had let a drag queen (although not in drag at the time) dominate, fist-fuck, and piss on him. I just said,

"Hi, nice to meet you." Chi Chi later whispered to me,

"He's a big drag queen too, he calls himself 'Claudette.'" It was all I could do to not say anything, but I never did, not until now. We sort of ended up in the same circle of friends later and were around each other a lot. While he was often evil and hostile to lots of people, (he had quite a reputation in the porn industry and around West Hollywood), he was especially hostile to me. Sharon Kane used to say she could never figure out why.

Hey Sharon, now you know!

MICHAEL MOORE

Michael Moore is incredibly sexy, and I wanted him the moment I saw him. I met him when I was living with Joey Stefano in 1990. He was just starting to do videos and was always talking about how much he loved to get fucked by dildos. He was just brimming with sex. It oozed out of him. I was beside myself. He always flirted with me, but it didn't seem to have any intention behind it; rather, flirting was a way of life for him.

One day, he invited Joey and me to go to San Francisco with him for a few days. He had a slightly older "friend" whom he apparently saw on a regular basis, who was going to pay for everything. We agreed, and were off.

We arrived at a fabulous, expensive hotel. I was anxious to get out to see the city, but we never made it out of the room in three days. Michael's sugar daddy, (Oops! I mean "friend") was into taking Xanax so he was asleep most of the time, so we helped ourselves to the honor bar and to the dildos that he had brought.

Finally, the moment I had waited for: Michael walked up to me, turned around with his ass in my face and pulled his pants down. He was wearing white underwear and was just waving his ass around. He slowly started to pull the underwear down as he bent over. I stuck out my tongue and licked his asshole. He actually squealed and pushed back on my tongue. I shoved it as far up his sweet ass as I could. It was squeaky clean. Joey handed me a lubed up dildo and said, "Stick it up his ass." So I did. I slid it in slowly, all the way. Then I pulled it out and pushed it back in again going faster and faster. Joey kept handing me bigger and bigger ones, until I was fucking Michael with a pretty huge dildo while Joey was sucking my dick. We all started to come at the same time. Joey sucked the cum out of my dick, then licked up Michael's and his own. That always drove me crazy; my dick wouldn't even go down, it just stayed hard when he did that. This one experience alone would have been enough, but it was only the beginning of several days of wild sex.

I spent hours fucking Michael and Joey with my dick and with dildos. We would fuck and fuck and fuck, then order room service and fuck again. I was high on sex and food. Joey and Michael were doing ecstasy, but I didn't need any, not with these two hot guys, one that had been my occasional lover for some time and the other that I had wanted so badly. I was high enough just on the sex.

A couple of times, we all got into the big jacuzzi bathtub together. Occasionally the sugar daddy would get up, stagger in to say "Hi" to us, then take some more Xanax and go to sleep again. I didn't understand...I mean, if I were paying for a room that was full of cute sex-crazed boys, I wouldn't be sleeping, but I guess this was his idea of fun.

We really were pretty cute; we were like little boys playing, only with slightly different toys. I loved watching a dildo slide in and out of Michael's beautiful asshole, and of course, as always, Joey's too. At one point they pulled out a huge double-headed dildo, and both plugged into it, bouncing their butts together, each trying to get more in. I wouldn't have minded getting fucked myself, but with perhaps the world's two biggest bottoms, it was obviously not going to happen.

Michael's friend eventually woke up, just as it was about time for us to go back to L.A. He was actually kind of cute, but he didn't seem to want to really get involved. He just enjoyed watching all of us, at least the few times that he was awake. He drove us to the airport and we returned to L.A.

After that trip, Michael did a few more videos and vanished. I haven't seen him or heard from him in years. He seems to have gone into that vast porn black hole where stars are almost never seen again, although sometimes, when you least expect it, they will come out of the woodwork. I hope Michael resurfaces. He was always really sweet, and I would love to see him and that cute ass again.

CHAD KNIGHT

I had seen Chad in a lot of videos, but my favorite was *Compulsion*. I had jacked off watching his ass get pounded over and over again. When Chi Chi LaRue cast me in the movie *Steel Garters* in 1990, she asked who I wanted to do my scene with.

"Catalina said you can have anyone," she said.

"Anyone? Really?" I asked.

"Well, anyone in this country."

"I want Chad Knight," I said. It was an instant choice.

"Perfect," Chi Chi said, "He's bisexual and he'll love you. Do you want to be bottom or top?"

"Both," I answered, "definitely both."

Then Chi Chi told me that Chad has a wife and two kids. A real live bisexual. We're always so much more fun, if you ask me! I was going to be in drag, so it was good that he was bi. He wouldn't be put off by the drag like most gay men, and he wouldn't be put off by my dick like most straight men.

The shoot was at my friend Paul Pelletieri's studio. A lot of the videos filmed in those few years were shot at Paul's. He had an enormous jacuzzi (seen in *Sharon and Karen*), a big steam room, a movie theater-sized projection TV system, on which we would watch movies and my early television appearances, a firefighter's pole from the second floor down to the first, and a huge shower. It was a magical place.

On the set, Chad didn't say much. He was incredibly shy, and so cute. I couldn't wait to get my dick in him, and his in me. This was going to be so much fun!

In the scene he was supposed to think that I was a girl. I

gave him a blowjob first then he pried my legs apart and my hard dick popped up.

"You're a guy!" he said.

"Nobody's perfect," I said, then persuaded him to suck my dick.

He was a great cocksucker. He worked up and down my shaft, worshipping my dick like he really loved it. He licked my balls and his tongue snaked back to flicker at my asshole. I squirmed around on it, letting him in deeper, as the cameraman got right under us to get a better shot of his tongue and my hole.

Some directors don't shoot a lot of footage, but Chi Chi usually does. When we got to the fucking, Chad fucked me for about an hour. He's usually a bottom in videos, but boy, can he fuck. I was loving every second of it as he plowed my ass on top of the clear plastic table. Again, the camera man moved under us, shooting up through the table to see Chad's cock plunging into my wet asshole. My dick was hard the whole time.

Then came the moment (or hour really) that I had been waiting for. It was time for me to fuck him. I loosened his ass up with a couple of fingers first, then started fucking him. As soon as I started, Chi Chi had an idea.

"Grab your wig and throw it off!"

I did, and it is pretty funny in the scene. It's like when I turn into a top the dude in me comes out and the wig comes off. Chad screams when he's getting fucked as if it's hurting but also as if he still loves it. I mean, he was screaming, but the words he was screaming were, "Fuck me, harder!" So I did.

I was pounding his ass as hard as I could, pulling my cock all the way out and shoving it back in. I kept watching his hole as I took it. It would sort of stay open and grab for my cock until I shoved it back in. I fucked him for at least an hour and could have gone on forever, but finally it was time for the cum shot. I sucked him off and we both came.

After the scene he was all shy again, which was really cute and charming. Usually people aren't so shy after three hours of sex. We both took a shower together in the huge bathroom of Paul's studio, then we got our checks, put on our clothes and left. I haven't seen Chad since except in videos. I have to have him in one of mine and see if he remembers me. And of course ask him,

"So...how's the wife and kids?"

DAVID ANGEL

I met David at a club called Arena years ago when I was living with Joey Stefano. By then Joey and I weren't lovers anymore, but we were still living together. It was just before he moved to New York near the end of Fall in 1990.

David was big and muscular and gorgeous with long hair and he was talking to Chi Chi LaRue. I sort of went up and stole him away from her. She was very annoyed, but eventually forgave me.

David and I talked for a while and somehow we ended up back at my house with Sharon Kane and Aaron Scott. We all started having sex on my bed. Aaron fucked David first, while David sucked my dick, and I licked Sharon's pussy. Then I went around and started licking and fingering his ass. He had the biggest muscle ass I had ever seen in my life. Something about a guy's ass already being lubed up from just being fucked by someone else always turns me on. I love a guy that's such a slut that he'll let everyone in the group fuck him, and David was definitely that kind of slut, I could already tell.

My dick throbbed in anticipation, bouncing up and down, and thickening even more as I fingered his wet slut hole roughly, twisting several fingers around inside it. I pushed my rod up inside him, feeling it go all the way in to the base in one thrust. David moaned in pleasure as I started fucking him while he lapped at Sharon's pussy and she sucked down Aaron's dick. Then Aaron fucked Sharon while I continued my rampage on David's bubble butt.

David rode my cock for a long time, as Aaron and Sharon watched, then Aaron got under him and slid his dick up that cavernous ass next to mine. Now we both were inside, stretching David's interior and feeling each other's dicks rub against our own. Sharon was so turned on by watching that she came, then one by one so did Aaron, David, and finally me. It was a very full evening.

I didn't expect to see David again, but he called me the next day wanting to get together. He lived in Riverside, and I drove all the way out there to see him. We started making out in his living room, then suddenly his doorbell rang. It was a friend of his, a girl name Regina. She apparently didn't know of his interest in men. They were talking forever and I went in and fell asleep on his bed.

Soon I was awakened by him sucking my dick, and almost before I knew it, I was shooting a hot load of jizz down his throat.

Very soon he moved into the house with Joey and I. We had three bedrooms, so David had his own, but sometimes he would sleep with me. By then he had started doing gay and transsexual videos for Chi Chi and for other companies.

David was completely bisexual, and so was I. We would get all dressed up in rock-and-roll leather and spandex and go out to straight clubs like *The Rainbow* . One night I got dressed up in drag and we went out to a straight club. We met two girls and told them that I was a guy. They thought it was great and were really into both of us. We were all dancing on the dance floor I was all over one of the girls. All of the other guys in the club were watching, totally turned on because they thought we were two wild girls together. We were kissing and grabbing each others tits (mine weren't real of course, but no one else knew that). All of the other girls were furious because all the guys were watching us.

Before a riot broke out we decided to all leave. We took the girls home with us and had a big four-way orgy. I woke up in the morning pretty hung over and with makeup still smeared all over my face. Not exactly a pretty sight. We didn't tell the girls that we were boyfriends until the morning either. They were a wee bit surprised, but then, one of them had just spent the night in bed with a drag queen, so they took it all in stride. They got into it as soon as they thought about it for a couple of minutes.

David was uncomfortable about being bi, and that soon turned into a problem. I was invited to his family's house for Christmas as his "friend." On Christmas eve, his dad almost caught us fucking under the tree.

Joey had long since moved out, and after a couple of other short-lived roommates, one of David's ex-girlfriends moved into the house with us. She didn't know about our relationship, and she wanted him back. One night, he was watching TV with her in the other bedroom. He kept making excuses to come into my room, and he would sit on my dick and bounce up and down on it until he was afraid that she would come looking for him, then he would pull up his underwear and run back into the room with her and then come back and do it all over again. The fact that she didn't know what was going on turned both of us on, but it also started to bother me. I had been living my life completely openly for a long time and I just couldn't have a boyfriend that wouldn't acknowledge me.

By then David had persuaded his ex and now again current girlfriend to do straight porn with him. She became Traci Wynn. She is on the cover of the bisexual video *Steel Garters* in which I have a scene with Chad Knight. Finally, I couldn't go on with the deception. I decided that I had to move out of the house and I moved down the street into Sharon Kane's house. I know David and Traci both stayed in the straight porn industry for a while, but I haven't heard from or about either of them for years.

BILL HUNTER

Before Bill Hunter became a director, he starred in videos such as *A Big Business* and *Size Counts*. I hadn't seen any of them, though. I met him when I was performing in videos, but before I was directing. Someone referred me to him in 1991 to be in one of his videos. I went to his apartment to meet him. He interviewed me and then asked me to get hard to take a Polaroid picture (See it is standard practice!). I was attracted to him and said that I might need help, even though I knew I was already hard in my jeans. He agreed.

I took off my pants and he started sucking my dick, without commenting that it was already hard. He took me all the way to the back of his throat and choked on my dick. He kept going though, sucking up and down with spit dripping out of his mouth. I grabbed the nape of his neck and fucked his face. I rammed my cock down his throat in and out, using it like a pussy that was just there to serve me.

Once again I was loving the feeling of putting out for a nasty porn director. He was a hot guy and I would definitely have done him anyway, but the situation made it even hotter, more delicious since it was taboo, fucking around with a potential boss. Pretty soon I was sucking his very large dick. I was on my knees down between his legs struggling to do as good a job on his horse cock as he had done on mine. It was, after all, an audition, was it not? I wanted to do my best to demonstrate my skill. I gagged but kept going, tears welling up in my eyes as I worshipped his dick the way it deserved to be worshipped. My throat was getting raw from the stretch, but I stayed with it, taking his dick all the way to the base each time.

Then he was fucking me. I remember looking out the window of his apartment that overlooked all of Hollywood while he was plowing my ass with his huge dick and thinking, "Hmmm, why would anyone complain about a casting couch?" I was loving it. He just kept slamming in and out of me until I was screaming.

"Slam it into my ass. I can take it."

He smiled and pounded harder, fucking me. Now I was the pussy-boy just there to service him. That was fine by me. Always glad to please. His hips thrust against my ass cheeks and he worked his cock around in circles, stretching my hole wider still. It felt incredible. He really knew how to fuck. Finally, I started to cum. Bill kept slamming into my hole as I shot all the way onto the window overlooking the city. He fucked me for a minute or two more, just to let me know he could and to remind me to take it no matter what. Then he shot all over my face. I felt his hot cum hit my cheeks and lips and drip off my chin. So hot! Bill immediately got all shy and embarrassed and told me that he didn't usually do this and that he was really sorry. I told him not to be, I hadn't done anything that I didn't want to do.

He said he would put me in his next movie, and would I like to go out with him? I said yes, he turned me on. I remember we went to see a foreign art film that neither of us liked. Then we went back to my place and fucked. We went out a couple of times after that and then I sort of lost interest and so, I think, did he.

When the time came for the video, he put me in a scene with Christopher Robbin, a beautiful blond boy that I loved fucking. Bill told me that Christopher used to be his boyfriend but they had broken up. However, soon after that video, they got back together.

The scene was shot outside, at the house where they used to shoot *Eight Is Enough*. Even though a lot of porn videos were shot there, I felt a little odd, but soon Christopher was sucking my dick and taking it up his ass like a pro and Bill seemed to really enjoy watching us. I was turned on even more when I saw Bill's huge dick snaking down his pants as he filmed us; he crawled under us to get close shots of my dick splitting Christopher's hot ass wide open for all the world to see.

Bill put me in a couple more of his videos and we remained friends. We would often see each other out at clubs. One night I went to a club that was popular at the time called Trade, on the Sunset Strip. Trade was historic in a few ways. In its few months of being open it was the first place that my band, The Johnny Depp Clones, performed, as well as the first L.A. performance venue for drag queen Jackie Beat, who would later move to New York and carve out her own little niche there. It was the first bar in L.A. to have go-go boy dancers. Not strippers, just go-go dancers. For a while everyone who was anyone in the gay and gay-friendly scene went to *Trade*. Porn celebrities like Joey Stefano, Matt Gunther, Sharon Kane, Chris Green, Chi Chi LaRue, designer Michael Schmidt, singers like Debbie Harry and Boy George, L.A. scenesters Christian Farrow, J.V. McAuley, April LaRue, and actors such as

Alexis Arquette, and even Harry Dean. Gail Brooks, (who years later became a director and put me in her MAC cosmetics TV commercial) was a cocktail waitress there.

Anyway, I was feeling particularly frisky that night and as I skipped into the club I saw Bill. I went over to him and said,

"I want you to fuck me."

"Now?" he asked.

"Yes," I said, and pulled him into the bathroom.

I was sitting on his dick in about fifteen seconds. I just sat right down on it with no lube and very little spit. It hurt like hell and I loved it. He was sitting on the toilet seat and I was bouncing up and down on him. Getting my insides scraped out by his monster cock. I was totally getting off on knowing that not only could someone walk in and catch us, but that his boyfriend was innocently waiting for him at the bar. (Nowadays, I would never fuck anyone's lover unless I knew it was okay with them, but I was less scrupulous then.) We finished and went back out as if nothing had happened. Well, except for me running up to Joey and Sharon and squealing "I just got fucked in the bathroom!" They demanded to know by whom but I wouldn't tell them and it drove them crazy.

One time after I was directing videos, Bill came over to my house to look at a picture of one of my models that he wanted to hire. Bill had done the camera work on one of my first directing jobs, and I didn't realize that there was any heat between us anymore, but before either of us knew it, his pants were around his ankles and his legs were in the air with me pounding his ass. After we both came, he said, "Um, we don't need to mention this to my boyfriend." I agreed. They eventually broke up (no it wasn't my fault), and later that year, Bill died. He was a sweet, kind person who was respected and liked by everyone I know in the porn business. He will be remembered and missed by many people for a long time.

PIERCE DANIELS

I met Pierce years ago, before I had begun directing videos. I think it was the end of 1991 or the beginning of 1992. We met in a bar and he came home with me. We both knew that the other did videos, but I don't think either of us had seen any of the other's. He was sweet and gentle and masculine and rough, all at the same time. He was a big hairy butch guy that just made you want to throw your legs up in the air, which I eventually did.

His dick was big, so he spit on my hole first, and loosened me up with his fingers. I squirmed around with his big fingers in me and couldn't believe they felt as good as they did. He massaged my rectum, rubbing his fingers up and down the walls, driving me crazy. Then he slid his cock all the way up my ass and started fucking me. It was heaven. He pounded my ass, and pounded my ass, stuffing his cock up it like it wasn't going to fit if he didn't force it. It probably wouldn't have, it was so big. I was moaning and writhing around and acting like it hurt, but I was lifting my ass up, thrusting back onto him, so the pleasure must have outweighed the pain. He fucked and fucked, using my ass for his pleasure, taking me just the way he wanted me, moving me so that his cock felt the best for him. I loved feeling like my ass was just there for him to use as he wanted. It turned me on more than if he'd demonstrated that he was just as concerned about my pleasure as his, which he really was. His concern became obvious when he leaned over to kiss me, even though he shoved his tongue in my mouth and nearly down my throat, taking it like he was taking my ass.

It seemed to go on forever, but that still wasn't long enough. If he were still fucking me now, I don't think it would have been long enough. It's not like you can be in ecstasy *too* long! I was moaning and screaming and kissing him and feeling everything in the world all at the same time. Finally, he pulled his cock out to come. It seemed like he took forever to slide out of me. My hole felt empty and abandoned and hungry once he was out of it. He shot one of the biggest loads I have ever seen—all over me. I was completely drenched in his come. The he stuck two fingers back up my ass and finger-fucked me until I came.

We got together once or twice after that, then we sort of just turned into friends. I would always hang out with him at parties and events when neither of us really wanted to be there. We made it bearable for one another. Better than bearable, we always had fun while everyone else played their "Hollywood" games. He was a very sweet, very sexy, hot man. Many people were deeply affected when he died a few years ago. He will always be remembered and missed by his friends and fans.

CHRIS GREEN

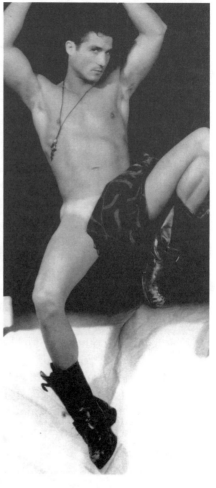

I met Chris in the middle of the street one night after the bars closed. I was with Chi Chi LaRue and we were going to a party at someone's house on King's Road. Chris came up to us and asked Chi Chi where the party was. She introduced us. I'm not sure where or when they had met, I think it was at a club that night, but I remember her saying, "Stop me now, I'm doing it again, I can tell." She meant falling for someone. Over the next few years she had a thing for Chris. I hadn't seen her like this with anyone since Joey Stefano.

We started hanging out with Chris and pretty soon he asked me, Chi Chi and another drag queen named Gender, to be backup singers in a band with him. We basically said, "Um...we're famous and you're not. We'll sing with you, but we won't be your backup singers. We'll all be equal." He agreed. He wanted to call the band *The Johnny Depp Clones*. We hated the name and insisted on changing it. Chris agreed, then turned right around and did interviews and got us a lot of press as *The Johnny Depp Clones*, referring to himself as the lead singer. We all were furious, but Chi Chi was in love with Chris so she wouldn't say much, and Gender didn't have much clout, so I assumed the position of Bitch of the Band.

I told Chris that what he had done was really underhanded and manipulative. Now we might be stuck with the name, the *Johnny Depp Clones*, but we were not his backup singers and I said if I heard him refer to us in that way again, I would quit . He usually didn't after that, but sometimes he would. Also, after a couple of years, Gender was picking fights with everybody and it just stopped being fun. I was about ready to quit anyway, and then I was pushed over the edge. After I had warned him again, Chris did it. He referred to us as "the backup singers" in front of me. I said, "I quit!" and I did. A few years later after they had kicked Gender out and replaced her with Bradley Pickleshiemer, they all asked me to come back to make an album. Chris promised that it would be different. I cautiously said yes, and the band has been fun. Our album *Better Late than Never* has done really well for an independent label. Chi Chi and I are both so busy and are so often out of town that we only get together to play about once a year, but whenever we do we always pack the house. People seem to love us.

Over the years Chris and I have hung out together, traveled together, and gotten drunk together. Despite the drama from the band we have always been pretty good friends. Chris is certainly very sexy. There have been a few times when we have had a few drinks and hung all over each other, groping each other and making out. We've never really had sex though. I think it would drive Chi Chi crazy and wouldn't really be appropriate. More than once we have had our tongues down each other's throats and hands in each other's pants and we'll look at each other and go, "We have to stop!" We both know that keeping everyone friends is more important than a quick fuck, no matter how much fun it might be.

Chris is a good friend. I don't see him very often, but when I was in the hospital for three months straight, he and his boyfriend Sal came to see me regularly. They were there more than anyone except my boyfriend, Babaji, who stayed almost every night. It's times like that when I know we are real friends, no matter what.

The appropriateness or lack thereof didn't really stop my ex, Sharon, from getting involved with Chris at one point. I think Chris probably did it partly to drive Chi Chi crazy, and it worked. She was furious for a while. Then Chris decided he didn't want to fool around with Sharon anymore, so she ran off with his ex-boyfriend to Las Vegas to get married, just to get even with him. Soon after that the ex-boyfriend decided that he was gay after all and they quickly got divorced. High drama, all of it. I try to stay just on the fringes of that group now. As dramatic as my life may seem at times, it looks like a Hallmark card in comparison to theirs!

CHIP DANIELS

I lusted after Chip Daniels in his Falcon videos. His scene in *Overload* with Ray Butler and Marc Saber is one of the hottest, nastiest scenes I have ever watched; one of my all-time favorites. At the beginning, Ray and Marc are slapping and fingering Chip's ass and then they all end up fucking each other. Hard. Lots of nasty cocksucking and butthole licking and in the end (no pun intended), Chip and Marc play with Ray's ass and Marc ends up fisting him.

When I saw Chip in this video, that did it. I had fallen deeply in lust. I finally met him in Palm Springs at the Mirage Hotel, while he was there filming *Mirage,* with Chi Chi LaRue. When I walked out of my room toward the pool, I was amazed to see him right there. I hadn't known that Chi Chi was going to be filming there that weekend, and I was just there on vacation. Chip looked at me like a hungry dog checking out a piece of meat. I couldn't figure it out. Sexy porn stars were swarming all over the place. Why would he want me? I knew who he was, but I didn't think he knew who I was. Too, I didn't think I looked good enough to inspire that kind of lust. Chi Chi introduced us,

"Chip, this is Rick Van." Chip said,

"I know who you are, I've been wanting to meet you. Why don't we go back to my room?" I gladly followed him with Chi Chi screaming after Chip,

"Don't you dare do anything, you haven't done your scene yet!"

By the time we made it to the door to his room, my dick was

hard and I was having a hard time keeping it inside my bathing suit. I didn't have to worry long. As soon as we were in his room, Chip pulled my dick out and sucked it all the way down to the base. He peeled off my swimsuit and licked my balls, then stuck his tongue up my ass. He was just as nasty and sexy as he was in the videos. People were walking by looking in his windows at me sitting on Chip's face, grinding my ass down on his tongue. A few stopped, their eyes widening. At one point, he took my whole cock down his throat and got my balls in his mouth at the same time. He was a wild man out of control, or maybe he was the one in control, I'm not really sure.

After a while he laid back on the bed with his ass up in the air. I started tonguing his hole, licking his balls, and sucking his cock. Pretty soon I was finger-fucking his asshole with three fingers while sucking his dick. He liked it rough, so I rammed my fingers in and out, twisting them around, abusing that hot hole that I had jerked off to, watching other guys abuse so many times. Finally I couldn't stand it any more. I had to be inside him. I stood up and shoved my dick all the way up his ass. He bucked down on it and said "Fuck me!" So I did. I fucked him long and hard, deep and fast. We were like crazed animals, it was so frenzied.

I would pull all the way out and look at his beautiful ass, wide open, waiting for me to shove myself back up inside. It stayed open like a hungry mouth, and that totally turned me on. I love the sight of a gaping hole. I crammed my dick back in and then I stuck a finger up his ass beside my dick He asked for more, so I stuck in two fingers, then three. He seemed like he could take anything. Finally I was about to come. I pulled out of his asshole and he went down on his knees again and stuck his tongue up my ass, while I shot all over the room. He didn't come. I asked him if he wanted to, and he said he couldn't, he had to save it for his scene.

What a good porn star!

We agreed to get together later that weekend after his scene, but it didn't happen. I was occupied with Dean Johnson, (see that chapter,) and I'm sure Chip managed to find a way to amuse himself— he could persuade anyone of nearly anything.

As the years have gone by we have become casual friends. He is now directing videos and co-owns his own video company,

Centaur. The videos he directs are as hot as he is. He is one of the few models-turned-directors that I think makes really good videos. We don't get to see each other very often, mostly at awards shows and at each other's birthday parties, but he always gives me a friendly grope and smiles at me like I'm one of the sexiest men alive. That is exactly what makes him one.

DEAN JOHNSON

    Dean was another guy that I had seen in Falcon videos. I happened to be in Palm Springs staying at the Mirage Hotel when Dean was there shooting the video, *Mirage,* for Chi Chi LaRue. It was a bit odd that I didn't know they would be there, since Chi Chi and I are good friends, and each of us usually has a general idea of what the other is doing. She joked that I was stalking her.

The night after Dean had done his scene, he and I and another tasty guy who was staying at the hotel were sitting in the hot tub. It was late at night and the air was heavy with the summer heat and sexual tension. Often after doing a scene I would feel horny, rather than satisfied. Dean was horny and he said so. He was grabbing my dick under the water and eventually lifted me up on the side of the hot tub to suck on it. The smell of the desert, the tropical plants and the chlorine from the hot tub combined into an intoxicating odor. The other guy joined in and soon they both were licking and sucking my cock, passing it back and forth. I said, "Let's go back to a room." We all agreed and then discovered that we all were sharing rooms with people and had no place to go.

We decided that this did not have to be a problem, and moved a little so we were behind some bushes and kept going. Dean started sucking the other guy's dick and I started licking his ass. I spread it with my hands and stuck my tongue as far up it as I could. He tasted delicious and he was loving my tongue up his ass. I started sticking my fingers up his ass, something I had wanted to do since I had first seen him on video. Pretty soon I almost had my whole hand up his ass, shoving my fingers in and out while he begged for more. The other guy reached around and stuck a couple of fingers in too and we both stretched his asshole open as I spit in it.

I really wanted to fuck him now. Luckily I had planned ahead and had brought condoms with me to the jacuzzi "just in case." I put one on and stuck my dick in his already stretched out ass. He thrust back to meet me. I started fucking his butt while the guy was fucking his face. I was pounding him harder and harder and he still wanted more. All of a sudden he started to come, I kept fucking him while he came then pulled out and shot all over his ass as the other guy shot his load all over Dean's face. We all got ourselves back together and after sitting in the jacuzzi for a little longer, went back to our own rooms. I saw Dean the next day as I was leaving and said good-bye; I haven't seen him since. I know he lives in San Francisco, so maybe I'll try to look him up the next time I am there. I wouldn't mind sharing him with another hot guy once again.

ERIC MANCHESTER

I met Eric several years ago. I've tried so desperately to remember exactly when, but I just can't. I know it was between 1991 and 1996, because I brought him home and I do at least know where I lived during those years, but our encounter was so intense I can't even remember if I was dating someone else at the time or was totally single.

It was a chance meeting, during the day on the street in West Hollywood, just blocks from my apartment. Within twenty minutes he was in my apartment ripping my clothes off. I knew who he was and he said he had seen a couple of my films and had wanted to fuck me ever since. I was happy to oblige. We sucked each other's dicks first (always the polite thing to do) but then quickly got into fucking. He didn't even have his pants off and neither did I, he just bent me over the back of my couch, shoved his dick in my ass and started fucking me. Hard. It was good. He knew exactly what he was doing and exactly every spot to hit in me with his dick. It wasn't very personal or lovey-dovey, just two guys fucking, which can sometimes be pretty great. This time it was.

We were both sweating and he was fucking me so hard it hurt but I still loved it. I started to come really quickly, and shot all over the back of the couch—the one that Chi Chi had given me. "Oh well, one more cum stain," I thought.

He kept fucking me and now it really was hurting, but I was still loving it. When getting fucked hurts so much, I just want to see how long I can take it. He was calling me his cocksucker and his pussy boy and grabbing my hair and pulling my head back so far my neck hurt and still, I wanted more.

He started slapping my ass—smacking it really hard. He

was wrenching my guts out with his cock, all the lube was gone by now and he was really hurting me, but I still hoped he would never stop. I felt like I was being pulled inside out with each thrust. Pretty soon my dick was hard again and I was so glad he was still fucking me, so glad I hadn't stopped him. I went past the pain and right into ecstasy, so high I couldn't believe I wasn't on drugs. Finally he came. He didn't fall down on top of me or lean over to kiss me or anything, he just pulled his cock out of my quivering hole, pulled up his pants and left. He took my number and said he would call me, but he didn't.

Isn't that just like a man?

CODY JAMES

Cody James was the hottest new star for a while at the end of 1991. Every one wanted him in their movies. He was a lithe, sinewy blond with a cute face and a huge dick. One of the longest I've ever seen. And by now, I've seen a lot.

Before I met Cody my friend Paul Pelletieri called me one day.

"Do you know who Cody James is?" Paul asked.

"No," I answered.

"Well, he's a new porn star. He's got a huge dick and a huge crush on you," he said, pausing for my response.

I was fascinated. Both of those things intrigued me. A porn star with a big dick, and a crush on *me*. It seemed that Cody had seen a picture Paul had taken of me on the wall at Paul's studio. Paul showed me pictures of Cody later. He *was* cute. He had odd eyes and gorgeous, perfectly shaped full lips. And a sweet little nose. And then there was the horse cock that looked like it had just been pasted on him; it was so big it just didn't seem possible that it was actually attached to him.

I saw Cody in person for the first time at a sex party at Paul's. I walked in after it had already started. There were a bunch of guys all around Cody and his dick. He saw me and walked away from the others over to me. As he got close, I dropped to my knees and started sucking on his dick. He gasped in surprise and all the other guys looked at me with envy. I sucked his dick all the way down. It was long, but not too wide to get down my throat. Soon, the other guys were crowding around us. We wanted to be alone. Paul let us go upstairs to his bedroom.

Cody slid his dick up my ass. It seemed to go in forever sliding and sliding, disappearing up my ass as I watched it in the mirror. It was fascinating. And God, did it feel good! He pulled it back out then slid it in some more.

"God, keep going slow, just like that!" I begged.

He did and my eyes rolled back in my head from pleasure. I couldn't watch the mirror anymore. I couldn't do anything except lie there and take his dick up my ass. He fucked me really slowly for a long time, then finally started going harder and faster. I was screaming and clawing at his back and telling him to fuck me harder.

We didn't realize it until later, but a lot of the guys were watching us. They just couldn't stay away once they heard all the noise.

All of a sudden the earth was moving. I thought it was an actual quake, but it turned out to be the bed breaking. We continued fucking at an angle, with me grabbing onto the side that was still intact. Finally we both came, shooting all over Paul's bed. We went to take a shower together and he fucked me again in the shower. This time we knew that we were being watched, but we didn't care.

The next week we were the hot item of gossip, in the columns and all over the porn industry. You would think two porn stars had never fucked before! It was partially because everyone had thought that Cody was straight until then. Allegedly, he had a girlfriend and only fooled around with guys in videos, although everyone had been trying hard. According to the rumors, he had been "gay for pay" until our liaison. I heard later that he said he had come to the party to meet me.

Cody had a friend that lived in my apartment building. He called me one day from his friend's apartment.

"Why don't you come down and fuck me," I said over the phone.

He was knocking on my door almost before I could hang up the receiver. I was already naked so I answered the door that way. He just looked at me and said, "Oh God." He started sucking my dick right there with the door standing open. We finally made it in to my bed and he fucked me again, just as good as the first time.

Later in an interview that he did with Dave Kinnick, he talked about me and it was so sweet. Dave asked him,

"What is good sex to you?"

He replied, "Good sex is [Geoffrey] Karen Dior."

We got together a few more times, then we just sort of lost track of each other. I saw him again a year later in Las Vegas at the Adult Video News Awards, but not since then. He seems to have vanished.

MADISON

I can't remember how I met Madison. I just remember knowing her and thinking that she was fabulous. She was tiny and cute and sexy as hell. She was gorgeous before she had her boob job, and she was just as hot after. I usually didn't like big tits on women, I was more turned on by smaller ones, but on her they drove me crazy. And hers were huge.

At first she treated me like one of her girlfriends, she didn't seem to realize that I was attracted to her. Women are that way a lot with gay men it seems. They don't realize that some of us are bi, and it doesn't seem to occur to them that we are fawning over them and grabbing their tits and asses and pussies because it turns us on. They just think it's cute. Which can be a good thing. I mean, how many men can just walk up to a woman and a minute after meeting her, grab her tits? Not many. I always can. They think I'm a big queen so they don't think anything of it. Half the time they grab my dick or my ass.

Finally Madison got it that I wanted to do her. We set up a three way with another guy. She came over to my apartment first. We sat and had a drink and smoked a cigarette each. I was a little nervous. She was nervous too, gulping down her drink and then having another.

I was always more nervous around women than men. Once it changed from playing around to being serious about fucking, I would start to get paralyzed, being afraid of rejection. With men I didn't seem to worry so much. If they rejected my advances I just went on to the next. With women it was different. I think it's partly because men are just easy. Come on, we are. At least most of us. It's just not that hard to get a man in bed, if you belong to the gender(s) that he is into. It's not always the same with women. In the past couple of years I have finally become more comfortable about the process with women.

Finally the guy showed up. He was a guy that I had done alone before and once with Sharon Kane. We started quickly. He took off his clothes and we started sucking his dick, passing it back and forth. Then while Madison sucked his dick, I licked down her body to her little, pink pussy. I licked around it timidly at first, but then when she got wet and started moving around a little, I dove right in. I licked up and down, thrusting my tongue in as deep as I could go. I sucked her lips into my mouth and pressed my lips together around them, pulling out a little. She moaned as she sucked on the other guy's dick.

I was getting really into it now, my dick was rock hard and I couldn't keep my hands off of it. I stroked myself as I flicked my tongue around her clit, pressing against it as her hole got hotter and wetter. She was starting to thrash around, pressing down onto my face with her crotch. I grabbed her legs and ran my hands up to her ass and pulled her down harder onto my face.

A lot of the time I thought of myself as gay, but whenever my face was buried in a pussy, I realized that I loved it just as much as when I had my face buried in a guy's ass. I am definitely bi. Thank God! I just wouldn't want to have to eliminate half the world from my list of potentials. Everyone in the phone book is fair game!

I reached up and grabbed her breasts, pressing down onto them. She didn't have the boob job yet, and I loved the feeling of them. I went up and started sucking on them going back and forth from one nipple to the other. Soon I was on one and the other guy was on the other. Then he was eating her pussy and I was sucking his dick. He had a big dick, really nice. He wasn't really all that hot otherwise, but that dick made up for the rest.

Before long, he wanted to fuck her. She was on her back with his dick fucking her pussy hard and fast as she sucked my dick. I looked down at his cock disappearing inside her. Damn it was hot! I wanted up in there!

As soon as I got a chance, we moved around and she got on top of me, sucking the guy's dick with me in her pussy. I fucked her as she rode me, grinding down on me hard. Soon we were all getting close. I started cumming and cried out. Madison started squealing and the guy started shooting all over her tits. We all collapsed in a heap together.

I got another chance with Madison, after she had her tits done. We had a scene together in *Bi Bi Birdie*. It was even better since it was just the two of us that time. Madison also has a song on the *Porn To Rock* CD, so we are together forever on the CD as well as in the movie.

DANNY SUMMERS

I met Danny after I had been doing videos for about one year. We were in several of the same videos, like *Fan Male* and *Immoral Thoughts*, but had never done a scene together. We were friends and would always see each other at parties and hang out, but we never got together until one night when I was doing a performance at *Highways,* a performance art space in Santa Monica. It was Friday, September 20, 1991. Sharon Kane and Chi Chi LaRue, Lex Baldwin, Matt Gunther and lots of other porn stars performed as well—it was a benefit for Act Up called *Highways is Burning.*

I was the last act. Sharon and Chi Chi had both performed with some of the porn stars as backup dancers, but everyone had remained at least partially clothed. However, as often happened, I got them all to loosen up. I did a lip-synch, in drag, to the song *Sex (...I'm a)* by Berlin.

About twenty-five porn stars, including three or four women, crawled on stage with me wearing only cellophane wrapped around them. There were several O Boys in the group so you can see part of the performance in my award-winning porn documentary, *The Orgy Boys.* I had told them to be wild but I really didn't expect them all to immediately rip off their cellophane and start having sex. The audience didn't either, but they were delighted. It was one of those things people talked about for the next year.

Anyway, Danny and Jeremy Fox were among the people on stage with me. They were right in the middle of the group sucking each others dick's. Somehow, before I knew it, Danny had pulled up my skirt and was sucking my dick as I was lip-synching to the song. I had waited for this moment forever but was a bit distracted by the fact that I was performing a song in front of three-hundred people while he was sucking me. Not too distracted to wet my finger and stick it up his ass, though, as you can see if you watch the video. By the time we finished the song, several of the guys had shot their loads into the audience.

After the show, Danny and Jeremy and I continued what we had started on stage. Jeremy and I took turns fucking Danny's perfect round ass, first backstage, until someone walked in and caught us, then back at my apartment. I pounded his ass as he cried for more, and now there was nothing to distract me while he sucked my dick. It was a pretty wild night. I shot my load all over Danny's ass, and Jeremy shot on his face, then we started in again and kept going most of the night.

Danny still comes in and out of the business, and in between, I see him around town. He is still one of the cutest and nicest guys in porn, and he still has that bubble butt that just can't be concealed by any clothing. Its perfect shape announces itself over and over and over. Who could ignore such a thing?

RICK DONOVAN

I met Rick Donovan in my early days of porn, back when I was still occasionally running around the clubs in drag in a bikini or a see-through fishnet bodysuit. That night, I was leaving a drag club wearing very little, and he pulled up on his motorcycle. I recognized him, but I don't think he knew who I was. I also knew he had a reputation for being into drag queens. I usually do not like having sex in drag; drag for me is more theatrical than sexual, but I thought, "For him, I'll make an exception." He was very charming, and we talked for a few minutes, then he asked if I wanted a ride. I said, "Sure," and jumped on the back of his bike (I grew up riding motorcycles in Missouri) and we sped off into the night with some very jealous queens staring after us.

He drove me home and I asked if he wanted to come in. He did. We barely got in the door and he had all of my clothes off of me. It was like a magician's trick, it was so fast. He kissed me, then started sucking on my dick. After a while he took out his huge dick and I tried to suck it. I could barely get my mouth around it, it was so big. I gave it my best effort though. Then he wanted to fuck me. I was hesitant. I told him I didn't think I could take his dick. Actually I was a little terrified of it, I mean it was *really* huge! He said he would go slow and would stop if I needed to.

I have never been one to run from a challenge and so I thought, "Why not?" He laid me on my back on the bed, and started opening me up with his fingers first, then he put the head of his dick up against my ass. He slowly pressed against my hole and the head of his dick finally made its way inside. I was taking deep breaths. It was really big. He waited a minute for me to adjust and then very slowly, inch by inch, started sliding the rest of his monster dick into me. It must have taken a full five minutes to get it all the way in but finally he arrived, with his balls pressed up against me. I could hardly believe it. It didn't hurt, it actually felt great.

He just held his dick inside me for a few more moments, and then slowly started pulling it out. He pulled almost all the way out and then slowly slid all the way back in. I was in heaven. It was amazing. I hadn't been fucked very much at that point in my life, and never like this, and never with a dick even half as big. He kept fucking me really slowly for a long time until I started asking him to do it harder. He gently started to increase his pace until he was slamming in and out of me, sometimes pulling all the way out and then shoving it all the way back in. I was loving it and I started to get really loud, screaming for him to fuck me harder. We started building up to a climax together. We both came at the same time, with him fucking me and me screaming loud enough that a neighbor complained the next day.

When it was over, he lay on top of me for a while, still inside me. When he finally pulled his dick out, it just kept coming out and coming out and I didn't think it was ever going to be all the way out. When it finally was, I felt so empty inside and wished he was back in me again. He kissed me again, got dressed and left. I went to take off my wig and wash off my face (Yes, I was still in drag; this was one of the few times in my life that I had recreational, non-video sex in drag.) For the next two days my ass was sore in the most delicious way. I thought of Rick Donovan with every step I took.

The only other time I saw him in person was at a gay pride parade. He rode up to the float I was on (the parade hadn't started yet) and winked at me. My friend, The Fabulous Phyllis (she impersonates Phyllis Diller and looks and sounds just like her), started flirting with Rick and then jumped on the back of his bike. I know that you might not think that a drag-fucker would be interested in someone who looks like Phyllis Diller, but they are often into the fact that you are in drag rather than caring much about how you look. They sped off, and I didn't expect to see her again, but in a few minutes they were back. They had just gone for a spin around the block. As Rick drove off, I asked Phyllis, "Girl, don't you know who that was?" She said "No," and I told her what she had missed and probably could have had. She was practically kicking herself. She just thought he was some straight guy driving around for fun. I said "Yes, he probably was looking for fun, but you came back here!"

The next time you are in drag, keep an eye open. You never know who might ride up on a motorcycle.

TONY BELMONTE

I met Tony on the set of *A Whole Different Ball Game* in January of 1991. We didn't have a scene together, but he gave me his number. When I got home that night I called him and asked him if he wanted to come over. He came over and we talked for a long time. We were lying on the floor in front of my couch talking and talking, looking into each other's eyes. We were both getting turned on, but neither of us really knew for sure if the other one was really interested. The sexual tension mounted for what seemed like hours. Finally I asked him if he wanted me to kiss him. He said "Yes".

As soon as we kissed, we started full-on making out and taking each other's clothes off, then began sucking each other's dicks. I loved his dick in my mouth. It fit perfectly and felt like it was made for me to suck. I wanted to fuck him, but he also wanted to fuck me. I decided that that both were good ideas. We went into my bedroom.

It was much better than okay; it was amazing. In fact, it was always great with us, even later after we had broken up but were still doing videos together. He pushed his perfect-sized cock into my ass and fucked me while I buried my head in the pillow. I had had sex earlier in the video, but not real sex, not like this. I got goose bumps all over my body as he ran his hands over my butt and kept fucking me. I grabbed the sheets and pulled them off the edge of the bed as he pounded my hole, making it his property. I flipped over onto my back and Tony shoved his dick back up my ass and kissed me. Now all I could grab was his back, which I clutched at like I had the sheets when I was on my knees a few moments earlier. We both came at the same time, screaming and shooting all over my chest and stomach. When it was over we fell asleep in each other's arms.

As often happened with me, once someone spent the night they just stayed indefinitely. He stayed for a month. It seems that he had several friends that were visiting him and staying with him at his tiny little house in Silverlake, so he stayed with me. Our sexual relationship was incredible.

Tony had not been fucked for a couple of years because he had had surgery on his ass, but he wanted me to fuck him. One night he asked me if I would. Of course I would! He very nervously turned around and stuck his butt up in the air. I started licking it and sticking my tongue in him. He started to relax and loosen up a little, so I worked a finger in. I pushed it in and out a few times then slid a second one in next to it, then started working them both around, stretching his tight hole more. I waited until he was moaning and writhing on the bed and then started sliding my dick in him very, very slowly.

Anyone who has seen any of Tony's many videos, knows that he has one of the most gorgeous asses in porn; seeing it today still turns me on. I fucked him slowly at first for a long time, barely moving as I slid in and out, letting him get really used to it. I waited for him to ask for it harder, and he did. I started fucking harder and faster, building up slowly until I was really ramming his ass. He was so into it, it was easy to believe that he hadn't been fucked for a couple of years, although I was slamming in and out of his hole pretty hard for someone with a two-year old cherry. After that time he loved getting fucked, and it was always hard for us to decide who would be top or bottom. We had sex at least once every day, usually more.

I can't imagine anyone not wanting to fuck Tony. He has one of the most beautiful, perfectly proportioned bodies I've ever seen. He could have been a huge porn star, taking his pick of the best and most lucrative projects, but instead, he did every video that came along. I think by now he has done at least two hundred videos.

In the month that he was staying with me, I was falling madly in love. He always made me laugh. He was a big Barbra Streisand fan. After sex, he would burst into a Barbra Streisand song, jump out of bed, run to my closet and don one of my wigs, which was a little scary, but still very amusing.

I was studying all sorts of metaphysical books at the time and had been writing affirmations, which I left lying all over. He found them. At the time I was writing affirmations about physical immortality, so I had to explain Sondra Ray's concept of physical immortality: that a person could achieve enlightenment in this lifetime and either live forever or just dematerialize. He said "Okay, my boyfriend thinks he is going to live forever and never die. Alrighty then!" But we had a really great time together, even though he thought I was nuts.

He had a boyfriend that he had broken up with in Boston. The boyfriend was now supposedly just a friend and was going to move out to Los Angeles. So he left and drove to New Orleans to meet him and then drove back. He was gone for a couple of days. I went out and bought tons of balloons and filled the whole house with balloons and flowers to surprise him. When he got back, he came into the house, looked around at the balloons, and said "Oh my god, this is horrible." Immediately, my heart sank, and I knew what he was going to tell me. He, of course, told me that he was going to get back together with his old boyfriend. I was crushed and thought I was going to die. I did not die, of course. We remained friends.

Over the years we did a great many scenes together. Whether I was in drag or not, he always knew the real me and was not affected adversely when I wore a wig. One of the best scenes is in the video, *She Mail*. I was in drag and he was wearing a bandanna with a fall under it (No, that's not his real hair.) In one shot he was fucking me. Then we were going to switch and I was going to fuck him. He asked if he could wear my heels. We decided that it would be funny and we would see if anyone noticed. Many reviewers and fans did, and I still get fan letters telling me that it is their favorite moment of all my videos.

Eventually Tony and I got to the same point I had reached with Sharon Kane: We decided that the last thing the world needed was to see another sex scene with the two of us, and so decided not to do any more scenes together. He has been in many of my videos over the years though, in scenes with others. He still always cracks me up on the set.

Tony and I are friends to this day, and he is still with the same boyfriend, so I'm glad that they did get back together. They seemed to be destined for partnership, and in retrospect, I wouldn't have wanted to stand in the way of that. Since it didn't work out for us, I'm glad it did for them.

(Last-minute note to fans: They just broke up, so he is fair game again as this book is going to press.)

CORY NIXON

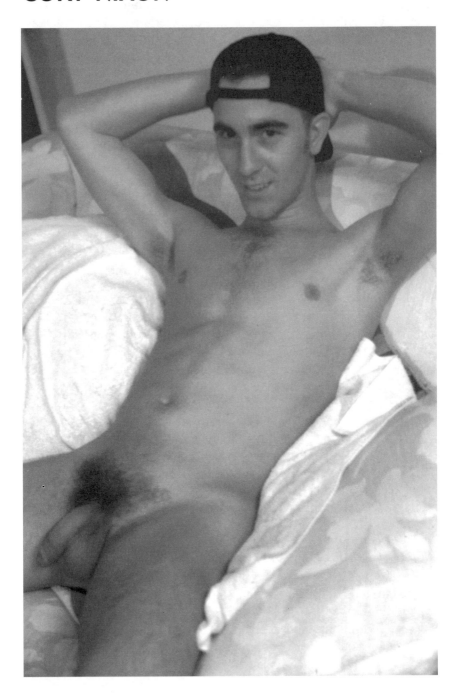

I met Cory at a fourth of July party at Tony Belmonte's house in 1992. He was wearing an orange Cat-in-the-Hat type headpiece which looked both quirky and cute on him. Unlike the rest of the band of porn stars and wannabe's at the gathering, he wasn't dressed the same as everyone else. I was instantly interested. We talked for a couple of hours and bonded on a number of levels. We ended up on Tony's bed talking with the bedroom door open one minute, and then making out the next minute. I shoved my finger up his ass without any lube and I could tell it hurt and that he liked it. I was intoxicated with lust. My head was spinning.

I pulled his pants down, rolled him over and started forcing my cock up his ass without any lube. It hurt and felt great and we were both going wild. I started fucking him hard. Since there was still no lube my cock was scraping all the way in and out of his ass. I had never dry fucked anyone before but this was really hot. We were getting really loud and didn't notice that people were peeking in the door. I guess we gave them quite a show. I was too caught up in the rush to notice. As I slammed into him, raping his ass and pulling his head all the way back by his hair. He was almost crying, but he was obviously loving it. Finally he exploded and I pulled my dick out and came with him. After that we just lay there looking at each other in amazement. I was hooked. I think he was too. Tony called me the next day and thanked me for providing entertainment for his party.

Cory lived with a "roommate" that turned out to be his boyfriend. Within a week he had moved in with me. We had wild hot sex all the time, both at home and in public, and nearly-public, places. Once at the beach under a blanket with other people around. Once in an elevator, where we almost were caught by a group of high school guys. The doors had opened one second after we had both zipped up our pants.

Cory and I also instigated lots of other mischief. We used to try to surprise people. We would show up at events with me holding him on a leash or something like that. One time I made him up in drag to look as much like me as possible. Everybody was freaking out because they thought it *was* me at first. Chi Chi came over to me and whispered, "You are sick, girl, you are really sick." I asked her why. "Because, drag queen's boyfriends shouldn't do drag. It's just not right." We both loved throwing people for a loop.

One time, on an airplane coming home from doing videos in

New York, a flight attendant recognized me. This turned Cory on. He looked at me with an evil grin and said, "Come with to me to the bathroom." My dick got instantly hard at the thought. We discreetly slipped away into the bathroom. I was expecting to fuck Cory, but he turned me around and fucked me. He just spit on his dick and shoved it up my ass. I stifled a scream.

I'm usually pretty loud when I'm getting fucked, but I tried to be silent. It was very hot, though. It seemed so nasty, being just a couple of feet away from the other passengers, standing up in the tiny bathroom with him fucking the shit out of me. I grabbed the sink and watched him in the mirror: his cock pounding into my ass and his hands gripping my waist and pulling me back on him. I shot all over the mirror and he kept fucking me until he shot up my ass. I felt his hot cum filling me up and it started to run out of my ass. He reached down and smeared some of it across my lips and made me lick it off. We composed ourselves and went back out and sat down in our seats. I still had an ass full of his cum. We looked at each other and smiled. We had pulled it off. No one had noticed! Just then the flight attendant came over and pinned wings on both of us. "I think you both deserve these," he said smiling wickedly. Cory and I burst out laughing.

Before meeting Cory, I had made plans to go to India to my guru, Babaji's ashram for a month. Without going into the entire story, which will be in my next book, I'll just relate the part that involves Cory.

Cory had reservations about me going, but I had the trip planned since before I met him. He didn't want to accompany me either, so I left and told him that I would call when I could. While I was gone, I called a couple of times and he answered the phone and acted very strangely. He wouldn't tell me what was wrong. He just said, "Come home."

When I got back to the airport in L.A., I started to feel that something was wrong. The feeling grew as I got closer to home. When I entered my apartment, nearly everything was gone. The TV, the VCR, the stereo, and even things like the vacuum cleaner were all gone. Cory was there and he weighed about 90 pounds. He had needle marks up and down his arms. He was crying and saying that he was sorry. He said that he freaked out because I was gone and he started shooting up crystal (speed). I knew that he drank some and sometimes smoked pot, but I had never seen him do crystal or even heard him talk about it before.

I was stunned. He had sold all of my stuff to buy drugs. It turned out that he had also taken all of my money out of the bank so that there was not only no money left, but the rent check and all of the other checks I had written for bills had bounced. As horrible as it was for me, and it was horrible, as I had no money coming in and no work lined up, I felt terrible for him. He looked half dead and was completely destroyed by guilt. He said that he would pay me back and that he knew he couldn't stay with me and that he knew there was no way I could trust him, but that he hoped I wouldn't hate him.

My heart was broken. I had been in love with him and I felt betrayed. I was hurt and angry, but I didn't hate him. I couldn't. A lot of my friends didn't understand why I didn't have him arrested. They hated him. I didn't want him to go to jail—I knew that wouldn't bring back my stuff or fix my heart. I tallied up how much he owed me, and over the next year he did pay me back all the money.

To earn some of the money, Cory ended up doing a couple of scenes with me, one in *Single White She-Male* and one in a gay video. The gay video was shot soon after everything had happened, so when I fucked him, it was sort of a grudge fuck. I was fucking him really hard and it was hurting him but he was taking it. It really turned me on in a slightly sick way. I realized that I was sexually addicted to him, and it scared me a little. After that I didn't see him much anymore.

Having all of my stuff stolen by someone I love was one of the most difficult things I have ever gone through, but I am a much stronger person now. Cory and I remained friends because I was able to forgive him. Unfortunately, he seemed to vanish about four years ago and no one I know has seen or heard from him. Cory, if you are reading this, call me!

CHRIS STONE

I had lusted after Chris' perfect butt in videos like *Big Bang, Sailor In The Wild 2,* and *Idol Eyes.* In 1992, my friend Paul Pelletieri was directing videos, and I came up with a title and concept for a video for him: *Bi Anonymous.* Paul cast me in the video and asked who I wanted to work with. I chose the two hottest guys I could think of that I hadn't yet been with: Chris Stone and Mark Steel. I couldn't wait for the shoot, I was so excited about both of them.

Chris is just as gorgeous in person as he is on video and I was a little intimidated because I was so attracted to him. I had met him once before, when I was hanging out with my longtime friend, Boy George, after a concert. Chris was backstage too, I guess he was also a friend of George's. Chris had flirted with me, but I thought it was just friendly flirting; he was with his boyfriend and there were other people around. Now his boyfriend wasn't there and I was naked in bed with him.

He soon helped me over my nervousness by giving me an excellent blowjob. He sucked my dick all the way down his throat while I did my best to do the same for him. I almost came while we were sucking each other, it was so hot. Then I started licking his tight beautiful brown hole.

I could have licked and sucked on his ass forever, but finally it was time for me to fuck him.

I pressed the head of my cock up against his ass and slowly pushed it in past the ring of his sphincter. He moaned as it popped in and he pushed back on my dick. I was trying to go slow for him, but he shoved himself all the way down to the base of my cock. He really gets into all of his scenes and isn't just acting like some people are. I could tell that his moans were real as I started to fuck his ass. I fucked him slowly at first, building up speed as I plunged in and out of his wet fuck hole. After a while we switched and Chris fucked me.

He stuck his finger up my ass first and loosened me up until I was squirming and begging for his cock. Then I took his dick. I was determined to take it all like he took mine! It hurt at first, but that just turned me on more, so I told him to slam into me as hard as he wanted. He pounded me until I almost couldn't take anymore. I did take it all though. I'm not sure if all of that scene made it into the video or not, but I loved getting fucked by him almost as much as I loved fucking him. He was very good, teasing me, sliding his dick in and out of me so slowly, that I was on the verge of coming for the final ten minutes.

Finally, I couldn't hold back any longer. I asked Paul, who was directing and holding the camera, if I could come. He gave the go-ahead. Chris and I both shot our loads and the scene was over.

As often happens, I haven't seen Chris since. But I haven't forgotten him.

RYAN BLOCK

I met Ryan Block in 1992 when we were supposed to do a video together. We were in Paul Pelletieri's studio, on top of a bar against a brick wall. It was one of his first videos. He was nervous, he said, because he was a fan of mine. I wasn't nervous, but I did think he was gorgeous; big and beefy. We started the scene taking turns sucking each other. I really got into sucking his cock. Then we were ready for fucking, or actually, not quite ready. He was supposed to top me in the video, but suddenly he couldn't get hard enough. Again, he said it was because he was nervous. He would be hard, then when he put on the condom, he would lose his hard-on. He would take it off, get hard again, put on another one, and then lose it again.

Finally, we decided that I would fuck him. I licked his ass first and then stuck a finger in. He was tight, really tight. He moaned and it sounded like it hurt him a little. It made me even harder. I believed him when he said that he rarely got fucked.

"Are you sure you are going to be okay with this?" I asked.

"Yes, definitely," he said.

I somehow managed to get my cock into his ass. At first I thought he was going to squeeze it out, but he eventually relaxed and I started fucking him and he started getting into it. I could tell he was really straining to take my cock, and that he really wanted to please me, and that turned me on and made me fuck him even harder, so that he would have to work harder to take it. He was starting to moan and grunt and sweat. Watching that big macho stud with his ass wrapped around my cock, struggling to take more and more, was driving me nearly over the edge. He kept getting louder and louder, and we were both totally ready to shoot when the director finally told us to. I exploded, and it was one of those mind-blowing orgasms in which you hardly know where you are when it's over.

Over the next few years, I would often see Ryan at parties, or at other events. He was dating an acquaintance of mine, Crystal Crawford. In her book, *Making It Big,* Chi Chi LaRue describes Crystal, as "the spawn of Margaret Hamilton and Mr. Ed." Not very flattering, but unfortunately an accurate description.

One night in 1993, a fuck-buddy of mine (the same one who introduced me to my best friend, Mark Allan), called me and asked me to come over. He asked if I was into girls. I said sure. He said he had a really hot, bisexual guy and a girl in his bed. I drove over to his apartment, walked in and who was in the bed but Ryan. He looked at me and I looked at him. My silent stare said, "Uh, that's not Crystal that you're with there." His returning silent stare said, "Please don't say anything!" I pretended I was meeting both of them for the first time.

Ryan and the woman and I all fucked while my fuck-buddy, who was totally gay, mostly watched and made sure he didn't accidentally touch the female. Ryan and I fucked him some, but mostly each other. After a while the woman left. Ryan stayed. We all got into a hot three-way then, with Ryan and I taking turns fucking my friend. Then Ryan fucked him while I fucked Ryan. It was a wild night. By the time we were done, the sun was coming up. We all came for the fourth or fifth time and decided that we were done. Before I left, Ryan said, "Whatever you do, don't tell Crystal!" He told me, "She (the woman) doesn't know I'm seeing Crystal and Crystal doesn't know I'm seeing other people."

I didn't tell anyone, but eventually he did. Crystal wasn't too upset because, as it turned out, she was cheating on him at the same time. I hate to moralize, especially in a book that is supposed to be getting you off, but for God's sake! If everyone is fucking everybody else, why can't we all just *say* so? Then it's all out in the open and nobody is cheating and everybody is getting what they want and nobody has to feel guilty or lie. If you really want a monogamous relationship, great; but why do so many people say they do when they really don't? I don't get it.

CODY FOSTER

Cody was one of those straight guys that does gay porn—as a bottom. I had seen pictures of Cody, he was on all the magazine covers as the hot new boy in 1992. One day I got a breathless call from Chi Chi LaRue. "Can you come over right now and be a stunt dick on a set?" They were shooting the video *Reunion* for Catalina. The big muscle guy that was supposed to fuck Cody couldn't get hard and they had been trying for three hours.

They were filming at the house where the old TV series *Eight Is Enough* had been filmed. In fact we were going to fuck on the front steps. This amused me greatly. I met Cody and dropped my pants and started fucking him. He was beautiful and had a great body and all that, but he seemed completely bored by what was happening. I might as well have been fucking a blow-up doll. A blow- up doll with a gorgeous bubble butt. And blond hair. And a muscular, V-shaped back...Okay, so it was still pretty hot. I fucked him harder and harder until I was pounding his straight-boy ass as hard as I'd ever fucked anyone. Hell, if he wasn't going to say anything, I might as well fuck him as hard as I want, don't you think? Chi Chi got all the angles he needed and then he wanted me to do a cum shot in case the other guy couldn't do that either (I don't know if he did or not). I shot my load all over his back and I left.

If you watch the video, it is pretty funny. Usually, stunt dick scenes are shot very close-up so that no one will notice the replacement. In this video, some of the shots were so wide that they caught my skinny little legs, so the video cuts from a shot of a big muscle guy fucking (or simulating fucking) to a shot of Cody's ass getting fucked by a big dick with some skinny legs attached. There were even pictures that turned up in magazines of my dick and skinny legs. Go rent the video and you'll see what I mean.

ROD GARRETTO

I had met Rod Garretto on many of Gino Colbert's shoots, although

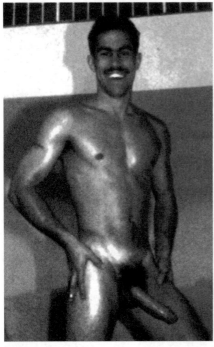

we had never done a scene together. He was always friendly enough, but I couldn't quite figure him out. He seemed to love fucking guys on film, but he had a wife and kids who would sometimes drive him to the shoots. ("Can you say *bisexual*, boys and girls? There, I knew you could.") I usually detest facial hair, but he was one of the few people on whom I liked it.

One day Gino called me and said he wanted me to do a scene with Rod. I said I didn't know, his dick was pretty big. Gino told me this was going to be Rod's first time bottoming on film and he (I'm not sure if he meant Rod or himself) wanted me to top him. I said, "Sure!"

On the day of the shoot, Rod was very nice, but a little nervous. We were shooting on Gino's bed, the same place almost every scene I ever did for him was shot. Between Gino's personal life and all the films he shot on it, I'll bet that bed has seen more action than mine!

Rod and I started sucking each other's dicks (Damn, his is long!) in a comfortable sixty-nine for a long time. I tried to get his schlong all the way down my throat, and at that angle, I found that I could. It was so satisfying, feeling a dick halfway down my throat. He sucked like the pro he was, too. The lights were hot, but it was definitely worth it, we didn't notice the crew at all and neither of us heard Gino the first time he told us to stop. We were just sucking and sucking, totally into each other, when I looked around and everyone was gone. Gino came back in and said,

"I said 'Cut, let's take a break,' but you two obviously didn't need a break, so I didn't want to interrupt you. Just keep going and we'll start shooting you again." We kept going, the crew came back in, and then we were ready to shoot the fucking .

I told Rod I would go easy, but he humped his ass right back on my dick and I started fucking him. My cock slid in with no problem and with just a minor grunt from Rod. If he had really never done it before, he sure was liking his first time! I pounded his hot Latin ass and he seemed to love it. I reached around and grabbed his cock as I was fucking him. It was rock hard. I started to get close and looked over at Gino to see if I could cum, or if they needed more footage. They needed more. Good. More fucking for us then!

It was over far too soon, we both came, got paid, and said good-bye. I told Rod it was great working with him. It was, but I could tell that he probably wasn't interested in getting together off screen, what with the wife and kids and all. I only ran into Rod once since then, with his wife and kids at the Universal City Walk. He doesn't ever go to the awards shows or industry parties or anything, but I know he's still around doing videos.

CHRISTOPHER RAGE

Christopher Rage was an intellect, a musician, a writer, an actor and many other things as well as being a huge sex-pig. He directed and starred in many videos—ones that stand out from others. He would often pick up guys and bring them home to film them. He would get fisted by them, pissed on, and even do things as wild as pulling a chain out of a guy's ass. No one else did videos this wild. Most other directors fear government censure, and with good reason: Many video distributors have spent time in jail over their films.

Christopher was a joy to know in so many ways, and of course, sex with him was never boring. He was the one person in the porn industry that I actually had to say "no thanks" to a couple of times. His sexual suggestions were too wild even for me.

We met early in my porn career, I can't remember exactly when. I do remember being surprised that he recognized me, especially in that dark bar. We immediately began what quickly became what is possibly still the wildest relationship I had ever had.

We had lots of ordinary sex of course, sucking and fucking, but there were also much more colorful times. The fistfucking. The pissing down his throat. The tying him up and gangfucking him with 10 other guys. The time I fucked him with a wrench, then shoved an enormous chain up his ass and pulled it out repeatedly.

He was someone that I could slap in the face, while looking into his eyes fucking him, and know that it was a very loving act. He was an amazing person who made a stand for freedom of expression and sexuality and was harassed a lot by the government for it. He beat them though, by dying before they could decide how and what to do to him, and by dying happy.

JAMIE HENDRIX

I'm not sure when I met Jamie Hendrix. I think it was around 1992, just after he did the video *Cruisin' II: Men On The Make* for Falcon. He looked good, incredibly good. He was blond and buff and sexy and had an air of being a naughty little boy. He was starting to direct his own videos, and Tony Belmonte had sent me to meet him, to be in his videos.

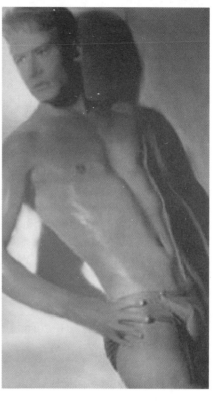

We met at his apartment. He came on strong to me, and I liked it. He was sexy enough, but I also liked the fact that it seemed a little forbidden. Of course models date and/or fuck directors all the time, but it still seemed naughty, like he was molesting me on the job, but in a really good way. We fooled around some at that meeting, then I called him soon after and invited him over to my house. He came into my apartment and said, "I'm really glad you called, I wanted a lot more of you than I got."

"How much do you want?"

"All of it."

He was still being naughty. We went in the bedroom and I unfastened his jeans. I pulled them down and saw that he was wearing his standard-issue porn jockstrap. I turned him around to look at his ass, up close and in person for the first time.

"You like that?" he asked.

"Oh yeah," I said "I like it a lot!"

Before I knew it, he had made his way into my pants and started sucking my dick. Then I went down on him, taking his cock all the way into my mouth and throat. It wasn't huge, but it was actually a perfect size. I like dicks that you can fit into your mouth or ass really easily. Admittedly, most fit pretty easily by now, but you know what I mean, not too big, not too small, just like the Goldilocks that he was.

Jamie was fucking my face and I was starting to sneak my fingers up to his hole. I slipped one in, then he turned around and I started licking his perfect, round, white ass. If anyone in the world had a perfect bubble butt it was him. He climbed over onto the bed and stuck his ass in the air and looked around at me. "Put it in," he said.

He didn't have to ask twice, I had been wanting to do it since he walked in the door, or really since the first time I saw him in that video. I started fucking him and I was in heaven. Once again, I couldn't believe that such a gorgeous guy was letting me fuck him, but he was, and begging me to do it harder and harder. I was going wild watching my pole disappear between his creamy white mounds of perfect flesh. It was hot and we were both starting to sweat, but Jamie still managed to look perfect, very Malibu Ken, I realized, much like Steve Fox, another porn star in this book, who I also call Malibu Ken.

Jamie was talking dirty the whole time, driving me wild until I just couldn't take it anymore. I finally pulled out and shot all over that milky white butt. He turned over and shot all over his stomach and chest.

"Thanks, that was really hot. You're a really hot man," he said. I told him that I thought he was, too, and that I hoped we could do it again soon. He left and I lay there on the bed, swimming in the afterglow of our workout.

Jamie started putting me in some of the videos he directed. It was always hot to have him telling me what to do. Occasionally he would demonstrate just what position I should be in and how the other guy should fuck me or suck my dick or even how to finger my hole. I loved being molested by him. It always seemed so nasty!

Jamie came over to my apartment several times. He really loved my ass, too, though, so we always wanted to fuck each other. We basically took turns, but I think we both loved being on top the best.

One time on New Year's Day, 1994, Sharon was over. It was an on-again phase of our on-again, off-again relationship. We decided we wanted a guy to come over and play with us, so we called

Jamie. He had asked me a few times about Sharon, aware that I sometimes dated her, and had told me he wanted to join us in bed sometime. So, when I called and invited him, he wasted no time making his way to our bed. He got to have the best of both worlds, fucking Sharon's pussy while I fucked his ass. It was really hot. In fact, Jamie and Sharon dated for a while—just the two of them. It's a big secret and I'm not supposed to tell anyone, but, oh well, that's what this book is about!

I still see Jamie at all the porn parties. We stay in touch on the phone and refer models to each other. He always tells me how sexy I am which I especially appreciate when I'm not feeling so sexy. Hmmm...maybe I should give him a call...

CHRISTIAN FOX

I met Christian Fox several years ago at a friend's house. I think it was right around the time that I had started directing videos. He was very cute and charming. I hadn't seen any of his videos, but we talked briefly about what it was like being in videos, the good aspects and the bad. He was very interested in me, but he didn't want my friend to know it. I think they were sort of dating or fucking or whatever; I never found out for sure. He very discreetly slipped me his phone number. I called him and we got together.

When he came over to my apartment, I continued our previous conversation by asking, "So, why are you a porn star?" "This is why," he replied, and turned around, hooked his thumbs into his blue shorts and pulled them down slowly. He reached back with both hands and spread his perfect ass cheeks to show me his tight pink asshole.

I felt all the blood rush to my head. Well, and to one other place, too. That wasn't exactly the answer I had been seeking, but now I was looking at one of the loveliest assholes I had ever seen. I took a risk that he wasn't just showing me, like in "show and tell." I hoped his plan was more "show and do," so I did. I leaned over and flicked my tongue over that pretty asshole. He started moaning

"No..."

"Do you want me to stop?" I asked.

"No," he said "don't stop."

I didn't.

I licked and sucked and stuck my tongue as far up his ass as I could. Then I started fingering him. He was really making noise now. Again, he was saying "No," and I asked him if he wanted me to stop. "God no!" he said.

I figured out later that part of the turn-on for him was pretending to resist some. Once he explained that to me, we got into more intense fantasies, always with him pretending to resist me, and me pretending to force him to suck my dick, get fucked, or whatever. He was such a good bad boy!

Eventually, I couldn't stand it any longer. I was dizzy with lust, my mind had ceased forming coherent thoughts.

I wanted that ass!

Ordinarily, I would have tried to be gentle, but this time, I was in no mood. I shoved my dick in and started to fuck him. He cried out and I pulled my dick almost all the way out and asked if he wanted me to stop once again. He whispered "No," and he squeezed my dick with his ass, gripping it tight like he was never going to let go. I slammed my dick back into his butt and started fucking him. He grabbed my bookshelf to steady himself. I was fucking him so hard that books fell off and rained down around us as I continued to slide in and out of his chute. His moans were getting louder and louder, which turned me on even more. We were our own mini-earthquake, complete with tremors. We finally came together, then fell over onto the tan shaggy carpet, our lips touching for the first time, in a deep passionate kiss.

We got together several times after that. Sometimes we would watch straight or bi videos together. He didn't want anyone to know that we were seeing each other. I think he was also seeing another friend of mine, a guy, and he told me that he also had a girlfriend. I was starting to fall for him, he was so sweet, the sex was so hot, and I loved cuddling with him afterwards. It finally got to the point where I told him I just couldn't see him anymore, not under those conditions. I was on the verge of falling completely in love, and I didn't want to get my heart broken again. I knew he didn't feel the way I did. He obviously liked me a lot, but he wasn't in love with me. This was difficult for me.

Before he left for the last time, we kissed good-bye for about twenty minutes. I missed him a lot after that. I never saw him again, and I was devastated to learn years later that he had died, possibly in a suicide. He was a sweet, beautiful angel. I will always miss him.

RANDY STORM

Randy and I met when we were to do a scene with each other in a video called *Express Male*. I was delivering packages on a dolly, and I think I was late or something like that. He punished me for being late by making me have sex with him (such cruel and unusual punishment). At one point, I was sucking his dick through the bars of the dolly (porn directors love that stuff, like it's so creative and gee, no one else would ever have thought of it).

Then we moved over to a couch. I remember him eating my ass and me not wanting him to ever stop. He was really good at it, licking all around my hole first, teasing me by not quite going in yet, then stuffing his tongue as far as it would go up my hole as I pushed down on it, trying to get further in. He plunged it in and out, fucking my pucker with his tongue, making it open up for him and for what was about to come.

After that, we fucked each other on the couch. I don't remember who fucked whom first, or why there was a couch in a post office, but I do remember loving all of it. His dick sliding home into my ass, pounding into me, and he was holding my legs up, with my ass draped over the edge of that postal couch. His pubic bone slammed in between my spread thighs as he pulled my legs farther apart, until I felt like he was going to split me open. I remember that wild look in his eyes; he liked being in control.

He liked being on the bottom, too, his balls drawn up tight to his dick, which was hard the whole time I took his ass. His knees were up against his chest and he whimpered a little as I grabbed his hair and pulled back as I banged him long and slow, then faster and faster. His hole gripped my meat as it made its new home deep inside him. Finally, we got all the shots we needed and were ready to cum. We were both worked up hotter than hell and we shot all over the place.

Randy was a good fuck and a nice guy. Someone perfect to do such a silly scene with. I hope we detracted from the ridiculous story line with our animal sex. We were in a lot of the same videos after that, but not in any other scenes together. I saw him around for a few years after that, but I haven't seen him recently. I wonder if he's gone into porn retirement, or if he is just waiting to resurface and make one of those oh-so-famous porn comebacks.

KEVIN KRAMER

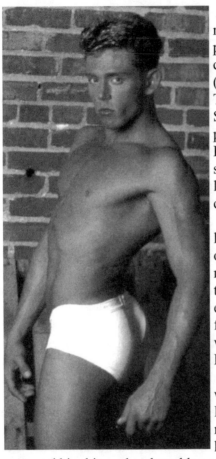

I met Kevin soon after he moved to L.A. and started in the porn industry. He was young and cute and sweet and innocent (really). We met at a barbecue at Tony Belmonte's house in Silverlake. It was a Fourth of July party, so it was hot outside and Kevin was wearing tiny little tight shorts, with a huge bulge. I learned later that he always wore a cockring. Always.

Kevin was flirting with me a lot, but porn stars do that as a way of life, so I didn't know if he was really interested. We hung out there most of the day, talking and eating and then watching the fireworks. Finally, I asked if he wanted to come home with me. He said yes.

He came over to my house and we were lying on the floor talking. I was very attracted to him, and now he was flirting with me pretty heavily. I was just about to lean over and kiss him, when he told me that it was so nice to just be talking to someone who wasn't trying to just get him into bed. He said that ever since he had been in L.A., everyone seemed to have ulterior motives and that he was really enjoying spending the day with me and getting to know me without wondering what I wanted from him. I realized that he needed a friend a lot more than I needed a good fuck (and I needed one pretty bad) so I didn't make any advances. He was certainly very sexy and flirtatious, but was also like a sweet little puppy. He was scared and insecure and alone in a new city. We stayed up half the night talking and then I gave him ten bucks for a cab home.

Those first couple of years he was a go-go dancer at the club Axis. He recently reminded me of it. Whenever I would go in, I would walk up and grab his ankles (he was up on a box) and get his attention and say, "Hi." I always worried that I was disturbing him, but he told me that I was the only person who ever said hello to him when he was up there. Probably most people are intimidated by the strippers, meanwhile, the strippers are lonely!

Over the years, we have remained very friendly acquaintances and are even growing into real friends. I have watched him become a confident, secure, young man. We have done a few AIDS benefits together. One night when we did a charity fashion show together, he thanked me for that first night. He said it was really helpful and grounding for him. I told him I was glad to be there and was glad that he was my friend now.

Some things are more important than sex.

Me, in the video *A Real Man*

Me, in drag

Me, from the photo shoot for the cover of my newest album, *S E X*

Me—an early porn
promo shot

Now I'm the Director

Becoming a director changed things a lot. Now I was interviewing and hiring models, and also in charge of entire productions. I was more responsible for my successes, and would have also been responsible had I failed.

I suddenly had a whole cast and crew depending on me, which made my role more stressful, but also ultimately more fulfilling.

JASON BRODERICK

I first met Jason Broderick, AKA Shadoe Thomas, in 1992 when I was just starting to direct videos. I thought he was the yummiest thing I had ever seen and I desperately wanted to fuck him. He was blond and small and shy and charming and sooo fuckable. He had the most sexy German accent. All I got to do that time was direct him in a scene, though. I watched him, trying not to let my hard-on show through my pants. I had him in a position with his ass propped up in the air for a long time, having it eaten, getting it fingered, and finally fucked. Then I rushed home to jack off and fantasize about him.

Soon enough, there was another video, *Apartment 69*. This time, I was to direct it *and* be in it. I asked Jason if he wanted to do a scene with me and he said "Yes." I told him I would be shoving big dildos up his ass and he said, "Great!" I knew for sure then he was my kind of guy.

The scene was actually shot horribly and edited even more horribly, but it was one of the most enjoyable scenes for me, ever. We started in bed, sucking each other's dicks, then I licked his ass and spat in it, sucking my spit back out and shoving my tongue up his delicious hole. I wanted more than my tongue up there, though, so I shoved a finger in. He squirmed and moaned and I shoved in another and twisted them around slowly. I graduated to finger-fucking him hard, abusing his pussy ass as he begged for more. When I couldn't stand watching him writhe and moan any more, I fucked him with my hard cock.

I made him beg for it before I shoved my dick deep in his hole and started raping it like there was no tomorrow. I pounded and pounded as hard as I could. He still wanted more. I'm not sure if it was him or if he was just in character, but I didn't care as long as I got to keep taking control of that pink hole. I started fucking him with dildos. I rammed the first one in up to the hilt as hard as I could. He screamed, but he was screaming, "Yes!" so I pumped it in and out, hard.

Then I moved on to a bigger one. I twisted it around and around stretching his now bright red little hole open more as he writhed and dripped sweat under the hot lights. By the end, I was ramming a huge dildo in and out of his ass, pulling it all the way out to look at his beautiful gaping hole, and showing it to the camera, then shoving it back in to hear him scream, as he clutched at the sheets on the bed, quivering and begging for more. I loved it. We both finally came, shooting all over each other. After the crew left the room, eyebrows and dicks raised, we fell over onto the bed laughing in each others arms, trying to catch our breath.

I cast him again as Gilligan when I shot *Gilligan's Bi-Land.* I played Ginger (in drag, of course) so our scene that time wasn't quite as wild. That is, if you consider a drag queen in a pink evening gown fucking a guy on a rock in the middle of a lagoon on the tame side. I personally preferred the bed though, fucking him with dildos— *without* the dress. Still, fucking Jason anyway, anywhere is still a good thing. A *very* good thing. We spent a long time shooting the scene. Usually I get the footage I need and then move on, but we were having so much fun we shot a lot more than we needed, just like we did in *Apartment 69.*

Jason also had a scene with Jarod Clark, who played The Skipper. I think Sherwood Schwartz --who owned the rights to *Gilligan's Island*-- sued the company and made them stop distributing it, (Does that mean he watched it?) so it may be hard to find, but check your local video store.

Jason stayed around in the business for a while and then, as so many others, seemed to simply vanish. I sure hope he's not stranded on an island. Or if he is, then maybe Jarod Clark is with him.

BRAD MORGAN

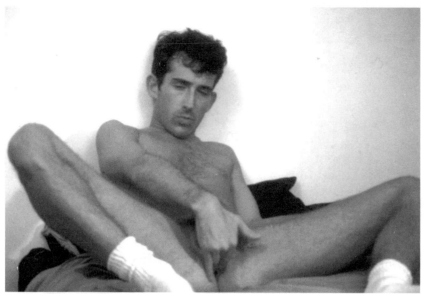

Brad was another guy I met through Tony Belmonte. Tony brought him over to my apartment one night in the spring of 1993. A couple of other people were there and we were all hanging out, but Brad and I couldn't take our eyes off of each other. I don't remember who else was there, and I'm sure I didn't hear a word anyone else said. For some reason, everyone wanted to go over to singer and Marilyn Monroe-impersonator Jimmy James' house to see him. Jimmy has been my friend for years and lived just down the street at the time, but I wanted only to be alone with Brad. We all went to Jimmy's and finally came back to my apartment. Eventually, everyone else left and Brad stayed.

We started kissing and quickly made it to the bedroom. We had both been waiting all night for this, to be alone, and we wanted to savor it. We kissed and rolled around on the bed and pulled each other's clothes off, laughing about how long it took to get rid of everyone. Finally I was in him, my dick slowly going all the way down to the base. I was on top of him looking in his eyes, hearing him moan, and I fucked him, sliding in and out as he moaned and clawed at my back. I looked down at my dick as it plunged into him and thought his ass, balls and dick were the most beautiful I'd ever seen. I looked in his eyes and saw that desperate look as he moaned.

I think that was when I fell in love with him. He was incredible. His face always looked like he was in pain when I fucked him, but when I asked if I was hurting him, he always said, "No". His face was just so sexy to look at! I loved holding him in my arms and fucking him. I moved in and out of him faster and faster, building the intensity, holding his gaze until we both came. We fell asleep in each others arms.

It turned out that Brad was visiting from Washington, D.C. He had come out to do some videos and was supposed to go back soon, but he stayed a couple of extra weeks with me. I was falling in love hard and fast. In retrospect, I think he was, too.

Just before he was supposed to leave to go back home he said that he wanted to move to L.A. and live with me. I thought that sounded great. He was cute, he was funny, he was absolutely brilliant and he was incredibly sexy. I was in love. Madly, stupidly, all-sanity-out-the-window in love. I realize now that I was having self-esteem issues. He would look at me and furrow his brow and say, "You are so cute!" I didn't believe him. I don't know why. Now I believe that he meant it, and looking back at pictures, I *was* cute. But I always felt like he was lying to me when he said that. At that time, I just couldn't believe that someone could really love me, could really think I was cute.

Brad went back to D.C. for three weeks to get his stuff together and to move out to L.A. It was just at the time of the 1993 March on Washington, so I decided to go see him and attend the March. Chi Chi and Chris Green were also there and we all ran around all weekend together. Brad and I went to the March, then back to his apartment to fuck. We went to dinner, then to fuck. We went to clubs and then we fucked. We fucked a lot. Finally, I flew back to L.A. and Brad loaded up his car and drove out. He called me every day on his cross-country road trip. In the beginning, we had lots of fun together. He was in lots of my videos while he lived with me and he also helped as production assistant.

One day, I was on my way to the set to direct a video and I stopped by a clinic to get the results of my HIV test. It was not the best idea in terms of how to do things. I was told that I was positive. I couldn't think, I went into a daze. Somehow, I drove to the set. When I got there he took one look at me and said, "What is wrong?" I took him in the other room and told him. I couldn't yet cry then. Somehow I managed to direct the video all day, although I don't remember doing it and I don't have any idea what video it was or even what kind it was.

That night in bed I cried and he held me. "I'm not going to leave you," he said. He was gone by the end of the month. I can understand—it's a lot to handle, and some people can't. After a month or so apart, we started our friendship again and we are still friends. In fact, he starred as The Professor in my video *Gilligan's Bi-Land* after we had broken up and he was great. Brad now lives in San Francisco and I occasionally get to see him.

DANNY BLISS

I first saw Danny Bliss in 1993 in a Falcon Video. He was one of the few people that I have seen in a video that turned me on so completely. I don't know what it was about him. He was so sweet and his ass was so perfectly gorgeous. He seemed to love getting fucked and seemed to love straining to take big cocks up his ass.

I asked some of my friends about him and they said,

"Oh, he's straight."

"Oh really?" I was skeptical.

"Well, he's straight, but he loves to suck dick and get fucked. He's strictly a bottom."

That was enough for me—I had to have him.

I cast him in a scene with me in *Bi Golly* (The same video in which Joey Stefano had the horrible scene with Tad Bronson). The video had bad editing, bad picture quality and our scene had no sound, just some cheesy music laid over the whole thing, but our mutual enjoyment of each other is quite palpable.

The scene started with Danny and I on a bale of hay in a barn, or rather, on a barn set at Paul Pelletieri's studio, with both of us in jeans, and me in a cowboy hat and boots. Very hokey. The set was left over from *The Best Little He-She House in Texas*, which we had just filmed the day before. I figured as long as there was hay all over, we might as well get our money's worth.

We started out kissing, and I have to say that he is an amazing kisser, especially for a "straight" boy. After a few minutes of very passionate kissing, he licked his way down my chest, then I licked my way down his. I grabbed his ass through his jeans and played with it for a while, then pulled the jeans down and stuck my hands in his underwear, playing with his ass some more. The lights and the smell of the hay, combined with the smell of him, took me into an altered state. When I slid my finger in his asshole, I felt his dick throb. I shoved my finger in his ass like I owned it. Then I pulled out his dick and started sucking on it. It was delicious. After a while, he got down on his knees and pulled my dick and balls out of my jeans and started giving me head. It was definitely one of the best blowjobs of my life. He took my dick all the way down his throat and wrapped his tongue and lips around it as he came all the way back up. He licked up and down, tonguing and sucking on my balls. I was in heaven and wanted it to never stop.

Except, I did want to fuck him.

Although it is edited out of the video, at that moment, I turned him around and stuck two of my fingers up his ass. He moaned and I nearly came right then and there. I finger-fucked his ass for a while longer, with him getting louder and me getting more and more turned on. I shoved my fingers into him roughly; the meaner I got, the more he loved it. I put a condom on and slid my dick up his ass. He didn't ask me to go slow, like a lot of guys do; in fact, as I slid into him, he said, "Push it in all the way." As I did, he stuck his ass out even more, so I immediately slid all the way into him, as deep as I could possibly go up his straight boy pussy ass. Then he said, "Fuck me hard." He didn't have to ask twice. I started pounding his ass.

I fucked Danny on all fours for a long time, then flipped him over on his back on the hay bale, grabbed his ankles and started pounding into him. His ass grabbed my dick like a pair of lips, pulling in and out as they held on. It drove me right to the edge; an asshole only does that if it's been fucked a lot, by big dicks. It turned me on thinking of all the huge cocks that had fucked that hole before me, stretching it out so that it was loose and rubbery for my dick. It wasn't long before he came. He wanted me to keep fucking him while he came and even afterwards. It's so hot when guys want to keep getting fucked after they come, like they can't get enough cock, ever. I just kept going as he looked at me like I was raping him, even though he was begging me to keep fucking him.

I couldn't stand it any more. I started to cum and I pulled my cock out, ripped off the condom and came all over his chest.

After the scene he giggled and kissed me and said, "Thanks!" I never saw him in person again, but every time I see his picture or a video with him I remember our time in the haystack. He was one of the best!

MARK ALLAN

Mark is one of my best friends in the whole world and we both love to tell the story of how we met. We always act embarrassed, but the story is too great not to tell over and over: We met in someone else's bed. It was a guy who was an occasional fuck-buddy of mine and whom Mark had just met that night. It was the first night of 1994, the day after New Year's Eve. I was seeing Sharon Kane at the time, and she had stayed over that night. On New Year's Day, we called Jamie Hendrix (*see his chapter*) to come over for a three-way. After both Jamie and Sharon left, my fuck-buddy called.

"Hey, I've got a hot boy in my bed, do you want to come over?" he asked. Of course I did. Just because I had spent the whole night having sex with my girlfriend and most of the day fucking her and Jamie didn't mean I was done! Sometimes I'm insatiable. I don't see it as a weakness. Let's call it a zest for life. And cock.

When I arrived, Mark was in the bed naked, sort of standing up on his knees with his ass just barely tilted out. I can still see him. He is pretty buff now, but he was really thin then, and still just as sexy, if not even more so. There was instant electricity between us. Everything except for him faded away. He was beautiful and Oh, that ass of his! Oh my God, his ass! I had to have it, and within a few seconds I did. I was fucking him before either of us could blink. I didn't even remember walking to the bed, I just saw him and the next thing I knew I was in his tight ass pounding it the way God obviously intended when She made it.

Mark remembers it the same way. Before we realized it, it was two or three hours later. My friend was watching us, sort of lying down on the bed, jacking off. He said he was tired (probably tired of us ignoring him), so I invited Mark back to my house.

I remember the drive over in my car: first I took Mark to get his car, a few blocks away, then he followed me home. It was late, and it was cold and damp outside. His body was so warm. Before he got out of my car and into his, we made out for ten minutes or so.

Once back at my house, we parked the cars, then we were ripping each other's clothes off in the elevator. We barely made it inside my apartment. Inside, we continued having wild, passionate, intense sex. I fucked him, then he fucked me, then I fucked him again. His dick was incredible, big balls and a thick shaft with a really thick head that felt so good pounding up inside my ass. I was clawing at him, grabbing his ass and screaming as I pulled him deeper into me. Then I flipped him around and shoved my dick up his ass again and fucked him until we came to another screaming orgasm. To this day, we both agree that it was one of the most intense, fantastic, sexual experiences either of us have ever had. I don't know how many times we came before we were done. We finally fell asleep holding each other, under my huge painting of Marilyn Monroe. (I'm not a huge Marilyn fan, but I loved that painting.) Mark, however, woke up in the middle of the night and got scared thinking someone was watching us, then realized it was just the painting.

The next morning (well, early afternoon, really) we went out for breakfast and talked. We discovered that we both really liked each other beyond the sex. It was a little scary. I knew then that it would be a lifelong relationship of some sort. We started (or continued) dating. We went for walks on the beach, out to eat, stayed in bed, watched movies, cuddled, and had *lots* of sex. Every time it was just as good. Then, on the day of the '93 earthquake, I couldn't get through to Mark's phone. Days later, when I finally did, he didn't return my calls. I didn't know what was going on with him. I finally decided that it was probably too intense for him and that the level of intimacy we had reached so quickly was freaking him out. That probably wasn't the real reason, but it made me feel better to think that, at least! I waited a few weeks, and then I finally called him and left a message.

"Look, we were really good friends and I know we love each other. I want you as a friend and it's okay if you can't handle anything else," I said, then hung up and waited.   He called me back and apologized for not returning my earlier calls, and admitted that yes, he had freaked, and yes, he did feel really close to me and wanted to keep our friendship.

We became best friends then; the only problem was that I was still in love with him.   My mind knew that our relationship was no longer about sex, but my heart and body didn't want to admit it.   Then Mark started dating someone and I had to really face my feelings and deal with them.   As soon as I let go of hoping that things would go back to the way they were with Mark, I met Jay [*see Jason Pride*], and quickly fell in love with him.

Mark's boyfriend wanted to do porn videos, and they both decided to do them together.   Mark used his real first name and his boyfriend chose the name Hawk McAllistar; I put them in some videos.   Their scenes together in *A Real Man* and *Earning His Keep* are two of the hottest scenes I have ever directed.   In *A Real Man*, they were in leather in a bar.   The fucking was intense and sweaty and wild. They also were in *Dildo Pigs*, having sex right beside me and Tanner Reeves.   While I was shoving dildos up Tanner's ass, Mark was shoving even bigger ones up Hawk's.   It was a best-friend male-bonding moment.   Sort of.

After about a year of us both being in relationships and living with (and mostly financially supporting) our boyfriends we both got dumped at about the same time.   We both needed a roommate, so Mark moved into the other bedroom in my apartment.   I met my next boyfriend, Dan, (one of the very few that never made it into the porn industry).   I dated him for about nine months, but we never moved in together.   I kept living with Mark.

When I got my guest-starring role on *Xena: Warrior Princess*, I took Mark to New Zealand with me.   He was even an extra in the big scene in which I kissed Lucy Lawless, but if you blink you'll miss him.   We had a great time in New Zealand, but were starting to fight some.   I met Anaru, a Maori guy who lived there in Auckland.   We had a whirlwind romance. I stayed for a whole month with him, and then he moved back to the U.S. to live with me.

When I brought Anaru back, things between Mark and I became unbearable.   I think the bottom line was we just both needed some physical and emotional space. He moved out, just a few blocks away. After a couple of months, we were getting along fine again and Mark is still one of my best friends.

Mark is a private chef for Charles Bronson, and I learned to cook while living with him. He is a great chef and a great teacher. Every Thanksgiving, he still talks me through the rough parts over the phone and everything turns our perfect.

We have been through so much together; I will always love him.

MARK ANDREWS

Mark has been in tons of videos over the years, including a lot of mine. I include him in this section even though I met him before I began directing. With his dirty blond hair, blue eyes and tight body, he was gorgeous. More importantly, he also reeked of sex in the way a lot of porn stars do. I always thought Mark was really hot, and his dick was ever ready, willing and reliable.

One day in 1994, he said to me, "Why haven't I ever done a scene with you?" That was all I needed. I scheduled us together in my very next video. Before the camera even began rolling, we had begun groping each other while the crew was getting set up. Usually, the stars are better behaved than this (and certainly *I* am!) but Mark and I had been waiting for each other for so long that we just couldn't hold off. Once it was rolling, we started with me sucking his dick, which I could have done forever, but pretty soon he worked his way down to mine. After a while he turned me around and started licking my asshole. He was incredible, I was in total bliss. I definitely could have gone on forever, and I think he could have, too, but then it was time to fuck.

I turned around and leaned over the edge of my couch and stuck my ass up in the air. He told me he had been waiting for my ass for years. It was definitely the right thing to say! He slid his cock in my ass and started fucking me. I was in bliss again. He fucked me harder and harder and I loved it. His dick was perfect: not too big, not too small. It didn't hurt, but it hit the right spot. He was really one of the best fucks of my life, he was so great. I didn't want the scene ever to end but it eventually did. He came on my butt and I turned around and came on my stomach. When we were finished, he said "Wow, why didn't we ever do that before?" I didn't know why. We agreed to do it again soon, but never did. Shortly after that Mark sort of vanished, "back to home" people said, wherever home is for him. Hopefully he will come back and visit, both on- and off-screen.

JESSE SKYLER

I met Jesse Skyler before I had appeared in any videos. in fact, I put him in his first few videos several months after we had met, in the summer of 1994. That seemed to happen a lot: meet me, date me, fuck me, eventually do a porn video.

We met through my best friend Mark. Mark and Jesse were friends, but Mark had a big crush on Jesse. I couldn't blame him—Jesse seemed to be the typical fantasy California boy. He lived in Venice Beach. He was blond and tan and trim and buff at the same time. He was always going roller-blading, in fact he taught me how, and we would skate up and down the boardwalk between Venice and Santa Monica.

Jesse and I were both interested in each other, I think from the very beginning, but because we were both aware of Mark's feelings for him, we didn't say or do anything about our attraction. There was always sexual tension in the air when we were together, though. I think we were both determined not to let anything happen, but we were always brushing up against each other. Every time we touched, sparks flew. Of course the inevitable finally happened.

We were all at a Fourth of July pool party one day and had had a few drinks. It was a beautiful, hot summer day, everybody looked great, and sex was in the air. I went inside to use the bathroom. When I came out, Jesse had just walked into the house. A few guys were in the bedroom fooling around. We looked into the room at them and then looked at each other. He said, "We shouldn't do this." I said, "I know," and then we were kissing.

We kissed with months of desire and repressed passion, our

tongues searching deep in each others mouths, our rational minds overwhelmed by the smell of Coppertone. Soon we found our way to the room and onto the bed in the middle of a bunch of other guys, ignoring them while ripping off each other's swimsuits and vigorously sucking each other's dicks. Of course just about then, Mark walked in. He looked at us and said "Oh," and walked back out. We stopped in horror for a minute, but then the passion overtook us again. We jerked each other off while kissing, and came. Then we sort of realized that there were other people in the room. I said, "I better go check on Mark." I felt horrible. I just knew he was going to hate me.

I found him and asked if he was okay. He said that he was. While the timing had been a little tacky, (I lowered my head and nodded) he had been waiting for it to happen. He said he knew all along that Jesse and I would eventually have sex, and that he was over Jesse anyway, although I'm not sure that at that time it was true.

Jesse and Mark and I all remained friends, and Jesse and I agreed that we should never have sex again. We talked about it and decided that we had gotten it out of our systems and that it was best for everyone's sake that we remain just friends. He did start doing videos for me soon after that though, and he was always a joy to watch getting fucked. That was the one thing I wish we had done that day.

Finally on one shoot, *Earning His Keep,* the top that was supposed to fuck him couldn't get hard. We decided that the only option was for me to be a stunt dick. We were both incredibly excited, because even though we had agreed not to fool around anymore, it wasn't because we didn't want to. As I started fucking him, he caught my eye with his and held my gaze. I couldn't look away except to occasionally look down at my dick slamming in and out of his asshole. We were finally finishing what we had started almost a year before. It was intense, hot, sweaty fucking. Sometimes when filming, especially a stunt dick shot, it is obvious that everyone is just going through the motions, but this time, everyone in the crew could feel our electricity. When we both came, I proclaimed, "*That* was worth waiting for!" Jesse said, "Yeah, for me too!" We never got together again after that. Still, for the reasons I mentioned above, there is always that sexual tension between us.

CASEY JORDAN

I met Casey in 1994 when he was hanging around with my ex-fiancee, Sharon Kane. After a party, he came back to my house and I threatened to put on some of his old FALCON videos, like *Spokes II* , but he was so horrified at the thought that I restrained myself. He said he didn't want anything to do with porn anymore. People should learn that that is the surest way to get back into porn: vow that you won't. Of course, shortly thereafter, he was making videos again.

I cast him in my award-winning video, *A Real Man*, which I starred in. His scene was to be with Troy Steele, whom I had not yet met, but had only seen in pictures. We were shooting that day in the living room at Dylan Fox's house in North Hollywood. Troy showed up and was nice enough, (In fact, over the years, he has turned out to be one of the most gentlemanly guys in porn, while still being a pervert; I love that!) but he was having a hard time getting his dick hard. After a few hours of trying, we finally decided that I would be the stunt dick and fuck Casey. This was something I had looked forward to and dreamed of for years, and it was nice, but my ideal setting for a great sexual encounter does not include a camera crew. At least not with them crawling up my ass. My cock popped right in past the ring of his ass and I fucked his gorgeous round bubble butt. He moaned and squeezed my dick with his hole, but it seemed more like it was from lots of practice than from real passion. Still, I was in the hot ass that I had wanted for so long, so I savored every moment. All too soon, the scene was over, or at least the footage that we needed of the penetration. I pulled out of his hole, which was pretty loose and sloppy by now, without coming. We finished filming the scene.

Casey and I remained friends through Sharon and hung out a lot together. We never got together again, though. He likes big butch, hairy men. Maybe me in 20 years, but not now! Anyway, he still has one of my favorite asses. One time we went to the gym to work out together. He pumped iron, sweating and flexing, while I and half of the gym nearly came just watching his ass through his tight sweats that had a hole in exactly the right spot. He would tell me stories of meeting guys through the phone lines, getting fucked all night with their huge cocks and then bigger dildos, and then would be nervous going in to teach his aerobics class. Nervous that his stretched out hole would just give out after having so much shoved up it. Every time he talks about getting things shoved up that pink hole, I can barely contain myself. Oh well—as I said, maybe in 20 years.

JASON PRIDE

When I met Jason in the summer of 1994, he was Jay. He hadn't started doing videos yet. We met at Dragstrip, a club that only happened once a month. There was a different theme every month, always with drag involved. When we met, I was in drag and he was in some sort of sixties costume with a headband and beads. I was attracted to him from across the room. He was instantly drawn to me as well. He wasn't into drag queens, that wasn't why he was attracted to me; there was something else. It seemed as if he saw through the drag to me, the real me. I had never been in a situation like this before: being in drag and having a strong attraction going with someone, but knowing that it was totally separate from the drag. The energy was jumping around between us, electric. We talked for hours about all sorts of things: God, sex, where we went to school, our past relationships, the state of the world, and much more. Finally, the friend I was with wanted to go. I hated to leave Jay, but it felt totally wrong to go home together that night, so we exchanged numbers and I left.

The next day, I went to a bathhouse with an outdoor pool so

that I could lie in the sun nude. There was a really cute guy that was lying about ten feet away from me, and he seemed to be sneaking looks at me. He never came over to me, though, and I didn't go over to him. After lying in the sun a while, I went into the bathhouse and had sex with a few guys. Later that night, Jay called.

"What did you do today?" he asked.

"Oh, I just lay out in the sun all afternoon." I didn't want to tell him that I had been at a bathhouse.

"Where?" he asked.

I didn't know why he was pressing me for more information. I didn't want to lie to him, but I still didn't want to tell him that I had gone to a bathhouse.

"Oh, just by a pool." I said vaguely, knowing that it must be obvious that I was trying to avoid telling more.

"Were you at a bathhouse?" he asked. How could he know this!? Was he psychic?

"And do you have a blue bathing suit?"

"Why do you ask?" I said, knowing that the jig was up but still not knowing how.

"Because I think I was lying next to you all day," he said.

Then I was silent for a moment, putting it all together. At first, I simply couldn't believe it. Then I thought about it. At the club, he was wearing not only clothes but a weird costume. Also, I hadn't noticed his looks so much, it was his personality and spirit that I had been attracted to. I, of course, had been in drag and looked completely different naked. We talked about how funny it was that we had been lying next to each other all day without recognizing the other. I asked why he hadn't come over to me and he said it was because he wasn't sure it was me and that he was shy.

On our first date, he showed up at my door with a huge beautiful bouquet of flowers. As I stood there, a bit overwhelmed, he just looked at me.

"I was right."

"About what?" I asked.

"I knew that you would be very handsome out of drag."

Now I was *really* overwhelmed, (he loved doing that to me, throwing me off.) I took a good look at him for the first time, and noticed fully how handsome he was. Beautiful, in fact.

He took me to a very nice restaurant, Chianti on Melrose, where the waiter led us to a table with a huge bouquet of flowers.

"Um, are these for me?" I asked.

"Read the card."

I did and they were. I didn't know what to say. No one had ever given me flowers before and this guy had just done it twice. I stared at him in amazement as we ordered. Before the food arrived, the waiter brought out another huge arrangement of flowers and sat it on the table.

"Okay, I'm starting to freak out a little. Why do you keep giving me flowers and are there going to be any more, because the table is getting pretty full." I said cautiously.

I was overwhelmed in a lot of ways. It was so romantic, but it also seemed like a lot for a first date.

"I like you a lot," he said. "I know you don't know this yet but we are going to be together."

"Oh, you think so?" I answered, skeptical.

"I know," he said.

A situation like this could have been very creepy, but it wasn't; it was very, very romantic. I looked in his eyes and couldn't pull myself away from them. We talked all through dinner.

After dinner we loaded the flowers into his car and went back to my house. We were sitting on my couch and began kissing. I really liked him and didn't want to have sex yet. It seemed like it was too soon and I wanted to get to know him better. Very often, I have sex immediately when I am attracted to someone, and I wanted to try a different way. I was also probably a little afraid that if I had sex with him he would leave and I'd never see him again.

He picked me up and carried me to the bedroom. I was overwhelmed by my passion for him, but I did manage to stick to my guns and we did not have sex. After some more making out, I made him leave, much to his surprise. I kept saying "No" but he kept going.

"Uh, is this thing on?" I said pointing to my mouth. He laughed. Then he left. It took him quite a while to get used to the fact that I did exactly what I wanted when I wanted, and it was impossible to manipulate or persuade me to do anything I didn't want to do. My stubbornness nearly drove him crazy on many occasions. He had been used to always getting his way.

We had a couple of more dates, each time with him bringing me flowers, and with long talks on the phone in between. I asked him why he was so sure that we would have a future together, and he said that he just knew. He said that he had never given anyone flowers before; he had always been the one who had been pursued, but he knew that we were meant to be together. I was still skeptical, but I liked him a lot

Finally one night, even though I was still determined to wait longer, I couldn't resist him any more. He had picked me up and carried me to the bed again and we were kissing, and I felt like I never wanted to stop kissing him. It was amazing, my entire body seemed to be on fire. He unfastened my pants, and even as I was saying "No", he started sucking my dick. Soon I was saying "Yes". It was amazing; I just can't describe the feeling. I had wanted him for so long, and he had wanted me and now we were making love. The waiting had made it so delicious, so special. I unfastened his pants and discovered that his dick was hard and *huge*! Really big around. Really, really big. Really, really, really...(you get the point!)

I struggled to get my mouth around it and barely could, but I wanted so desperately to suck him all the way down my throat, that I managed to. I took him down my throat in long strokes, while my hands ran over his chest, pausing to tweak his nipples before moving on. I licked his balls and all around his dick, flicking my tongue up and down his dick, teasing him until he begged me to suck him again. I did. I was delirious and we were naked and kissing and on top of each other, and I was in heaven. He started playing with my ass.

"I want to fuck you," he said.

"Um, I don't know if that's going to be possible," I said. "You're pretty big." I knew I would take his dick no matter what, but I wanted to still resist a little. It still felt so good to flirt with him, even as we were having sex.

"I'll go very slowly," he said.

He worked my ass open first with his fingers, then put the head of his dick against my asshole and just held it there for a minute. Now he was teasing me, making me show how much I wanted him inside me.

"Put it in," I finally whispered.

He pushed just the head of his dick into me, past the ring of my ass. I took deep breaths for a minute, then was ready for more. He slowly slid all the way into me and started fucking me. It was bliss. The physical feeling combined with my emotions made me unable to think.

"Fuck me, fuck me, fuck me harder!" was all I could say.

He did. He fucked me for an incredibly long time. I'm sure it was hours, and I was in ecstasy the entire time. I didn't ever want it to stop. Finally, we both couldn't hold back any more. We came together with him fucking me, then lay holding each other for a long time. I was hopelessly in love.

Jay had the most gorgeous ass. It was perfect and of course, I wanted to fuck him, but he said, "I haven't been fucked for a long time," so I didn't push him. Finally, one night, I met him at the door wearing my tuxedo. He loved suits on guys. I had made him dinner (pasta, hoping we would need the carbs later,) and put a single red rose on the plate. After dinner I led him to the bathroom. I had drawn a bubble bath. Beside the tub were strawberries, champagne, and another red rose. I undressed him slowly and we got into the bath together. It was very romantic. After the bath, I led him to the bedroom. I had lain rose petals all over the bed. We started making love and he said he wanted me to fuck him. I asked if he was sure, and he said "Yes".

"I want you to fuck me," Jay whispered.

"Are you sure?" I asked, "Because I don't want to hurt you."

"I'm sure," he responded.

"I don't want to do anything you aren't ready for," I said.

"You want it so bad you'd sell your grandmother," he joked.

"Well, yes, but—" Jay stopped me.

The first time I slid my dick up his ass and I heard him moan, I fell in love with fucking him. If it had been a long time, it wasn't because he didn't like getting fucked. He loved it. I loved fucking his beautiful butt and hearing him moan. From then on, it was always hard to decide who would fuck whom, we both liked it so much. It was about fifty-fifty.

Pretty soon he started staying over (I only went to his house once and we didn't even sleep there.) As soon as he started staying over, it was like he moved in. His house was about forty-five minutes from me and his work was only five minutes from my apartment, so he just stayed with me every night.

After about three months of him staying over continuously, I said, "Why don't you just move in? You're here all the time anyway, so you might as well bring all your stuff and help pay rent." He was nervous about taking that step but he did it. I don't think that he was totally ready, and I think I pushed him too soon, which caused some discomfort for a few weeks, but eventually we got used to officially living together.

Eventually the inevitable happened. He decided he wanted to be in a porn video. At that time, I was not only still appearing in them, but was directing and producing as well. I swear, it was completely his decision and his idea. My friends always joke that once you sleep with me, you will eventually end up in a porn video, but that is not always the case (okay, it usually is) and I have never once tried to coerce anyone into doing porn. Jay really wanted to do it, and I saw no reason for him not to. He was a gorgeous man with a huge dick who loved sex, and on top of that, he was an exhibitionist. He was a porn star waiting to happen.

We decided that his first video would be with me, although his first scene ended up being with Dallas Taylor. I felt the tiniest bit of jealousy as they did their scene, but basically I was okay with it. The video was *A Real Man*. He wanted his stage name to be Jason Pride. I didn't really like the name, but it was going to be *his* name, so I didn't say much.

The video got great reviews. It was the first video ever to have a character that was HIV-positive, which I played. I was preparing to eventually come out publicly as being HIV-positive, but I wasn't quite ready yet.

A Real Man won one award that year at the AVN awards, and was nominated for several more. That was also the year that I was inducted into the Adult Video Hall of Fame along with Ryan Idol. Until then, the only gay porn star who was in the Hall of Fame was Jeff Stryker. I was thrilled. I was now not only the second (Ryan was inducted a minute after me) gay performer inducted into the Hall of Fame, but also the youngest director ever inducted. It was a great honor. Especially so early in my porn career. Sharon Kane (who was also in the Hall of Fame) and I always joked that the Hall of Fame award was the "Thanks for being in our industry, you're old now, so get the fuck out before it really starts to show" award. I was only 25. Where else are you old at 25?

Anyway, Jason's and my scene together in the video looks really hot. I had just put on a lot of muscle and it was the first time I didn't look like a 16 year old boy. (Chi Chi showed it to Falcon without telling them it was me and they didn't recognize me and wanted me to be in their next video.) It was difficult for us shooting though. We didn't realize it then, but it was because our sex together had always been very intimate and it felt really fake and uncomfortable performing in front of a camera together.

Still, we decided to be in the next video together, *More Than Friends*. We played boyfriends who broke up because my character was a call boy and his character couldn't handle it. After we both had new lovers, we remained friends or rather, more than friends, and decided that we were family. Sharon Kane had a hysterically funny non-sexual role that she completely ad-libbed. She plays an airy-fairy, way-out-there metaphysical freak who corners Jason at a party and tells him about all of her experiences being abducted by UFO's and with gurus who materialize and de-materialize, and also about re-birthing and all sorts of other things. These were all true(!) stories that she had told me before. I told her to just camp them up and before each shot I would just say, "Now tell the one about..." She was brilliant. She had an excellent sense of humor about herself.

I was nominated for "Best Groaner" at the Gay Video Guide Awards for this video (which was an interesting honor, I guess) as well as being nominated for Best Screenplay, Performer of the Year, and a bunch of other things at the AVN awards. Sharon was nominated for best non-sexual role. Although the scene looks really good, it too was very difficult for us and we decided that we wouldn't do scenes together anymore. Our sex life would be private; just for us. We were soon off to Hawai'i together, and when we came back, we moved down the hall to a bigger apartment, the one in which I still live today.

Soon after we moved, we started having problems. I was getting clean from drugs and I was pretty insane. We kept fighting more and more.

After a while, although we were still having problems, I felt that things were starting to get better. We had now been together for one year, which was my record for a relationship. I thought we would make it and that I would spend the rest of my life with this man I loved. One day I bought him flowers and stopped by his work to surprise him. He started crying and told me that he had decided to break up with me. I was shocked and my heart broke. I couldn't believe it.

Jay lived in the apartment for another month before he moved out— and directly in with another boyfriend. I was depressed for months. I had been so in love with him, and now I was terrified of being alone. A few weeks later, my best friend, Mark Allan, moved in with me. He had just been dumped by his boyfriend, too, so we decided we would take care of each other.

Jay and I are still friends or, perhaps I should say, friends again. Our relationship problems were not all the fault of either of us and we both realized that. Jay now lives in San Francisco and I see him whenever I am there. In fact, he comforted and counseled me when I was having a fight with my girlfriend, Jill, just before she and I broke up. More recently, he and his boyfriend had lunch with me and my new boyfriend. It was really nice that we felt so comfortable. He is a good friend.

TANNER REEVES

When I first met Tanner in 1994, I thought he was really nice and very sexy. Then when he was in one of my videos and I saw his ass, the only thought I had in my mind the whole time was how much I wanted to stick a dildo up his ass. Very soon, Pleasure Productions told me they wanted me to make a video called *Dildo Pigs*. It seemed like the perfect opportunity. I called Tanner and asked if he wanted to do a scene with me, with us fucking each other with dildos. He gave me a very firm "YES."

My friend, Mark Allan, and his boyfriend, Hawk McAllistar, were in the video with us. They were right next to us, in fact. We turned my dining room into a dungeon with black plastic everywhere. We tied my chandelier up out of the shot and moved the table into the living room. Finally, we were ready to shoot.

During the video, I fucked Tanner with various sizes of dildos. His ass was sticking up in the air and he was begging for more. I fucked him harder and harder with bigger and bigger dildos. Between takes, I kept asking him if he was okay, just to make sure he really wanted what he was asking for. He said he was fine, I could fuck him as hard as I wanted, so of course I did. You don't have to ask me twice to fuck you hard with a dildo!

By the end of the scene, I was ramming it in, pulling it all the way out and slamming it back in again, harder and harder. I decided that unless he said he needed me to stop or slow down, I wasn't abusing his hole enough. I mean, the video was called *Dildo Pigs*, so that's what we should be. After slamming it in and hitting bottom hard a few times he gasped, that maybe I should slow down a little.

Good. I did it hard enough! Finally we both came. I loved every second of it. His ass just seems to me to be made to have things shoved up it, but then I guess I feel that way about most asses. If something isn't bolted down it should be shoved up someone's ass. That's just sort of my motto in life.

Tanner has been in several of my videos over the years, like *Palm Springs Cruisin'* and *More Than Friends*. He is a good performer, and also a friend. He is another gay man that fell madly in love with my ex, Sharon Kane, and maybe our closest bond aside from that is that he loves Hawai'i as much as I do. I can tell when he talks about being there.

A few years ago, he had an accident: a truck ran into him while he was riding his bike, and it took him a year to recover, but soon he was back again, just as sexy as ever, first with his arm in a brace, and eventually without the brace. As gorgeous as his ass is, he is also a good top, as you can see in many videos. But I know how I'll always remember him: as my dildo pig!

KEN RYKER

That name seems to be the hottest name in gay porn right now, the one that sends shivers down the spines of gay men everywhere. Ken himself sent shivers down my spine, and the spines of most people who met him even before he was famous. He showed up at a party after the Gay Video Guide Awards in 1994. Everyone else was all dressed up from the show, in tuxedos or gowns. He was wearing jeans and boots. He would have stood out anyway, but the jeans, boots, and plaid shirt completed the picture, and made him look like a wet dream.

He had dirty blond hair and big puppy-dog eyes and seemed larger than life. I don't know how tall he is, but he's definitely several inches taller than my six feet. He's several inches larger elsewhere, too.

I noticed him standing outside the party, in front of some bushes that seemed to have been planted for the sole purpose of framing him. Sort of like his later videos, in which the guys he fucks seem to be a frame for his huge cock. Everything looks planned out to display him in the best possible way. But it might just look that way because he is so compelling.

His eyes followed me in as I walked past him. "Hmmm... One of the bi boys," I thought. I could just tell. I wandered around for about thirty seconds, made a quick circle through the party, then wandered quickly back outside to the front yard. I casually walked up to him, and flirted immediately, running my hands all over him, from his chest down to his enormous dick snaking down the side of his jeans. It was half hard already, and about a foot long. I surprised and flustered him by being so forward, but he obviously liked it, from the growing serpent in his pants.

He didn't grope me back, but he didn't pull away, either. He looked like he didn't know what to do, like a huge deer in the headlights. I realized he was probably new and maybe wasn't used to being groped by strangers. I thought I should give him a break, so walked away into the party without even saying a word.   He was gorgeous, but it was a big night, and there were lots more people to grope.   I didn't really know for sure then that it was his first appearance on the porn scene. If I had, I wouldn't have mauled him. Well, maybe I would have. Or at least I would have spoken to him while I was mauling him.

Soon enough though, I was inside dancing and making out with straight porn star Jeanna Fine, while Ken and the other bi/straight boys looked on jealously and I forgot about Ken, until I saw his picture popping up everywhere.

Years later, after Ken disappeared from, and then returned to, porn, reviewer Jordan Sable and I were on our way to a movie at the Beverly Center. He said

"Guess who's in love with you?"

"Who?" I asked. I was so not expecting his answer:

"Ken Ryker."

"What do you mean!?"

"He talks about you all the time. He wants to fuck you."

I was flabbergasted. I didn't know what to say. It was definitely an interesting situation. Jordan brought it up a couple of other times. I never found out more about it, and I haven't run into Ken again, but I certainly intend to. Again and again and again...

RYAN IDOL

Most people who have seen very much gay porn know who Ryan Idol is. They knew even *before* he made headlines by falling four stories to the sidewalk nearly naked in New York, and then making it out of the hospital barely scraped. I always say life isn't about how far you can throw or how fast you can run, but rather how well you can bounce. I usually don't mean it quite so literally, but I guess it works that way, too.

Idol's fall was widely reported and analyzed, and boy, did everyone speculate and come up with different stories: Some said he jumped; some said he was pushed in a drug deal gone bad; some said he was high on drugs and fell. Even *he* seemed to give different reports at different times. In most stories, he said that drugs were involved, and he felt that God saved him. It certainly was dramatic, no matter what really happened.

Ryan and I met unofficially when we were both running around West Hollywood one night with Chi Chi LaRue. I usually am discreet in West Hollywood; I try to blend in, and I don't think Ryan knew who I was then. I was just some guy with Chi Chi. We all had a lot of fun, going from one bar to another.

We met more officially on stage when we were both being inducted into the Adult Video News Hall Of Fame at the 1995 Awards. Before us, the only gay star had been Jeff Stryker. Ryan and I hung out together that night at a party thrown by his agent, David Forest. Over the years, we got to know each other and interest grew. Ryan seemed especially impressed the first time he heard me sing, and told me he thought I had a great voice. He has always sincerely congratulated me on my mainstream acting roles, as well.

He and his on-again off-again girlfriend, Ellie, were always flirting with me, either separately or together, whenever we would run into each other at the bars and parties. One night, we were all out at The Love Lounge, and they were both hanging all over me. They both smelled great, like cookies or fresh-baked bread or something. I wondered if they had been baking, and how they managed to both smell like that, even in a smoky bar. It was intoxicatingly sexy.

The three of us started making out and groping each other, hands down pants and up skirts, causing quite a scene. I was getting totally into it, until I suddenly realized that people were watching, then I realized that my dick was hanging out. Oh well, it's not like no one has ever seen it before, or like I'd never caused a scene in the Love Lounge before. I think every porn star I know has made a scene there at one time or another. Ryan and Ellie wanted me to go home with them, but for some reason, it just didn't feel right.

This sort of thing has happened a couple of times with the three of us, and each time it has seemed somehow off—not quite right. Ellie is absolutely beautiful, and it certainly isn't because I'm not interested in her. Maybe it has been because Ryan was always a bit of a loose cannon. Recently, since his accident, he has calmed down a lot, but he's still a little wild. Not too long ago, we did a charity fashion show together and we had a lot of fun hanging out back stage, cracking each other up.

I think if he asks me to go home with him again, next time, I might just say "Yes".

DINO PHILLIPS

I met Dino when I was directing the video *Earning His Keep* in July of 1995. We were up at a house in the hills on Mulholland Drive by a pool that overlooked the whole San Fernando Valley. The guy who was supposed to do a scene with Jesse Skylar didn't show up, and we were in a panic. Jesse said he knew a really hot guy that had just started doing porn, who had just done a scene with him for someone else. I asked Jesse to call him. I was a little nervous; whenever someone says that someone else is hot, it could be their own taste, and the guy might not look that great to anyone else, but I had seen the guys Jesse had been attracted to, (hell, I had been one of them,) so I knew it would be okay. Still, I would feel better once the new guy showed up.

Dino walked in while I was directing a scene between my lover, Jason Pride, and Dallas Taylor. He was gorgeous. Dino is one of those guys that looks so much better in person. He looks great on film, but in person...*Woof*! He stared at me from across the room with those incredible eyes of his. Jesse came over and told me that Dino had asked him who I was. He thought I was one of the models on that shoot, and that I was cute. I was surprised and excited to hear that. It made me flustered all through the shoot.

"Do you still appear in videos, or do you just direct them now?" Dino asked.

"I'm in them sometimes," I replied, hoping he wasn't just asking out of curiosity.

"Good—we should work together sometime," he purred.

"Uh, sure," I said, nervous all over again.

According to my live-in lover Jason's and my rules, I couldn't ask him out, but I could do a scene with him. Video scenes or casual sex were okay; planned formal dates weren't.

I mentally cast Dino with me in my next video right on the spot, but waited a day or two before calling him to make the offer. He accepted. It was called *Hard On Demand*.

The scene was shot in my bed. I was nervous and excited. We were both hard and throbbing as soon as we started. He sucked my dick first then I sucked him. He put on a condom and slid his fat cock up my ass. I loved the feeling of his dick in me. It was really hot and we were both into it, but I think we both felt a little inhibited, since Jason was there. Jason lived with me and was also in the video. Of the three of us, Jason was the only one that *didn't* feel weird. He never seemed jealous of me being with another guy.

When the stills mysteriously vanished, Dino and I had to fuck again (how sad for us) while Jason took the pictures. Jason was completely fine with it all, and we were too by then, so the second time was much better than the first. During the video, Dino held himself back a bit during the fucking, but when we did it the second time, he didn't; he fucked me all over the bed, hard, just the way I love to get fucked.

Over the next few years, Dino and I became friends. I was a stunt dick a couple of times and fucked him in videos like in *3-Some*. When you see what looks like Morgan Allen pounding Dino while Dino is nailing Grant Wood, it's really me fucking Dino.

We never got together off camera. The timing was just never right and eventually we were the sort of friends who aren't sexual. It's too bad, because Dino is so hot and really sweet at the same time. We probably would have made a good couple. Or at least a good couple of tricks.

Dino has been in a lot of my videos. My girlfriend, Jill, was madly in lust with Dino when he flew to Hawai'i in the Spring of 1998, to be in my video, *Hawai'ian Vacation*. We were all staying in my friend's mansion just outside of Honolulu, and Dino was walking around the whole time in underwear, or a swimsuit, or just a towel. I told Jill that as far as I knew he was incredibly gay. I couldn't really imagine him with a woman. She was jealous when I told her about Dino fucking me in the video, jealous that I got his cock in me and she didn't, until she realized that if it was on video, she could see it. She borrowed my copy of *Hard On Demand* and never gave it back. Jill and I broke up, but are still friends. She asks about him now whenever I talk to her.

SPENSER ALLEN

Spenser didn't stay long in the porn business. I don't know why, and I haven't seen him for a few years, but the scene I was in with him is one of my most vivid memories in the porn industry.

I met Spenser in June of 1995, and he asked me to go out with him. I had a boyfriend that I was living with at the time, Jason Pride. I had a video coming up that weekend, and I needed another person for a scene with me, so I told him I couldn't really go out with him, but I asked him if he wanted to do the scene. He said yes. The video was *The Streets of L.A.*, the first of two videos that I shot for Pleasure Productions outside in the streets and alleys. We just went outside with the guys and a little camera and shot sex all over the place. The videos were narrated by me, and I had scenes in each video. Both videos got really good reviews and I think that they are two of the hottest videos that I have ever made, since there was always the possibility of getting caught. When we were shooting that scene, it wasn't just a possibility.

First thing that morning, we shot a scene with Tony Belmonte and Jesse Skylar in the alley behind my best friend Mark Allan's house in Venice. They were fucking in the alley, and no one noticed. We were done by 1:00 p.m., and then Spenser and I and the camera person, John Simms, went out to the beach in my Mustang convertible to film the scene that I was to be in.

We found a big empty parking lot right in front of the ocean, not too far from the Santa Monica pier. I don't know why it was empty on such a beautiful day. It was odd, now that I think about that. My dick was hard the whole time we were driving to the parking lot. I just couldn't wait. Spenser started giving me head while I was in the driver's seat. He gulped my whole dick down his throat, then slowly slid back up my shaft. My head leaned back as I moaned with pleasure. Spenser's mouth was driving me wild.

The top was down on the car, and John stood outside, shooting down into the car. It was a gorgeous sunny day, one of the first real Summer days that year. It was hot, but there was a cool breeze blowing in from the ocean that smelled fresh and salty. We were all so into what we were doing that none of us noticed the police car drive up about 20 feet in front of us. If you watch the video, the shot pans up from my dick to the police car then the picture goes out.

We all panicked. The policeman walked over to us (my shorts and Spenser's head were up by now) and made us all get out of the car. I got out wearing my tiny tight red stretchy shorts showing a big bulge still trying to look innocent, but not pulling it off. With the big, burly, absolutely-hot stud cop looking me up and down, my bulge was growing again. I started to fantasize about him frisking me.

"What are you all doing here?"

"Uh...we were just looking at the ocean," I stammered.

I was trying to talk us out of trouble, but I was so freaked out that I instantly made the situation worse by lying, an incredibly stupid lie too. I've never been good at lying, which is one reason I don't generally do it.

"We're visiting from Missouri," I said.

I thought I still had my Missouri ID. When the policeman asked for my ID, I discovered I was wrong.

"What were you shooting on the camera?" He asked.

I knew I was just making it worse by lying, but I couldn't seem to stop. I'm a terrible liar. I just can't do it convincingly. I always get caught.

"The ocean!" I said, sounding like a pathetic five year old with his hand in the cookie jar, who keeps insisting he wasn't stealing cookies.

"Then why was the camera pointed down into the car?" he asked.

I panicked and froze. I didn't have an answer for that one, and it was obvious that he knew what we were doing. All I could think was that we were all much too pretty to go to jail. Even with officer Studly Do Right taking us in, it wasn't what we really wanted.

"Look, you can either tell me now or we can all go down to the station and play the tape, whichever you want," the policeman said.

"Look...we were just fooling around...we didn't mean to hurt anybody...we'll never do it again," I whimpered.

I probably sounded so pathetic and looked so terrified, that he felt sorry for me.

"Well, all right, just move along then, and don't do it again!" the officer said.

I couldn't believe it. He was letting us go. Some guy named Snake wasn't going to make me his prison bitch after all.

We realized that he had believed me, that we were just some perverts filming each other with a camera (it was a small one that looked like any tourist's camcorder). If he had realized we had been making a professional porn video, this book would probably be my prison memoirs. Then again, if he'd seen the footage, maybe this story would be even better concluding with him fucking us all.

We were all pretty shaken, but we went back to my house and finished shooting the scene there. It was just what I needed to calm me down. If I could just get fucked every time I got upset, life would be great. Spenser had been really scared too, and the sex was an incredible release of tension for both of us.

We started again with him sucking my dick, then I sucked his. It was really long, but not too thick to get all the way down my throat. I was really going wild on it and also proud of myself that I was taking it all the way down my throat. I wanted it all the way up my ass though, and soon it was. He slid it in and it seemed to just keep going in forever, until finally it was lodged all the way up my hole. I love getting fucked by long dicks, fat or not. The feeling of it sliding in and in and in forever and then all the way back out again was making me think that maybe I should go out with him after all. I mean, you can have a boyfriend and still date other people can't you? Or maybe we would just be fuck-buddies, yeah, that's it. As Spenser fucked me faster and faster, I soon lost the ability to think. I couldn't do anything but fuck. Eventually we both came, shooting our loads all over each other. The scene and the long day were over.

I came back to reality and realized that while I had an open relationship with Jay, and I fucked around with other people, I didn't really want to date anyone else. Spenser did do a few more films after that one, so at least I know that it wasn't the trauma of the near arrest that got him to retire from the business. He probably just moved on as most do. I'm sure he won't forget me, and I sure won't ever forget him or that day!

I didn't know what became of Spencer until just before this book went to print in 2000. I was on Maui at a party and I walked past him. Of course I recognized him. He didn't recognize me, but when I gave him a few hints he did, and we laughed about our adventure and close call together. He has been living on Maui for a few years and loves it there. And he's madly in love with a lover he's been with for a year. That's equal to seven in heterosexual years, you know. It was nice to run into one of my film fuck-buddies that had vanished. He is a really nice guy and we had a great time hanging out on Maui. He looks even more handsome than before, and definitely is just as sexy. I love his big nose. It's unique and so hot. And his other big body part. Maybe sometime he and his lover will want to have a three-way with me. I can always hope can't I?

MARC SABER

I had seen Marc in a few videos, including one of my all-time favorite scenes, the one with Chip Daniels and Ray Butler in *Overload*. Watching him sucking dick, fucking and getting fucked in that scene, made me come many times. Especially the look on his face as he is getting fucked. At one point, he gets a dildo up his beautiful ass, then he fist-fucks Ray.

Somehow, Marc got my number and called me in September of 1995. He wanted to be in one of my videos. I said, "Sure", I would love to use him, he didn't have to come over, but he said he wanted to; he liked to meet the people he was going to work for before he did a video. He came in and said, "I know you need to see me naked." Before I could stop him, he had his clothes off. When he pulled down his pants, his dick popped out rock hard and *big*. He obviously got off on people seeing him and wanting him. He turned around and spread his gorgeous ass showing me his delicious looking hole. It was puckered out and looked wet. He squeezed it and it winked at me.

"Why don't you stick a finger in and see what it feels like?" he asked.

He was obviously horny, and wanted my finger in his ass. Since I had already told him he was hired for the video, I figured if he wanted to play, then I did too, after all, I had jacked off watching him so many times. Here again, I felt like God was giving me a little gift on a silver platter. I wondered what I had done to deserve this, but only for a second, then I stuck my finger up his asshole. It was already all lubed up. He was prepared. He was really nasty and

I loved it. I had a feeling that he woke up every morning and lubed up his hole, and probably never in vain.

"Stick three or four up there," he ordered. I stuck in three and started finger-fucking his hole. He was humping back on my fingers and moaning like a dog getting fucked. He had that same look on his face that he had in videos. I shoved another finger in and stretched his hot, wet, welcoming hole a little more.

"Harder!" he barked. So I shoved them in and pulled them out, twisting my hand inside his ass and abusing his hole like it was a toy just there for me to play with. It was, after all.

"Gimme your cock," he said and turned around and practically ripped my jeans off me. He swallowed my whole dick all the way down his throat and wrapped his mouth around my balls, too. Then he just held it there for a while. Finally, he had to breathe and he started sucking hard and fast.

"I want this dick up my hole," he said and spun around and sat all the way down on it in one move. His asshole was still all wet and warm up inside and felt great wrapped around my dick. He reached back around and pushed my balls inside his ass, too, then gripped his hole down around them all so that nothing would come out. I started fucking him with my balls up in his ass. It was the wildest feeling

I fucked him on his hands and knees with his gorgeous ass up in the air for a long, long time, then he asked if I had anything bigger. I smiled and got out some big dildos. He picked the biggest one, almost as big around as my arm, and said, "Shove this up my hole." I did, and it went right in, all the way to the base. I started really fucking him with the dildo, pulling it all the way out and then shoving it back in. I was twisting it around in him and abusing his hole the best I could. He couldn't get enough.

All of a sudden, he said he wanted to fuck me. Almost before I knew it, he was tonguing my hole to get it wet, and then loosening me up with his fingers. In one fell swoop, he shoved his dick all the way in. I gasped. It hurt like hell, but it felt great. After he had taken all that abuse from my cock, I was determined to take whatever he gave me. As he fucked me, the pain melted into ecstasy. Out of the blue, he popped his balls inside my ass, just like I had with him, and kept fucking me. It was an amazing feeling, being totally filled like that, with my asshole clamped down hard around his cock and balls. Just as quickly as he had begun, he pulled everything out of my stretched-out hole and shot all over my face. I shot on his ass with my asshole clenching and squeezing, already missing the feeling of his dick inside me. He leaned over to kiss me and smeared the cum all over both of our faces. Then he said he had to go. I asked if he wanted to take a shower and he said "No, someone else is waiting for my ass." He pulled up his jeans and left, with cum still on his face. It totally turned me on to think of the next guy that would find his lubed, up stretched-out hole and be up inside it soon. I wondered how many there were before me that day!

Marc was in my video, *Leather Lover*, in a scene with my then-boyfriend, Jason Pride. I loved watching Jason fuck him. He made all the same sounds and faces all over again. Marc was supposed to be in my video, *Sex Trigger*, which we filmed in October. He showed up the first day and was in a dialogue scene where some guys are sitting around talking about what gets them off. The next day he was in my convertible with Jay and I going to the set. Suddenly, he said,

"I've gotta go." and he threw his bag out of the car. Before I had completely stopped the car, he had jumped out and ran off. Jason and I looked at each other in amazement. I turned to Jason,

"Um...you don't suppose he's coming back, do you?"

"I don't think so," Jason said. We ended up getting a replacement for him, and we never heard from Marc Saber again. He never returned my calls, and no one seemed to know whatever became of him.

It was a very bizarre departure, but as you can tell from reading this book, I am used to the bizarre. In fact, I seem to be a magnet for psychos and fruitcakes. And not just in the porn industry. My experiences with TV and movie stars and recording artists top even the most freaky porn star encounters. You'll have to read my next book for those stories.

As for Marc Saber, who knows? Maybe one day I'll be driving along and he'll jump back into the car.

RICHARD REYES

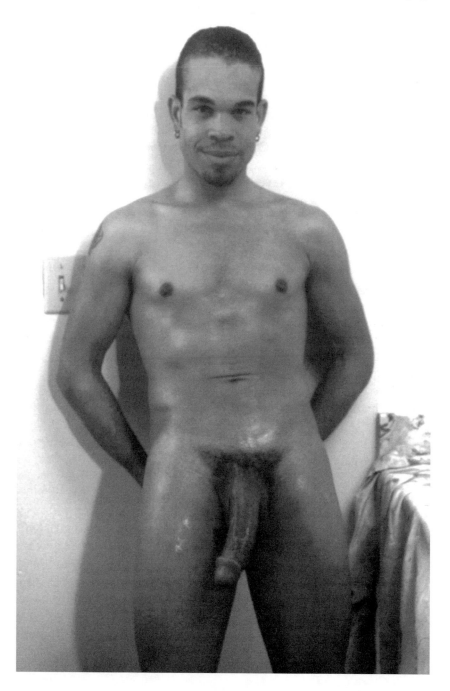

I met Richard in a bathhouse, the infamous Hollywood Spa, in 1995. A cute blond guy had been sucking my dick for about an hour: we had the door of my room open, and Richard came in. I didn't know who he was at the time, and he didn't know who I was. He started sucking the blond guy's dick and stuck his gorgeous ass up in my face. I started licking his juicy asshole and then fingering it. I pulled his huge cock back between his legs and sucked it down my throat. By then he was moaning for me to fuck him, so after shoving a few more fingers up his ass, I did. I slid my dick into his perfect ass ever-so-slowly and fucked him. He let out a low moan as my cock slid up his wet chute. The other guy eventually came and left, but we kept going for a long time.

I fucked him in every position we could think of. I kept getting close to coming, but didn't want to stop fucking him. I would hold back until the urge had passed, my dick still embedded in his ass, then continue fucking him.

The loud, obnoxious music of the bathhouse, the smells of Crisco, poppers and sex layered into the walls of the building were all working together like alchemy with Richard's moans. He moans in this way that sounds like a cat being drowned. I know that sounds like it would be weird, but it is actually incredibly sexy. Finally I pulled my dick out and came in his face, I couldn't hold back anymore. He licked my cum off his lips and shot his load onto my chest, then smeared it around.

As we were getting ready to leave, Richard gave me his number, and when I went home, I copied it into in my book. I called him once to get together with him, but he had a mysterious reason why he couldn't come over right then. He told me later that it had been a porn video that he was shooting.

The next time I saw him, again, I didn't recognize him. I was at The Love Lounge in West Hollywood performing the song *Sex* (*I'm a...*), wearing only shaving cream, with the Showboys (Kurt Young, David Thompson, Dino Phillips, and Grant Wood) and Marshall O Boy as my backup dancers, or backup sex sluts, really, since they were all wearing only shaving cream and came crawling onto the stage and started sucking and fucking and didn't exactly dance. At one point I sucked, Grant's dick and the crowd went wild. (I was banned from performing at the club for one year after this performance, but everybody talked about it for that entire year, so it was definitely worth it.)

Near the end of the song, Richard, whom I still didn't recognize, came up on the stage and dropped his pants. Then he pulled down his underwear. I thought, "Perfect! Cute guys from the audience are joining in!" I started sucking his dick. The crowd went wild again. Later, in the dressing room, I flirted with him and thanked him for coming up on stage and letting me suck his dick. I told him I would rather do it in my bed, though. He gave me his number.

When I got home, I realized that something seemed familiar about the name and number. I looked in my book and of course it was already there. I called him up immediately.

"Hi, do you remember me? I just sucked your dick on stage," I said.

"Of course I remember you," he replied.

"Well, I also fucked you in the bathhouse a year ago, and we talked on the phone once after that but never got together."

Richard started laughing.

"That was you? Oh my God!"

He came over that night.

We got together many times after that, either from him calling me, or me calling him, or me fucking him at an O Boy party, or us running into each other in a nightclub. We would always end up making out passionately, right in the club, until we were on the verge of fucking right there, and then rush back to my house and fuck all night.

We got really wild together. I would always shave his asshole first, and then shove my tongue up it once it was nice and smooth. He loved getting fucked with big dildos, too. Sometimes he would fuck me, and once or twice we invited another guy over, as well. Sometimes we would play out fantasy scenes: A couple of times I tied him up and blindfolded him before I fucked him. He was always up for anything. Until recently, when I repainted, his bootprint was on my wall above my bed, as a constant reminder of him, his big dick and his hot ass.

SONNY MARKHAM

My favorite experience with Sonny Markham was at one of Chi Chi LaRue's birthday parties. We had met several times before, but only casually, in large groups of friends. I never knew before that he was a drag fucker (or tranny chaser, whatever phrase is your favorite.) I had gone back and forth trying to decide whether or not to go in drag. I really hated getting in drag, it took so long, and even though it was late Fall, I was afraid it would be hot at the party since Chi Chi's parties were always so crowded. Being in drag is hot already; the wig on top of that feels like wearing a big teased wool hat. However, I thought Chi Chi might be offended if I didn't show up in drag. At the last minute, I decided to go in drag, after all. I wore a tiny little short slip dress in case it was hot. It was, in more ways than I had anticipated.

I hadn't been there very long when Sonny came up to me and grabbed my ass.

"Who are you?" he asked. I was amused that he didn't recognize me.

"Geoffrey Karen Dior," I answered.

Sonny recoiled as though he just realized just pinched the ass of the Queen of England by mistake.

"Oh my god! I'm so sorry! I didn't realize it was you. I wouldn't have done that if I'd known it was you," he said.

"Why not?" I asked, confused.

"Because you're Karen Dior!" he stammered, as though he were saying "because you're the First Lady!" You would have thought I was a nun or something. I mean, you're reading this book: I've done a lot more than being groped at a party!

"It's okay, really," I said. He smiled and seemed very relieved. A few minutes later, I went into the tiny bathroom and he followed me in.

"Look" he said. He pulled his dick, rock hard, out of his pants. He just looked at me and stroked it.

"I'd love to um... but I can't," I said.

"You don't like me," he whined.

"No, I do like you, What's not to like, am I crazy? It's just that I can't mess up my lipstick. I have to go back out to the party, and people will see me, and there are photographers..." He looked like a sad puppy.

"You don't like me," he said again.

I didn't want him to think I didn't like him—I liked him a lot, and it was beginning to show from under my short dress. I decided that I had been in all those videos without messing up my lipstick, and anyway, I was in the bathroom with a mirror, I could always fix it. Besides, he was grabbing my cock by now, and there was no way I could stop. He sucked on my dick first, gulping it all into his mouth. Now the puppy was happy, he had a bone. He sucked it furiously, and was really good. He pulled all the way off my cock and flicked his tongue at the tip. Spit stretched between his tongue and my cock for a second, then it was back down his throat, again. I grabbed the back of his neck and pulled him even closer. Damn, he had a big neck!

Way too soon, I was about to come, but I didn't want to yet, not without sucking on that gorgeous dick that had lured me into this situation in the first place. I went down on him. I looked up at him and he was watching me intently. I think he had the hardest dick I have ever seen. It perfectly suited his hard body. His thighs were incredible, they were so thick, like tree trunks growing up into him.

I suddenly realized what I was doing and was momentarily horrified. I thought, "I'm at a party, down on my knees in a dirty bathroom *in drag* sucking someone off with about five-hundred people outside the door. What a slut I am!" Then I got turned on again by how incredibly nasty and trashy the whole situation was. I decided that it was a good kind of trashy, not a bad kind and kept sucking. Sonny was really getting into it now and was about to come, I think, he was getting so loud. He leaned his head back and touched his nipples as I licked up to his navel, then slowly back down to his cock. I sucked his balls into my mouth one at a time, then let my tongue wander all the way up the underside of his dick before sucking it into my mouth again.

Just as we were both about to shoot, Chi Chi barreled in like a freight train. "Hrrghhii!" I mumbled, Sonny's dick still in my mouth. Damn! She was always doing this—interrupting me right in the middle of good, trashy sex! Marshall O Boy had been watching the door for us, to make sure no one came in, but he obviously couldn't keep out the host.

"My turn!" she said and pushed me aside. She must have heard us. It was clear that there was no way I was going to push a 6'3" two-hundred-fifty pound drag queen away from that dick, so I checked my lipstick (it was still perfect), tried to hide my still-hard dick (not an easy task) and discreetly exited the facilities. I don't know exactly what happened in there after that, but it was quite a while before they came out, with Chi Chi looking very happy. She walked by me and said,

"Thanks girl! Now *that's* a birthday present!"

KIP KASEY

Kip sent pictures to me in the mail. Not just a few Polaroids, or even small snapshots. Color 8x10's, nude, mounted on poster board, with his phone number on the back. Of course I called him. I had to hand it to him, it definitely is a way to get your picture noticed! Not that I would have ignored his picture anyway—he was hot, with dark wavy hair, a tight, well-muscled body, dark hair on his chest and a friendly, sexy grin. I quickly got as hard as the poster board-mounted picture I held in my hand.

Kip had been in the business for several years, and had been in lots of videos. He knew who I was, but for some reason we had never met. He had gotten my address from someone, and was sending me pictures so that he could be in one of my videos.

When I called, he came over to meet me and we talked. We somehow decided that even though I had the nude pictures of him, it would be fun to take some Polaroids, and of course he wanted help getting hard. Thank you God, Thank you God!

We went from my living room into the bedroom, and I went down to suck on his dick. It was already pretty hard before I even got my mouth around it, but I was certainly not going to say "No" to this gorgeous stud asking me to suck his dick. I was able to get the entire thing in my mouth: I love that! I reached around to grab his ass and pulled him into my mouth over and over. Then my hands wandered up to his chest, through the soft fur and over to his nipples. God, what a sexy chest he has! I cupped his huge pecs like they were tits on a woman. They were big enough to be breasts, but very, very firm. I couldn't remember ever having seen a guy with pecs like his. I was really getting into sucking him when he pulled me up and went down on my dick. He was good, definitely a pro. I rolled my head back and closed my eyes as he moved up and down my cock, waves of pleasure washing over me. I looked over in my huge mirror and watched him down on his knees. The sight of his swarthy, hairy, muscled body down there sucking me off made me ready to come almost instantly.

I pulled him up and we took some pictures, and then decided to finish by jacking each other off. We came at the same time, shooting all over each other's dicks. Just after he came he said, "My roommate will never believe that I just had sex with Geoffrey Karen Dior." He said it wasn't what he had planned, it just felt right at the time. It felt right for me too!

After that day, Kip and I began to run into each other all the time, at parties and porn events. It was a long time before he ever actually made it into one of my videos—he always seemed to be unavailable when I was filming—but he did finally do one.

He is a very friendly, easy going guy, and is very popular among other porn stars and directors. What's not to like?

LEO MASTERS

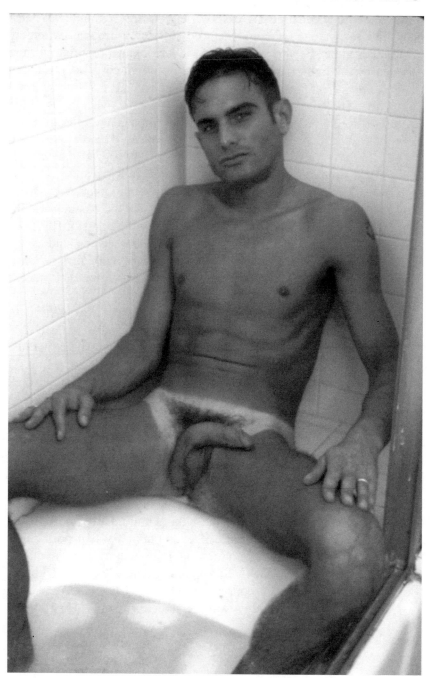

Leo is another guy that I first saw in a Falcon video. I knew he was gorgeous and sexy, but not much else. I met him a few years later when he was dating my ex-boyfriend, Tony Belmonte. When I saw him in person, I thought he was so sexy I became extremely distracted. Since he was dating Tony, it seemed inappropriate for me to even flirt with him, but I did put him in my videos. Lots of them, like *Behind His Back, Desert Maneuvers, Desert Paradise*, and *Sexcuses*. The beginning of his scene in *Sexcuses*, when he is in the bathtub (my bathtub, by the way) fucking himself with the dildo, is sooo hot!

In two of my videos, *Behind His Back* and *Desert Paradise*, I had to be a stunt dick and fuck him. I swear I didn't plan it! In fact, in *Desert Paradise* he is supposed to be getting fucked by York Powers, who is one of the most reliable dicks in the business. York was just having a bad day; it happens to everyone occasionally. But the funny thing is that that video got great reviews which said things like, "all of the fucking is way above average, especially York Powers' huge cock pounding Leo Masters." Not only was it *my* dick in *that* scene, but I also did *all* the fucking in *every* scene in that video, except one. We were in Palm Springs and the heat just was getting to everybody else, but it certainly didn't keep me from fucking Leo! I love the heat anyway, and Leo has the most amazing asshole that just grabs your dick and stretches in and out as you are fucking him. I don't see how anyone could even notice anything else with their dick up that hole. I sure couldn't. I pounded Leo's ass while he looked up at me smiling, as if he had somehow planned this all along. We definitely had waited a long time for this moment.

One time after he and Tony were no longer dating, but were still friends, we all went to a bathhouse together. Leo came into my room and we got each other warmed up before going out to cruise the rest of the guys in the bathhouse. It was the only time I was alone with him without cameras, at least so far, although at a party not too long ago we made out madly in front of everyone. (It was a porn star's birthday party—no one even notices making out at events like that— you pretty much have to fuck while spinning plates or juggling knives or something to stand out in our crowd.)

Anyway maybe there's still a chance for more. What do you say, Leo?

From Behind the Camera

These stories largely came from after my retirement from appearing in front of the camera. I had begun appearing in television and mainstream movie roles, but a couple of times, I jumped back in front of the porn camera. I will probably never claim to be completely retired; I may or may not return to appear in porn videos. If I do, it will most likely be in response to my fans, who continue to write asking to see more of me. To all of you I say again: *I love you!*

GORDON LEE

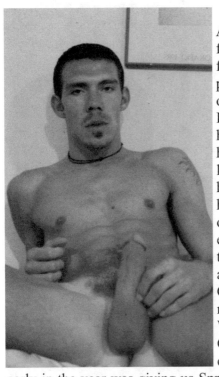

I met Gordon at a party in April of 1996, through a mutual friend, Bill. I was there with my friend Tony (who wasn't in the porn business), and another friend of Bill's, who had ridden with me. I offered to give Gordon a ride home. I took my other friend home first, although he actually lived closer to me and it would have been more practical to drop him off last. He kept pointing this out to me, but I kept finding excuses as to why I was doing it the way I was. I was really horny and could definitely tell that Gordon was too. It was a warm night, even though it was April. We sped through Silverlake to Gordon's house with the top down on the car. The warm night so early in the year was giving us Spring Fever, and there was just one cure.

When we got to his house, Gordon invited me in. He was showing me all around the house, and when we got to the kitchen, I turned around and started rubbing my ass up against him. Within seconds both of us had our pants down around our ankles and he was fucking the shit out of me. Once again I had a huge cock rammed up my ass with no lube, no spit, nothing. He just rammed it in. And I loved it! I was standing bent over, grabbing my ankles in the middle of his kitchen. I think we both had expected the tour of the house to end in sex, but not in the kitchen. But then, why not?

He fucked me mercilessly and I ate it up. As he slammed in and out of my rear, I grabbed at the edge of the stove but couldn't quite reach it. I just grabbed my ankles again and continued to take his fat cock up my hole. I hadn't been fucked for a while and not only needed it, but needed it hard and nasty. And that was just how I was getting it.

At one point, we somehow moved to the living room and continued on the sofa. Gordon's dick is pretty big and I was loving getting plowed by it. Finally, we couldn't hold back. Just as I started to come, he did too. When we were finished, I was a bit dazed.

Just then, his roommate came home. I was ready to be embarrassed, lying there with my hole stretched out and pointing right up at him, but he just walked in and said "Hello", as though he were quite accustomed to finding Gordon with naked guys in the living room. (We became very good friends later and I learned that this was indeed not uncommon. Gordon was very, shall we say, *friendly*.)

Gordon has since appeared in many of my videos and is still one of my best friends. He has a biting, brilliant sense of humor and is also my biggest fan.

When I moved into the apartment I live in now, Gordon helped me decorate it. We always joke that I am missing the gay decorating gene. Then again, we always joke about everything; that is one of the reasons I love Gordon. If I am taking something too seriously, he will snap me out of it. He is a great friend. We have been through many, many adventures together and our friendship has survived him moving from L.A. to Phoenix, to San Francisco, and now back to L.A. I'm sure it will endure much more.

MICHAEL VISTA

Michael is another guy that I met through our mutual friend Bill. I saw him originally at a dance performance in 1995, but didn't actually meet him at that time. He was in a chorus line, but he stood out among all of the other dancers. There was something about him that was so sexy. When I did actually meet him face-to-face a few months later in the Spring of 1996, I was in drag backstage before a performance. I talked and flirted with him as best I could in drag. It was obvious that he was quite gay and was not sexually interested in a drag queen, although he was very friendly and said that he was a big fan of mine. I was a little nervous because I was attracted to him.

The next time I ran into Michael was at an audition for the Braun razor commercial that I eventually was in. I didn't go in drag, I just brought an array of pictures and a demo reel, so Michael didn't recognize me. He, on the other hand, *was* in drag, so *I* didn't recognize *him*. We sat in the waiting room, not recognizing each other, until someone came over to say good-bye to me and called me Karen Dior. Michael then reintroduced himself to me.

We talked while waiting to be called in, and he told me that he was interested in doing porn videos. I told him that I thought he was very sexy (not in drag) and to just either send me some nude pictures or drop them by my house, or if he didn't have any I could take some for him. I said that if he looked as good out of his clothes as he did in them then he would do well in porn. I could tell that he really wanted to do it, not just for the money, but for the sexual thrill. Those types of guys make the best porn stars.

He slid some Polaroid pictures under my door a few days later. He did indeed look good nude. I wished that he had needed

211

me to take pictures rather than just dropping them off. I called him up and asked him if he wanted to be in my next video. He did, and in fact would be in many other of my videos.

An amusing bit of gossip about him is that he picked his last name by the street that he used to live on. It's an old drag queen trick: you take the name of your first pet and the name of the street you live on and you have your drag name. People end up with names like Fluffy DeLongpre and Bitsy Martel. And Chi Chi LaRue. If I did that, I would be Charity Kings. As time went on, Michael and I became friends, but I was still developing a crush on him and I didn't know how to tell him, because I wasn't sure if the feelings were reciprocal.

Finally, the inevitable happened. We were in Palm Springs shooting the video *Desert Paradise* and the guy that was supposed to fuck Michael couldn't get hard to save his life. We decided that I should be a stunt dick. The moment I had been waiting for! Sometimes when stunt dicking, it is pretty mechanical, just fucking for the angles and shots that the camera needs. This was definitely not the case with Michael. I stuck my fingers in his hot ass first "to help me get hard." It worked—I got hard instantly, put on a condom and slid my boner up that hot little ass. I was slamming my dick into him and he was looking into my eyes the entire time. I pulled my dick all the way out and shoved it back in as he looked at me in amazement. He was obviously seeing me in a whole new light. I was very sorry when it was over, and he said he was too.

A week later, our mutual friend Gordon Lee told me that Michael had told him that I had fucked him, that it was really good, and that he hoped it happened again. Not only did my heart and dick leap, but I got the courage to call him and tell him my feelings for him. He was very sweet and said that although, yes, he had loved getting fucked by me, he valued our friendship too much to get involved, and he was afraid that if we did get involved our friendship would be damaged because normally his relationships didn't last very long. I was disappointed, but appreciated his honesty.

Michael and I have continued to be great friends. I can call if I am really depressed or just feeling crazy. We go to porn events sometimes together or to movies or dinner or just hang out. He is a great guy, and in my and many others' opinions, has been very underrated as a porn star. His performances are always genuine and very hot. You can read more about him in the Brian Dean chapter.

COLE REECE

Cole Reece was referred to me by another model and came to my apartment to meet with me in May of 1996. I was instantly attracted to him, but wasn't sure if he was interested in me. When we tried to take a Polaroid, it turned out that my camera was out of film. I told him it was okay—I wanted to use him in my next video and I didn't have to have a picture.

Throughout his scene in the video, I was aching to fuck him. I thought that he was also interested in me, but I couldn't tell for sure.

I didn't want to make the first move; I'm normally very cautious with models. It's a strange situation: On the one hand, they are working for me and therefore it seems inappropriate for me to make any sexual advances. On the other hand, I was at the time still a model in videos too, and before I was a director, we (the models) all fucked around. Most of us are in this business partly because we are big sluts, and our business is sex, not something like banking, so I'm not always sure where to draw the line. Since becoming a director, I usually wait for a model to make a first move. Luckily for me, Cole did.

Cole called me the next day and said that he wanted to come over for me to take a Polaroid, since I hadn't had film the other day. I told him that it wasn't necessary, but he insisted. When he got to my house, he took off his clothes and immediately asked if I would help him get hard. I started sucking his dick and then his balls and then as he rolled onto his back, licking his asshole. I shoved my tongue up his ass, just like I had wanted to the entire day before. He wanted me to fuck him. I had been ready since I met him so I stuck my dick in and started fucking him. It was amazing, one of those times when I knew that there was more of a connection than just sex. As I fucked his hot little ass, I went wild. He was a deeply sexual being, and we were connecting on a level much deeper than the purely physical.

I kissed him and fucked him, and kissed him and fucked him until we both came into a delicious frenzied explosion. As he was putting on his clothes, he asked me if I would go out with him. He said that he had wanted to ask me from the beginning but had been shy. I said "Yes".

We never actually got together. He called to postpone three times, and after the third time, I said "Um...this isn't going to work for me. We can still be friends, though, and I still want to use you in videos, I just don't like having dates constantly canceled." He later told me that he understood and explained to me that he had been going through a particularly difficult time and had no hard feelings.

Soon after that, he started dating Nick Collins and they moved to San Diego together and both do videos occasionally. As far as I know, they are still together. They are both really nice guys and certainly deserve each other, but you still can't help but wish they would share themselves with the rest of us more often!

MORGAN ALLAN

I met Morgan one July night in 1996. My friend, Jason Nikas, brought him to dinner. Joining us were my transsexual friend, Christy McNicole, from Australia, whom I had recently met, and my good friend and ex-boyfriend, Bill, one of the few that never did porn. Morgan and I really hit it off. He was new to the porn industry, and I found him to be fascinating. He had been a Mormon missionary, he was currently a geophysicist, and he was absolutely brilliant. He was also just getting over a divorce from his wife, whom he had really loved.

Morgan and I became good friends, and started going out together all the time. He was going through what he called his "slut phase" and wanted to (and did) have sex with nearly everyone he met. It happened to be at a time when I was not in a slut phase (believe it or not). I was really wanting a boyfriend to settle down with, and Morgan seemed perfect. We were very attracted to each other, but I think Morgan didn't want to just have sex with me because he was afraid that it would be like leading me on, and he had no intention of dating just one person. Morgan was funny, intelligent and sexy, and I just couldn't figure out why he didn't see that we would be perfect together.

One night in November, we went out together. I was singing at a club, The Love Lounge, and was also celebrating because I had just found out that I had gotten a part on *Xena: Warrior Princess*. Well, I hadn't found out *officially*, but I was sure I had it. The director, Marina Sargenti, came to the club to see me sing, and I felt sure that after seeing me perform live she would want me for the part. I knew I had done well at the audition.

Morgan and I both had a couple of drinks, and decided that neither of us should drive. Another guy (who would much later become James Perry's boyfriend) who really wanted both of us, kindly volunteered to drive us home in my car, so off we all went.

The next thing I knew, we were all in my bed (It's like a magnet sometimes). Pretty soon the other guy left, (I think he called a cab) because Morgan and I were totally into each other and were completely ignoring him. The months of desire and repressed passion were finally being released. It was so delicious, especially because we had waited so long. I loved kissing him, and holding him, and being inside his delicious ass. I fucked him literally for hours. We would stop, fall asleep for a while, and then wake up and continue. This went on until the sun came up. In the morning we looked at each other and said, "Wow!" It had been really amazing. After that we still hung out together and occasionally fucked. I continued to hold myself back from falling in love.

Morgan and I and an entire cast and crew went to Palm Springs to film the video, *Palm Springs Cruisin'*. Or I should say, almost an entire cast. Three people canceled at the last second, we didn't find out until we were actually in Palm Springs that they weren't coming. There was a cute guy at the resort that most of us got around to fucking that weekend. I asked him if he wanted to be in a video and he said "Yes". That was one down. We called around and managed to find one model from L.A. to drive right out for the other scene. We still needed one more person. I hadn't been in a video in a while, and had no intention of doing it, but I decided that there just wasn't anyone else. I asked Morgan if he wanted me to do the scene with him and he said, "Of course."

The scene was outdoors at night under a full moon. Morgan sucked my dick and then I sucked his. Then I fucked him. The scene looks great; really hot, but Morgan and I agreed that it was a little weird for us. Our sex had always been private and personal and it felt awkward with the camera there. I also remembered why I had stopped being in videos: It had become old to me. The excitement was gone. I much preferred being alone with someone (or ones). The scene we shot didn't make it into that movie. I finally did put it in a video though, as an extra scene for my recent video *Island Fever*, most of which I shot in Hawai'i.

Soon after that video, Morgan met a friend of mine and they became lovers and eventually moved in together. I was very happy for them. They started a business together and keep quite occupied with it, so I don't get to see them very often, but Morgan is still one of my very best friends. In fact, he and his lover helped me set up programs on my laptop computer that I am using to write this book.

DREW ANDREWS

I met Drew Andrews when I was singing at a club in the summer of 1996. It was the premiere of Jamie Hendrix's video, *The Rush*. Jamie had asked Sharon Kane and me to sing—at that time the two of us were recording music and singing gigs under the name "Goddess." He shyly came up to me.

"Uh... I heard you sing tonight and I saw you at another show, and um...you are really great," he said.

"Thanks, you're very handsome." I smiled.

"Uh...thanks, I heard you sing before after the Porn Star Softball game, you were great!" he said.

"Thanks!" I said again.

Then Drew ran like a rabbit in the headlights of a car. He seemed totally starstruck and I was shocked and thrilled to have a gorgeous man whom I never met before show such obvious interest in me. I thought I completely scared him away, though. Knowing him now, that incident was so unlike him and his on-screen persona. He is always so self-assured.

My friend, porn star Jason Nikas, called me the next day.

"Drew Andrews really likes you. He also wants to work on a video with you and he wants to work with Sharon Kane," he gushed, breathless with excitement over passing on hot gossip. I felt like I was in high school again, but I loved it.

"Should I pass him a note in gym class?" I joked

"Maybe, he's pretty hot for you." he replied.

"What exactly do you mean, 'hot for me?'" I wanted to know for sure. Or maybe I just wanted to hear it said out loud. I was practically giddy. I hadn't dated anyone since a painful breakup a few months before. I was happy to be considering someone again, it had been so long since I'd had any interest. When I had gone to New Zealand for my guest spot on *Xena*: *Warrior Princess*, I met and fell in love with a guy named Anaru, who came back with me to the U.S. I broke up with him a few months later when I learned he had stolen thousands of dollars from me. In any case, I was practically giddy.

"I mean he wants you bad," Jason emphasized

"Really?" I asked.

"Yes! Call him, he told me to give you his number."

I wasn't feeling brave enough to ask him out, but I was producing a transsexual video for Kim Christy at the time and so we put Drew in a scene with Sharon and my tranny friend from Australia, Christy McNicole. He seemed very excited about it.

All day on the set, he flirted with me. I finally worked up the nerve to ask him out on a date. He said "Yes." A couple of days later we went out to dinner. I didn't want to have sex right away—I was still shell-shocked from my last relationship. Drew said he didn't either, so we made out like schoolboys on my couch. He shoved his tongue down my throat as he grabbed my ass. It felt so good we kept at it for a while, rolling around the couch on top of each other. Then he left. We had a couple of other dates and still both felt like waiting to have sex. (Don't ask me how I waited, I certainly wouldn't wait now, but at the time it seemed right.)

Then came the night of the Gay Video Guide Awards. We ended up making out in the bathroom at the club after the show was over. Half the porn industry kept walking into the bathroom and catching us.

Soon after that, Drew started canceling plans, and either not showing up, or being very late for dates. After about three times, I decided that this was not going to work for me. I liked him a lot, but someone not showing up drives me crazy. We stopped seeing each other, but the rumor mill didn't stop. People told me he said that he had never dated me. People told him that I said we were boyfriends. The story changed from us kissing in the bathroom the night of the awards announcements to us fucking in the stall with Bo Garret. The gossip columns were all writing about it and the hysterical thing was that we had only ever had about four dates, never had sex, and parted on good terms. People thought that we were enemies for a year or two, however. I would arrive at an awards show or something like that and someone would scurry up to me.

"You'll never guess who is here!" they would whisper, or, "Sorry, I know you're going to be upset, but..." Neither of us was ever upset. But no one would ever believe it when I told them.

In the past couple of years, Drew has been in several videos that I directed. He was always reliable and on time and the guys he worked with always liked him a lot, whether they were getting fucked by his huge dick, or fucking his hot ass. He is still always very friendly with me, groping me playfully at every opportunity.

When I decided to be in another video, *Trannyville,* for Vivid , I asked Drew if he wanted to do a scene with me. He said "Yes," and his eyes lit up. He showed up early for the shoot. We did our dialogue and then I went down on my knees and pulled his huge dick out of his pants. Finally! It was already getting hard before I could get it in my mouth. I licked up and down the shaft then swirled my tongue around the head before I sucked him as far down my throat as I could.

He moaned as I forced his dick farther down my throat, almost to the base. I started stroking it with my mouth, up and down. I loved having his cock bouncing against my tonsils and stretching my lips wide open. I wondered again why we had never done it before. I sucked his balls into my mouth as I kept his cock, still slick with my spit, going with my hands. We switched then and he was sucking my cock. Drew is an excellent cocksucker. I leaned my head back and thrust my hips out so he could get at it better. He licked all around my cock and balls, tonguing the crevice between my legs and the base of my dick. I grabbed the back of his head and fucked his face, forgetting about the camera, the crew and everything else in the world. All I wanted to do was be in his mouth.

Finally, I fucked him. I watched my dick sliding up his hole as he knelt on his hands and knees on the floor. I plunged in and out of him with the video camera looking over my shoulder. The still photographer was hetero, and was watching us with a mixture of revulsion and fascination. I don't know why Vivid insisted on using a straight still photographer who obviously did not want to be there. He only took a couple of rolls of film for the whole video. We were kind of into making him squirm though, and we fucked harder and louder. At one point I stopped.

"Don't you want to get some close-up shots of my dick up his ass?" I asked.

"Uh, no, I already got everything I need," he said.

I winked at Drew and kept plowing his ass. Finally we both shot our loads. After the shoot, we kissed and got in the shower. We both had a great time, I think, and I don't know why we never did it before. He gives great head, and I loved fucking his ass. And we still aren't fighting. Really!

GRANT WOOD

I put Grant Wood in his first video in October of 1996. Someone had referred him to me so I met him in my apartment for an interview. He had gorgeous long hair then. I told him that eventually some of the companies would tell him he had to cut it to get more work. They did, and he did, and he is still gorgeous, but I loved his long hair.

As I interviewed him, he was very friendly and it was obvious that he was intelligent. He wasn't one of those guys that just wanted to do videos to make money, he already had a serious career. He wanted to do videos to have fun and to explore his sexuality. Guys like him are the best porn stars, because they are fucking for the sheer joy of doing it and being watched. We talked about how we were both bisexual, and lots of other things. I could tell that this was someone who would become my friend; we really connected on another level, even though he didn't seem sexually interested in me.

When he took off his clothes for the Polaroid, it was all I could do not cry out loud at his gorgeous, perfect body. Great abs, great chest, beautiful dick and delicious ass. It was a struggle to remain professional, but remain professional I did. I have never fooled around with a model when I am in the position of producer or director unless they initiated it. Unfortunately for me, he didn't.

I cast him in my next video, *Threesome*. His first scene was with Dino Phillips, who is always a reliable top. The first fucking position went fine but by the last one Dino was having trouble staying hard. At that time, I didn't understand why, but I think I do now. Dino and Grant started dating immediately after that video and I think Dino was a little thrown off by his feelings for Grant.

At any rate, we decided that I would have to be a stunt dick. (I know, poor me, having to fuck this gorgeous man.) I fucked him as he was lying on his back on a lawn chair. His ass is one of the most perfect asses I have ever seen and I was getting really turned on. His ass practically has lips and they gripped my dick as I was fucking him. I couldn't hold back very long. I pulled out and came, partly because I just couldn't help coming and partly just in case the come shot was needed for the video. I can't remember for sure but I think it was and we used it.

I put Grant in many more of my videos and then cast him in *Desert Paradise*. He played one of three guys that were trying to pull an insurance scam and were hiding out in a hotel in Palm Springs. His scene was to be with Donovan Cory and they were going to be flip-flop fucking. When it came time for the fucking they both decided they couldn't top. I said, "Okay, I'll be a stunt dick. Who wants to get fucked?" Grant immediately said, "Me!" I smiled at him and said, "I thought you'd never ask." I fucked him on the bed in the hotel room doggy-style first, and then face to face. I leaned over and started kissing him as I was fucking him. He is a great kisser. We got all the shots we needed, finished shooting the scene, came, and went back to being friends. Though we really are just friends, whenever he sees me, he always gives me a big kiss or grabs me or pulls me onto his lap. I never resist. I'm not the only one that can't resist him. Once he had a three-way in the bathroom with Giorgio Falconi and with my ex-fiancee, Sharon Kane, at one of my birthday parties! He later asked if I was upset and I said I was only upset that they didn't do it in the middle of the party so that we all could watch!

SHAWN JUSTIN

Shawn is big, beefy, hot, sexy, studly, manly, juicy, has an enormous cock...need I go on? I like him, get the picture? I had seen Shawn in videos such as *Hologram,* and *Abduction II: The*

Conflict. I don't remember exactly how I ended up meeting him, near the end of 1996, but of course I started putting him in my videos. He is another one who, though you wouldn't know it from his nasty scenes, is a really nice guy.

In one of the first videos, *For His Own Good*, he was in two scenes. The first one we shot was with Jesse Skylar. It went well because they were really into each other. The second scene was with Giorgio Falconi and Shawn was just not into him, and who could blame him? Giorgio was stretching his on-camera career a few years longer than most people really wanted to see him and he had an especially bad attitude that day. He arrived late and haggard and was just being completely obnoxious to everyone. The owner of the house was about to kill him.

Shawn was trying to be a good sport about it, but just couldn't get hard with Giorgio. He asked me if I would help him. I said, "Sure, what do you want me to do?" He said, "Let me suck your dick." We got into a sixty-nine position and began sucking each other off. Suddenly it seemed like a blessing in disguise that Giorgio was being so bitchy. Shawn got hard, and we shot some footage, but his hard-on didn't last long with Giorgio, so we had to keep stopping for me to help him. I was glad to be of service.

Shawn was in several more videos before my lucky day arrived. When he was doing his scene with Justin Case in *I Am Curious Leather*, (nominated for Best Leather Video that year, and if you don't remember the mainstream movie, *I Am Curious Yellow,* then you are too young, put this book down and go back to playing your Nintendo) they were really into each other, but when it came time for the fucking, Justin just couldn't get hard enough to fuck Shawn. While on the one hand, I am never glad that someone is having trouble getting hard in my videos, I certainly don't mind being a stunt dick when it is someone like Shawn that I have to (get to?) fuck.

Shawn was hanging in a sling and I fucked him for a really long time. We were looking into each other's eyes and both really enjoying it. He was holding onto the chains and urging me to plow his ass harder. All the times I had seen him top other guys on video went flashing through my mind. I love fucking a big, butch, top. I was sorry when it was over. Shawn said that his boyfriend likes to watch him get fucked, and that I should come over some time. I haven't yet, but I definitely intend to take him up on that offer.

CHAZ CARLTON

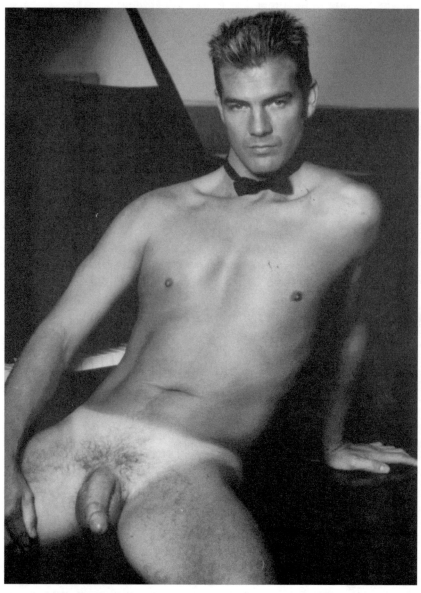

The first time I saw Chaz I had the same reaction anyone who likes blond California boys would: Yum! He's a cutie, and very sweet also. I have cast him in several of my videos. Of course, the inevitable eventually happened on a shoot. It was April of 1997, at Mickey Skee's house. The video was called *Virgin Territory*. The top that was supposed to fuck him couldn't get hard and I had to be the stunt dick.

I didn't understand what the problem was, since the top's dick looked hard. He said he couldn't get it in. After seeing Chaz bottom in so many videos I was surprised when I couldn't get my dick in his ass either. It was clamped shut. The video was supposed to be about guys getting fucked for the first time, and he sure was getting into his role. I could have sworn his was a virgin asshole! Suddenly I remembered that everyone that had ever done a scene with him had a hard time getting in. The boy has a tight asshole. I didn't want to force it in, but all of my efforts at coaxing it open weren't working.

I finally put a lot of lube up his butt with my finger, a lot of lube on my dick and just rammed it in. He cried out but he didn't say to stop, so I didn't. The fucking went fine for about two minutes and I was starting to really get into it then he started complaining that it hurt and he had to stop. Now my dick is big, but it isn't *that* big. Then I remembered that this had happened on all of the other shoots too. Chaz had the reputation as the bottom that can't stand to get fucked. The scene took what seemed like the rest of the day, with us getting one minute's worth of footage at a time before he would have to stop again. Finally it was over. I don't know when I have worked so hard.

I forgot about what happened until a couple of years later when I was directing a scene in *Big Deposit* with my boyfriend at the time, Paolo Centori. The same thing happened. I told Paolo to just not worry about it and fuck him hard. If Chaz needed to stop he would tell us, and he did about every two minutes. The scene took forever and I and Paolo and the cameraman were all getting a little annoyed with Chaz. I have to admit that I enjoyed watching Paolo's huge cock slamming into Chaz, who was whimpering and trying to run away from it. Chaz is a nice guy and really cute, but don't expect to fuck him for more than three minutes, and the next time you see a scene with him, know that it probably took all day!

BRIAN DEAN and TY DAVENPORT
(top left)

Brian is a good friend now. I first met him and his boyfriend, Ty Davenport, in the early Spring of 1997 in my living room. Ty had been referred to me by someone, and said that his boyfriend, Brian was really cute and did videos, as well. Brian came over with Ty; I interviewed both of them and took Polaroids. I really liked them both, not just for the video, but they both seemed like really nice people who would be fun to hang out with.

They were both in that video, and they were great. I called to offer them roles in my next video, but Brian couldn't do it because of his regular job. He is one of the

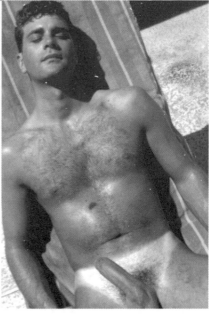

guys in porn who has a career outside of porn. Doing videos was just for fun and extra money. Ty was able to do it though, so he was in the video. I fell in love with his ass shooting that video. His scene was with Patric Ives and was shot in my office in my apartment. Ty was on a massage bench with Patric massaging his ass, then fingering it, then fucking it. I was turned on the whole time, my dick tenting out my shorts, as I directed Patric to "Stick another finger up his ass, then twist them around." Yum.

Though Ty did a few more videos for me, Brian was never available. I cast Ty in my video, *Doggy Style*, because I knew he could act and the script required a lot of acting. It was really funny. I had actually written it three years before for *me* to star in, along with my best friend, Mark, and Vince Harrington (AKA Lana Luster), but when I started getting TV and mainstream movie parts, I stopped appearing in porn for a while, and the script just lay around gathering dust in a desk drawer. It was one of the only videos for which I actually had people audition by *reading* for the parts.

By then, Mark was no longer doing videos and the studio didn't want me to use Vince (who in their minds was Lana Luster, his drag persona). I had also written a big part for Mark's dog Orca. Orca was a big, long-haired Alaskan Malamute, whose charm could be resisted by no one. Often Mark or I would be driving in my convertible with the top down, a hot guy would pull up next to us, and just as we were sure he was going to ask us out he would say, "You've got such a beautiful (yes?....) dog!" The bitch always got more attention than any one, which proved she had star quality. Orca was still willing, but two weeks before filming, we found out that she had cancer of the uterus, so we decided that it would not be the best thing for her. The part was played by Chaney, the dog of my good friend, makeup artist Mr. Ed. Chaney has her own charm and played the part well.

The first day of shooting went great, but the last scene of the second day didn't go so well. We were in a house in the valley with a living room leftover from the seventies. It was a three-way between Ty, a new kid from Canada, and Brett Williams. Brett was being a bit of a bitchy diva that day, I don't know why, maybe he had a bad day, or maybe he was just getting too old for the porn business. (Ooooooh! Did I just go there!?) Anyway, on top of everything, he couldn't get hard to be a top and he refused to get fucked. Finally, he ended up fucking himself (just what everybody felt like telling him to go do after keeping us all waiting for hours) with a dildo while the other two guys fucked each other, or rather while I fucked the other two guys as a stunt dick, since by then, after languishing under the hot lights for hours waiting for Brett, no one could get very hard. I fucked the cute Canadian kid first. He was really hot, but I couldn't wait to get to that butt that I really wanted: Ty's.

Even though circumstances were not ideal, I loved fucking

him. I slid my dick all the way up his ass in one swift motion and held it there, pressing inside him, and he moaned. He looked me in the eye the whole time I fucked him, whispering "Yeah, harder!" I was happy to fuck him harder and harder, pulling my cock all the way back out and ramming it back in. Sweat was dripping down my face. I hardly noticed the cameraman and the other people on the set. Ty was turning me on so much, I couldn't help myself. I pulled out, pulled off the condom and came all over him. He said, "Thanks" and I said, "No, thank *you*!"

The next time I saw Brian and Ty was at a small sex party in the Hollywood Hills at the home of Mickey Skee's boyfriend. Brian came up to me and said, "My boyfriend said that you fucked him, and that you're really good. I want some." I felt a little nervous at first, like I had been caught with someone's boyfriend, but then I realized that Brian really was glad that I had fucked his boyfriend, so I said, "Sure!" and started playing around with both of them. I was shoving my fingers up Brian's butt and he was loving it. I was also kissing him and falling in love. There was a real connection between us beyond the sex, which made the sex great. I fucked him while Ty and everyone else in the room watched. I didn't notice anyone else, though. I was completely into him and his hot ass. I was insatiable; I couldn't get enough of him. It was rare for me to be with someone sexually who could be so wild and uninhibited, yet at the same time totally present, not off somewhere else while we were fucking. It was incredibly intimate. All three of us finally came together, and then they left the sex party, but not before we agreed to get together soon, just the three of us.

The next two times I called, both Ty and Brian were available. They were in my videos, *Desert Maneuvers* with my ex-boyfriend, Tony Belmonte and in *Sex Toy Story, Part II*. In the second video, they had a scene with Michael Vista, whom I think is equally hot. They were both dominating him and shoving huge dildos up his ass. I was rock-hard the entire time directing the scene. It was one of those rare times when all of the models were completely turned on to each other. If you haven't seen it you must—it is one great scene. Unfortunately, the video company made me edit out the biggest dildo that they fucked him with and the parts where they both had most of their hands up his ass—they feared legal repercussions. I got to watch it though.

Even though Brian, Ty and I had all agreed that we wanted to get together again, it never happened. Brian and I went out for dinner one night. We talked for hours. He told me about his life. About his ex-wife, and his lover, Steve Summers, who had died. They had lived together in Palm Springs. Steve had owned a video company in the 80s. He would make a couple of videos that were really bad but had great boxcovers, and sell them by mail order. By the time the customers discovered that the videos were crap he had already dissolved that company, and started a new one with a new name and a reputation that wasn't bad and he would do the same thing all over again. In the meantime, Steve was pulling scams on banks, writing bad checks on one account, depositing them into another bank account and withdrawing the money before the bank discovered that the first account had no money. Both of them were doing lots of drugs and Brian didn't really pay much attention to what was going on. They had big beautiful houses, lots of cars and spent money like it grew on the cactus in the backyard. Steve told Brian that he wanted to put everything in Brian's name because he loved him so much. Brian believed him

Then Steve got sick with AIDS. On the day Steve died, the police showed up with warrants for his arrest. Brian was informed that "Steve Summers," the name his lover had been using for years, was a false identity; his real name was Wayne Matovich, and he had been hiding from the government. The police made Brian leave the house. There was a huge debt and since everything had been put in Brian's name, the debt was now his. He lived out of his car for weeks, still unable to get off the drugs.

At one point Brian went up to a cliff with a gun. He was going to shoot himself in the mouth and fall backwards into the ravine. He figured his body would never be found, so his family would be spared the ordeal of his death and a funeral. However, a passing truckdriver spotted him and pulled over to stop him—right into Brian's car. The crash startled Brian and he shot himself in the foot. His car somehow ended up on top of him pinning him down. Now he was trapped under a car, shot in the foot, and had to explain to the police and his parents why he had been about to kill himself. He finally told them about the drugs. He got help and has been clean and sober ever since. He got his life together and even managed to pay off all of the huge debt that his lover had created for him. He told me that he paid the last of it with the money he made on the last video he did for me.

I thought his story was amazing and it really inspired me. Brian was an incredible person to go through so much and to discuss it with such dignity, the dignity that comes with turning your life around. I told him a lot about my life and my struggle with drugs. About my best friend, Paul Pelletieri, who had died of AIDS and my friend and lover, Joey Stefano, who had died of a drug overdose. I shared with him how I felt when Joey died. I broke down and cried. I think Brian was the first person I had been able to talk to about Joey. I had been holding the pain for so long.

Brian and I became very close, very fast. We also were intensely attracted to each other. I desperately wanted him. His agreement with his boyfriend was that they only fooled around with other guys together, though, and we both knew that if we had sex it would not be casual. We agreed that it would be out of integrity to have sex, and that we shouldn't even get together with his boyfriend because of our intense feelings. It was so hard to let him walk out of my apartment that night without ripping his clothes off.

As our friendship developed, we both realized that we felt so strongly about each other and really loved each other. We went to dinner, we went to the movies, but of course we never had sex. Occasionally we would get into my bed to watch TV and cuddle, but still, no sex, not even kissing. For a while it was hard for me and I really wished that he would break up with his boyfriend to be with me, but as time went on and that didn't happen, I got over it.

Then, finally he and his boyfriend did break up. I kept waiting patiently as time went on for Brian to figure out that I would be the perfect boyfriend for him, but he never did. We remained good friends.

As it turns out, he did get back together with his boyfriend, so if they are happy together, I am happy for them. Brian and I remain good friends to this day, and I love him a lot.

PETER DIXON

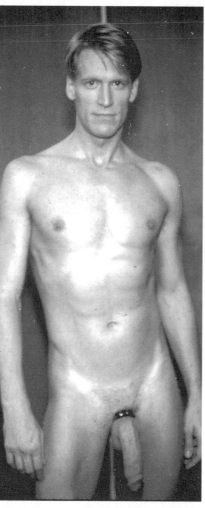

I always call Peter Dixon my Chicago boyfriend, because he lives in Chicago (duh) and he's my boyfriend when he is in town. We aren't and never were *boyfriends* exactly, but it was always fun to pretend that we were. Does that sound confusing? Let me put it another way: We like each other and we like to fuck.

I met Peter in my trailer backstage just before I was going to sing at L.A. Gay Pride in 1997. I had just flown in from San Francisco from doing a concert with Nina Hagen the night before, and was a little frazzled. I had been staying in San Francisco with my friend, Falcon star Greg Ross, whom I hadn't seen in a few years, so I had been really busy for several days between running around with Greg and singing three nights in a row with Nina. One night, I even sang at two clubs, one right after the other. The big concert was the last night. Greg and my ex-boyfriend Jason Pride were there, as well as lots of fans and other friends I hadn't seen for a long time. I had been up pretty late, then got up, flew back, took a shuttle home from the airport, barely had time to shower and change my clothes before dashing down to the festival and rushing to get ready backstage. Allan, my manager, brought Peter in to meet me.

"This is Peter, he's going to be one of your backup dancers in the Hare Krishna number."

I was going to sing my friend, Boy George's, song "Bow Down Mister." While I had been in San Francisco, Allan had recruited about twenty porn stars to dance around in orange robes with me and throw flowers into the crowd.

I didn't have time to pay much attention to him; I just noticed that he was tall, blond, and handsome. I would have been intimidated, but I was too busy getting ready. He danced with me and the others on that song. Later that night, the infamous O Boys had a sex party at the nearest hotel. I stopped by and was fooling around with some guys when Peter came in. He took his clothes off and for the first time, I got a really good look at him. He was gorgeous! Probably about 6'3", with blond hair and cobalt blue eyes. He had a beautiful body, a great ass and a huge dick. They don't call him Big Peter Dixon just because he's tall, that's for sure.

I couldn't take my eyes off him; there was a hot guy sucking my dick, but I suddenly lost interest. I didn't know if he was going to pay attention to me or even if he recognized me from earlier, but he came right over to me and we started groping each other. I was surprised that he was so into me, but he told me that he had been looking forward to meeting me and had thought that I didn't like him. I explained that I had just been focused on getting ready for the show and proceeded to show him just how much I *did* like him. I started sucking his dick with the other guy still sucking mine. After a while, we decided we wanted to leave the party and be alone. We took the other guy with us.

The three of us came back to my house and started to really have fun. Peter and I took turns fucking the hot dark-haired guy. We were fucking the shit out of him and he loved it, one of us down his throat and the other up his ass; then we'd switch. Before long, though, we were ignoring the other guy because we were so into each other. He wanted to leave, so we gave him a ride home and went to Peter's hotel room.

Once there, we got even more wild. I was dominating him and making him fuck himself with big dildos while I watched.

"Shove that big dildo up your pussy ass, boy!" I ordered.

"Yes, sir!" he said and shoved it in deeper, in and out.

"That's it, show me that fucking pink hole."

He was making me crazy, he was so into it. I told him to stand up, turn around, bend over and spread his ass for me. I made him finger-fuck himself. I jacked off and watched him as he rammed his fingers into his own ass, spreading it wide for me to see. There was some fruit on the table, and I picked up the grapes and shoved some up his hole. He pushed them out one by one, then I shoved a banana up his ass and fucked him with it for a while.

Finally, I slammed my dick up his hot hole and fucked him. I fucked him for hours in the bathroom, on the bed, on the floor. All over his hotel room.

Then he fucked me with his huge dick. It was amazingly thick and long. It seemed to slide out forever and then slide back into me forever. We took turns fucking each other the rest of that night, the next day, and for the next two days, until he had to leave town to go home. We also went out to dinner and spent some time talking and getting to know each other, but mostly we fucked. I really missed him a lot after he left. He is a sweet, smart, goofy, sexy guy. Why did he have to live in Chicago?

We get together every time he comes to town. I guess there's nothing like only seeing someone a couple times a year to keep things fresh and exciting. The last time I saw him, he got into town and came to my house when a friend of mine was using my computer. We kept sneaking into the kitchen to kiss. I just couldn't keep my lips off of him. I love kissing him, he's very good at it. We waited impatiently until my friend left. Then we ripped each other's clothes off.

We lit some candles and put on some music and got in the bathtub together. It was very romantic although once we were both in the tub there wasn't room for much water. We didn't mind. We started kissing again and were both hard instantly, his huge cock sticking up out of the water. He was so cute, like an overgrown little boy playing in the tub with me. A six-foot-three little boy, that is.

There's something about being in water with someone that I love. I'm an Aquarius, and I love to be in and around water. It's very sensual for me. Sometimes if it's raining, I just go outside and lie down and let it fall on me. I used to do that in our driveway growing up, though my mom thought I was crazy. "Don't you have enough sense to come in out of the rain?" she would ask. I go to Hawai'i whenever I can, and just lie on the edge of the beach and let the waves wash up over me. Maybe it reminds me of the womb, I don't know. I feel safe and warm in water, especially if I'm holding someone as sexy as Peter.

After a while, we went to bed. We made out for a long time, rolling around on top of each other. Finally, he lubed up his huge dick and very slowly worked it into me. It was perfect. I had said before that a dick that big is too big to get fucked with, but I was so wrong, and his dick was so right. I don't know what I could have been thinking, saying a dick could be too big!

He fucked me slowly at first, then faster and faster, finally pounding into my ass. I looked in the mirror and watched his huge cock slamming into me. He flipped me over on my back and within a minute or two of him fucking me in that position, I came. I didn't want him to stop fucking me though, it felt so great. I told him to keep going and he did, for about fifteen minutes more. Finally, he pulled out and shot all over my stomach, chest, and face, as I shot again with him. Then, believe it or not, a couple of minutes later, my dick was hard again and I fucked him until he came again. The next forty-eight hours were equally great. Whenever we would go out, I couldn't wait until we could get back to my house and I could get his cock up my ass again.

Peter has been in some of my videos like *Red Hot And Safe* (see the Tony West chapter for that story) and *Sleeping Booty* and he always performs well and is well-liked by his co-stars. A friendly, horny, gorgeous, blond hunk with an enormous dick. What's not to like?

REX CHANDLER

Rex Chandler and I had met briefly at parties, but our official introduction was when someone referred him to me to shoot stills on one of my sets. At first I said, "Oh yeah, I'm sure he can really shoot good stills. Doesn't he say he's straight? He's probably just another former porn star trying to cash in on his fame to get work." My friend said, "Uh, look who's talking." I called him up and hired him.

It was an outdoor shoot in Silverlake and he showed up in shorts. Short shorts. Tight shorts. Short, tight, black, spandex shorts. When it got hot that day, he took off his shirt and everyone nearly swooned. He knew exactly what he was doing, too. It was hot, but that wasn't why he took off his shirt. Beautiful people know that their beauty works for them. They know how to work it, and honey, he was workin' it with his shirt off and those tight shorts with that huge bulge in them. Even without the bulge he would have been a bit intimidating. He is about six-three and has very broad shoulders. He's a big guy. A lot of the big stars in porn who are known for having big dicks are actually quite short, (e.g., Jeff Stryker) so it doesn't take too much to make their dicks look big in comparison to their heighth. I realized just how big he must really be elsewhere if what I was seeing in front of me was so huge and his dick still looked so big on screen in proportion. I had a hard time paying attention to the video and the guys I was directing that day.

I was actually expecting him to be a jerk, but he is one of the nicest guys I have ever known. He is friendly, funny, (he always has a new tasteless joke) and has absolutely no attitude. We have become good friends. He is a great photographer and is wonderful with the guys. He really gets into taking the pictures. "Oh yeah! That's hot! Show me your ass just like that! That's it, grab your dick now!" He makes the guys feel really attractive and sexy and that is the most important thing in getting good shots. They love having Rex Chandler telling them they look hot and sexy. Very often, the guys will say to me, "I wasn't turned on to the guy I was doing my scene with at all, but because Rex was shooting the stills I was totally turned on the whole time we were shooting." Who wouldn't be? He even shot me once, for the cover of *Frontiers*, with Seth Black and my then-boyfriend, Tony West on either side of me.

He doesn't like to hear the name Rex; I and all his other friends call him by his real name. He says that he regrets doing the videos years ago. He was young and needed the money, and later felt misled about how much money he would really make. He thinks being in gay porn ruined his chances for a legitimate acting career. I always tell him he's saying that to the wrong person, but he points

out that I play very different parts than he would be up for. That is true, but I still think he can make it if he can just forget about the past and believe he can do it. As I said before, he is one of the nicest guys I've ever met and I would really like to see him succeed in acting, or whatever he wants to do. And no, we've never had sex and probably never will. Why?

Because he really is straight.

SETH BLACK

Leo Masters brought Seth Black over to my house in the late Spring of 1997 for me to meet him. He was another one who immediately walked in and I thought, "Oh my god, is he gorgeous!" As he sat filling out the paperwork, I got really nervous. I needed to take a Polaroid of him and I asked him to take off his clothes and get his dick hard. He went in the bathroom and tried and tried, but couldn't do it. He said he was nervous, and he asked me if I would suck his dick. Of course, being the helpful person that I am, I couldn't say no.

We went into my bedroom with Leo still waiting in the living room. I started sucking his dick and he still couldn't get hard. I kept sucking and sucking, not really minding that he wasn't hard. He was sweating so much it was dripping down on me. I looked up at him and he looked so hot! I finally stuck my finger up his ass and that seemed to help. We took the Polaroids and decided that we should stop since Leo was waiting.

Seth ended up starring in several of my videos. I always loved directing him while he was getting fucked. One time we were in Palm Springs shooting the video, *Desert Maneuvers*, and performing at a club, CC Construction Company. I was singing and Seth was one of my backup dancers. Seth was in a scene with Paul Morgan, who was his boyfriend at the time, sort of. They started their scene outside at night, but we had to move inside because the neighbors complained.

There are a bunch of gay clothing-optional hotels in Palm Springs, all in the same area on two or three streets. Occasionally, there is a house or an apartment complex next to one of them. I certainly wouldn't move in next to one if I didn't want to see naked guys, but sometimes people do. There was a fence, so I thought we were okay, but at one point while Paul and Seth were fucking, someone next door started yelling.

"Take it inside!" Then we heard two people fighting.

"Leave them alone!" came a man's voice.

"They're right out there where I can see them!", this time from an older woman.

"Gladys, you were standing on a chair to see them!"

We were amused, but still thought it best to go inside. Once in the room, Paul fucked the shit out of Seth on a little kitchen table. It was really hot.

The next day, we went to perform the show. After the show, we ended up getting a little drunk. Seth managed to get thrown out of the bar. He, Gordon Lee, and another friend of Seth's that happened to be out in Palm Springs, all went home with a guy we met there. Gordon left after a while, and Seth's friend passed out, asleep. The other guy was really hot, and was into both of us. We took turns fucking Seth all night. He couldn't get enough. I loved shoving my dick in his ass, ramming him while watching him choke on the other guy's dick. We both fucked him hard from each end, with Seth's arms flailing, grabbing the green comforter on the bed trying to stay impaled on both of our cocks. Then we switched. Now Seth was choking on my cock while the guy fucked his asshole. We kept going back and forth like that until we both came all over Seth and we all fell asleep in our cum, just before the sun rose over the mountains. We slept half the next day.

The next time Seth and I had a sexual interaction was the video, *Behind His Back*. Seth had a scene with Alex Carrington and Alex was supposed to fuck him with a huge dildo. Alex had a problem getting the dildo into Seth and fucking him with it; I think he was afraid of hurting him. Seth finally said, "Geoff, will you just do it!" We got close-up shots of my hand holding the dildo and fucking Seth with it, which of course I didn't mind. Okay, so I always love shoving big dildos up the asses of cute guys, shoot me! If you ever see that video, you might recognize my hand.

While Seth is a great person, I also tell him he is a pain in my butt. He is the person that will call up every day before the shoot with a different question, then ask me why I don't like him. I always tell him, "Honey I love you, but you drive me crazy!" One year I proved it (the love part) by singing for him at his birthday party. He can be obnoxious, but he can also be sweet and you still gotta love him. And of course, he is always sexy.

PAUL MORGAN

Seth Black brought Paul Morgan to my house to meet me. They were boyfriends, he said, and he wanted to work with Paul in my upcoming video. I had just met Seth and we had fooled around. He obviously wanted to make sure that did not happen with Paul and me. Seth was really possessive and quite jealous if Paul fooled around with anyone. Which of course he did nearly on a daily basis in videos. He was in more videos in 1997 and 1998 than any other gay porn star. He was in so many because he is gorgeous, and is one of the best sexual performers ever. He is definitely one of the best of all time and I and all the other directors of course wished we could use him in every movie we made. Paul also fucked people off camera and when Seth would find out he would be furious. Paul always told me and other people that he and Seth were "just buddies."

I met Paul, and Seth sat beside him, very, very close as Paul filled out the interview form. Paul seemed really nice and was obviously a pro. I could tell already that he would be great in the scene with Seth. I still needed a picture for the files anyway, so Paul went in the bathroom by himself with his little video camera he had with him. He said he had taped him fucking a girl and he wanted to look at that to get hard. He came out in a couple of minutes and his dick was rock hard. I took a Polaroid and then we scheduled the shoot. Seth and Paul were great in the scene. I think the video was *Desert Maneuvers*, which we shot in Palm Springs.

Paul was in a lot of my videos after that. On one set Paul was flirting with me a lot and brushing up against my dick. Seth was really upset later and said that Paul told him that we had been having sex in the bathroom. We hadn't though. Not that I wouldn't have wanted to, but I certainly wouldn't with Seth there, and without being clear about what their relationship really was. I wouldn't want to hurt Seth's feelings in that way. I think maybe Paul wanted to make Seth jealous. Eventually he and Seth "broke up" and they didn't really want to be in the same videos, but I alternated back and forth using them. They both were always great performers.

Eventually there was a video and the person Paul was doing his scene with couldn't cum. Finally my opportunity to lie under him naked had come. The scene was on the couch in my living room. I slid under Paul in the place of the person who couldn't cum. The cameraman, John Simms, got a shot of my dick and Paul's dick and stomach. He was hot from the scene and I could feel the heat from his body. A drop of sweat fell down onto me. Paul played with my balls while I jacked off and shot my load for the camera. The scene was saved. I was just getting warmed up though, really.

Soon enough I had another chance with Paul. We were in Palm Springs shooting a video, *Desert Paradise Part 2*, I think. After we finished shooting that day, I was relaxing in the jacuzzi and Paul came and got in next to me. He started grabbing my dick. Since he and Seth were completely broken up by then I didn't feel guilty grabbing back. His famous always-ready pole was there, just as hard and ready as it always is in his videos.

We pawed at each other under the water for a while, then some of the others from the shoot got into the jacuzzi with us. We got out and went to my room. We lay down on the bed with each other's dick in our mouths. He sucked my cock as furiously as he always does in videos, and I gulped his down with equal vigor. He tasted freshly chlorinated from the jacuzzi, but still delicious. Before I knew it, I tasted something else. His hot load shooting into my mouth. He shot so much it dripped out the sides and onto my chest as I tried to gulp it all down.

STEVE PIERCE

I first met Steve Pierce over the phone. He was living in San Francisco at the time. Someone had given him my address, and he sent me some very hot pictures. I was preparing to direct a hard-core video with dildos and fisting at the time.

We talked over the phone, and he seemed really nice, and just as sexy as he looked in the pictures. That video ended up being canceled however, and I eventually forgot about him. A couple of years later, I got a call from Giorgio Falconi who now was Steve's agent, or so he said. He wanted to send Steve over to meet me. Steve lived in L.A. now, very close to me, so he came over. We talked for a couple of hours and he told me all about his boyfriend who was a chef, moving to L.A., how he used to work in department stores, and many other details of his life. He seemed genuinely sweet, and, as many porn stars are, constantly flirty.

When we were ready to take the Polaroid, he took off his clothes and sat down on the edge of the couch with his asshole pointing out at me and legs spread. He couldn't seem to get hard so I asked him if he wanted a magazine or a video, some lube, some help?

"Some lube, and definitely some help," he said. Well who was I to say "No"? This gorgeous nice guy was naked on my couch, looking me in the eye, and asking me to help him get hard. It would be rude to refuse, especially after I had just offered. I got some lube.

"Suck my dick," he said. I did.

"Oh yeah, I could do this all day," he confirmed. Then he wanted to suck my dick. The whole time he kept saying things like

"It's really easy for me to get fisted. It just goes right in. I love having things shoved up my butt." I finally took the hint.

"Do you want me to fist you?" I asked.

"I really shouldn't, not without more lube," Steve said.

He slid his ass out more to the edge of the couch. I stuck a finger in his ass, then two, then three. In less than a minute, I had my whole hand up his ass. Soon I couldn't take it any more. I came and asked him if he wanted to.

"No, I have two escort jobs to do, and I usually get $300 to do this anyway," he told me. I wasn't sure what to say. I took my hand out of his ass.

"OK, well um, I'll call Giorgio and tell him that I definitely want you in the next video I'm doing. It's not a fisting video, but I would love to have you in it."

He was acting a little weird and I wondered if he had expected me to pay him, too, since he had mentioned the thing about usually getting money. The vibe had suddenly turned very strange. As he left, though, he said good-bye in a very friendly way, so I decided that I might have imagined the weirdness.

The next day I called Giorgio and told him that I wanted to use him in my next video, and I also told him what had happened and what we had done.

"Yes, he told me, and he said that he thought that it was very inappropriate and he said he does not want to work with you," Giorgio said in a scolding tone of voice. I was shocked.

"This guy asked me to suck his dick, asked to suck my dick, and practically begged me to stick my fist up his ass, so I did, and now he's upset? What's up?!" I asked.

Giorgio said he didn't know. I felt confused and horrible, like a disgusting dirty old man pornographer (which is pretty funny, considering that Steve is older than I am), I knew that I hadn't pushed myself on him, but I still felt like I had. I knew I had to try to find out what was going on.

Steve had given me his home number. I called and got his machine. I left a message saying that I was sorry if anything we had done had bothered him or made him uncomfortable and to please call me. He never called me back, and I never found out why he acted so weird. Maybe his boyfriend found out, and he is only allowed to fool around for money. Maybe he expected me to pay him. Maybe he was crazy. I will probably never know. I was constantly reminded of the incident every time I opened any local gay magazine—Steve's face stared out at me from his hustler ad. It was very unsettling.

The next time I saw Steve was a few years later, for a documentary of a performance art piece I was going to be in called *Men Loving Men*. Steve, his lover, myself and some other guys were supposed to express love however we wanted, (like by fucking) while we were being filmed, then the filmmaker, Heilman-C, went out to show people on the streets the tape, and filmed their reactions. She also interviewed us one at a time. Gloria (Heilman-C) has become a good friend of mine now. She is a brilliant artist and has a huge studio, called Blue Studio (it's painted blue) in West L.A.

Before we actually did the performance, we all met one night at Blue Studio. It was May 12, 1999. I hadn't known that Steve was going to be in it. I didn't know if he recognized me, he didn't say anything, but I thought he must surely know who I am. I decided that if he didn't have a problem, then I didn't either. I wasn't paying much attention to him, because that was the night I met my boyfriend, Babaji, who had been named after my guru, by his guru. I was totally into him, and not thinking of much else, although we all were rolling around on each other and making out.

On Saturday, May 22, the night we finally shot the documentary, Gloria sent a limousine to pick us up. We didn't even know where it was going to be filmed; the whole thing was very mysterious. Steve and his lover both were being very friendly, and everything seemed to be fine with him.

The location was a beautiful house in the Valley with a big sculpture of a bull in front. Inside, there was gorgeous art all over; it was fabulous. Soon we all were having sex in front of a roaring fire on a big, fuzzy rug. Cautious, I sort of waited for Steve to make the first move with me during the almost-orgy. Pretty soon, he was sucking my dick, as I was sucking someone else's. I fucked Steve, (I think actually I fucked everyone, as I seemed to be the only top,) as well as fisted him. He and his lover were both really sweet, and I didn't feel odd about him anymore. I guess he got over our past and everything is fine now—I've never asked. I have assumed it might be something private (well, private until I wrote this book,) and he would tell me if he wanted to.

DANY BROWN

I first saw Dany Brown in Falcon videos like *Deep In Hot Water* and *Made For You*. He was one of the few porn stars to whose image I had jacked off over and over. The look on his face when anything was up his ass (a finger, a dick, a dildo) made me come many times.

One day in the fall of 1997, I got a call from a friend and he casually mentioned that Dany was back in the business. My heart leapt up to my mouth. He had vanished before I had started directing and no one seemed to know where he was. Now he was back? I was almost afraid to hope that it was true, but my friend said he would tell him to call me. I told him to tell Dany to call me immediately because I wanted to put him in my next project.

Within days, Dany called to say he could come right over to meet me. I was very nervous. He arrived and it really was him. We talked and he told me that he had gotten tired of L.A. a few years ago and had gone home to Canada. He was back for a while and wanted to do as many videos as possible, because he loved sex and he loved getting fucked. He had a lot of pictures from magazines and box covers that he showed me. "I know who you are, you don't have to convince me of anything," I said.

The whole time I was talking to him I was freaking out inside. He was so sexy. I really wanted to rip his clothes off and fuck him. Instead, I acted like the professional I was.

"Usually I take a nude Polaroid of the guys, but the companies all know who you are so it's not necessary."

"But I want you to!" he exclaimed.

God was obviously rewarding me for being so good. If he really wanted to take off his clothes in front of me, gosh, who was I to protest? It would have been rude, and my mother definitely taught me not to be rude. I went to get my camera.

Slowly, he undressed in front of me, taking off his tank top and shorts, then bending over to remove his shoes and socks. His white underwear was the last to go. Just watching him take off his clothes would have been enough to let me die a happy man, but Dany wasn't finished with me.

"Will you help me get hard?" he asked.

I couldn't believe he was asking me this. This was another

one of my fantasies for the last few years coming true. I asked what he wanted me to do.

"Let me suck on your dick," he said.

I pulled out my dick, which had been hard since he walked in the door.

"Wow, it's big!" he gasped before he started sucking on it.

The reason it looks in the videos as though he gives great head is that he does. It was one of the most delicious blowjobs I have ever had. Pretty soon his dick was hard so I pulled my dick out of his mouth and got the camera and took a couple of pictures. He turned around and bent over and said,

"Take one of my ass," so I did.

"Do we have to stop now?" he asked.

"Definitely not!" I said.

I started sucking on his dick, and then he lifted up his legs and I licked his ass. I loved shoving my tongue up his sweet asshole, the one I had watched so many times. I licked it as it relaxed a little more.

"Stick a finger in me," he begged.

I obliged immediately. I started finger-fucking him with first one, then two, then three fingers. I was really getting off on playing with his ass, shoving my fingers in harder and harder. He seemed to like it more as I used his ass for my pleasure. He started sucking on my dick again and jacking himself off while my fingers fucked his sweet loose hole. I started to come and so did he. I shot all over his face as he shot on his stomach.

He asked if I could give him a ride home and I said, "Sure." In the car, he said, "Next time we get together, you have to fuck me." I promised that I would, but it never happened. The next time I talked to him he said he was sorry that he hadn't known that I was so famous, he had just seen me on television and hadn't known who I was before that. I guess his roommate must have filled him in. After that he always seemed a little shy around me. When he called, he treated me like some huge star, apologizing for bothering me. I always told him not to apologize, that he was never bothering me.

Dany was in several of my videos including *O Is For Orgy*, parts I and II, and *Big Deposit*, in which he was fucked by Paolo Centori, who was my boyfriend at the time. I really got off on watching him getting fucked by Paolo's huge dick, in fact, I was always hard when directing Dany in a scene; and after 10 years of porn that doesn't happen often.

After a while, Dany called and said he was returning to Canada. He was in one last video and then he was gone. He came back soon, though, and when I was in the hospital recently, he visited me several times. As attracted as I am, I don't think I can go through with our planned fuck. It always makes me uncomfortable when people treat me differently because of my fame. I liked my time with him better before he found out "who I am."

At any rate, he is still doing videos and is still a total hottie.

TONY WEST

Tony Belmonte sent Tony West to me in August of 1997. He wanted to be in videos. Tony walked in and my heart stopped. I was so attracted to him I could hardly stand it. I interviewed him, then it was time to take a photo. He took off his clothes and tried to get hard but couldn't. He asked me for help. I almost didn't, but at last I couldn't resist, and I started to suck his dick.

I ran my hands up over his chest and my mind turned to mush as I played with his nipples. I wet a finger and slowly started to work it in his ass. He was hard by now but there was no way we were going to stop to take the Polaroid. I finger-fucked his ass with one then two then three fingers. Then I went around behind him and bent him over, rubbing my cock against his cheeks, up and down the crack of his ass, teasing him until he told me to put it in. He grabbed his ankles and I slid my rod into his ass. Tony moaned as I pushed all the way into him with my dick until I was pressed up against him.

I started pumping in and out, hearing gasps from him with each thrust. I pounded him as he watched us in the mirror on my wall. I really got into him getting into watching us. I grabbed his hair and pulled his head back as I fucked him harder, really nailing him. I finally flipped him over on my couch and started really slamming my cock up his ass. We were both sweating and he was staring at me with wide eyes and an amazed look on his face. He started shooting, cum pumping out of him each time I pumped into him. I kept fucking him for another couple of minutes as his gasps grew to cries. Finally I pulled out and my load joined his on his stomach.

We just lay there for a minute, both stunned and out of breath.

I asked him if he wanted to rinse off, and we got in the shower together. I was totally nervous again now that the sex was over. I felt like I never wanted him to leave and it was scaring the shit out of me.

"Wow, you're a really hot guy. I was expecting a porn director to be an old fat man," he said, his words echoing in my ears.

"He thinks I'm hot! He thinks I'm hot!" I screamed inside.

"Thanks, I wasn't expecting this either. I don't usually have sex with models during an interview." I said, feeling a little guilty. (Well, I don't always!)

When we got out of the shower we realized that I hadn't taken a Polaroid. I told him not to worry; I would remember him and I didn't need a picture, he would definitely be in my next video. I wanted to ask him out but I was too afraid. I walked him to the door and watched him walk down the hallway to the elevator. I closed the door and collapsed on the couch.

I was standing in my kitchen when he called the next day and asked if I was sure I didn't need a picture of him. He was sort of stammering a little, like I do when I really like someone. I said I didn't need a picture, but I could tell (at least I hoped) that he sounded interested in me. So I gulped and took a big breath and asked him if he wanted to go out with me. He said "Yes". I danced all around the kitchen quietly while finishing the phone conversation.

We went to a premiere screening of a movie that I was in called *A River Made to Drown In*, starring Richard Chamberlain. We went out to eat with my publicist and my assistant, Eddie, after the movie. After the date I took him home. We just kissed and said we would see each other soon. I started thinking that I wished I hadn't taken him to the premiere, because now if he wanted to see me again, I wouldn't know if it was because of me, or because he wanted to date someone famous. People can get caught up in the glamour of Hollywood and fame and stuff like that. Not that I'm that famous! I wished that we had just gone out to a movie that I *wasn't* in. I convinced myself that he already knew who I was before we went out anyway, so it didn't really matter where we had gone. He either liked me or he didn't. I could already tell that I liked him way too much and that this could be dangerous.

We were going to have another date but Tony was sick on the day we were supposed to go out. A couple of days later he somehow made it over to my house. He stayed in my bed for about a week. Not having sex, of course; he was still sick. We watched videos and I made him soup; we cuddled and I took care of him until he felt better. After he recovered, he just sort of stayed with me. Like they always do. He had been living with some friends, so he occasionally went to their house to get more clothes, but he stayed every night and most days with me.

I was falling in love. He was too, he said, and I think I believed him. Something about it was strange though, I couldn't quite understand it. Once again I realized that someone I had just met was suddenly living with me before either of us really knew it.

How did this keep happening?

The first video that Tony was going to do was *Red Hot and Safe*, the AIDS charity fundraising video that I produced, and in which I and four other directors (Wash West, Sam Abdul, Mike Donner, and Jamie Hendrix) each directed a scene . It took over a year before it came out because we kept waiting for other directors (Chi Chi, Jim Steel, Jerry Douglas) who had promised to shoot scenes but never did. In spite of the delays, the video won the Safer Sex Award at the 1999 GayVN Awards Show. All of the models and directors and crew worked for free and all of the proceeds of the video have gone to the AIDS charities.

I was impressed that Tony was willing to do his first video for free and was so quickly willing to help the project. His scene was with Peter Dixon [See his chapter] whom I was sort of dating long distance. We always got together whenever he came into town. The scene was going great, it was really nasty, with Peter making Tony finger-fuck himself, then fucking him with a big dildo, then finally fucking him with his dick. Or actually with my dick. For some reason about halfway through the fucking Peter lost his hard-on and just couldn't get it back. I had to be stunt dick. It was really weird. I was very turned on and loved fucking Tony, but it was odd to be filming it. Fucking someone I had strong feelings for in front of a camera was almost always a little weird for me.

After we finally finished the scene, we all came back to my house and started fooling around. We all had gotten really turned on from doing the video. Peter and I took turns fucking Tony, and each other. I was surprised that Tony's ass wasn't sore from the way Peter had been abusing it with the big dildo in the scene, but he took a lot more abuse from both of our cocks and more dildos. We had sex for hours and hours. We finally rested, but the next morning we were all still horny and we fucked half that day, too.

Peter stayed for one more day, then he had to go back to Chicago. Tony continued to stay with me and we decided that we were boyfriends, although it still felt very weird to both of us. He was in several of my videos and I always got totally turned on watching him getting fucked. I still do. The time I remember the most was a scene we shot in my office with Paul Morgan fucking Tony. Paul kept cumming all through the scene, he couldn't help it. He would fuck Tony for a while, but every time he looked down at Tony's stretched out hole puckering around his dick he would try to hold back but he couldn't, he would start to shoot again. He came four times in that scene.

In October Tony and I decided to go to Hawai'i for a vacation. It was where Tony grew up, but it was where my relationships used to break up. I love Maui, it is my favorite place on Earth, but, for some reason, my relationships seemed to fall apart there. I think Maui is spiritually very powerful and it can speed things up—including a relationship, and it can bring it to its conclusion peacefully. I broke up with Tony the second day we were on Maui sitting in a restaurant. I didn't want to break up with him, but I finally realized that he wasn't in the relationship in the same way I was. We would make better friends than lovers, I said, and he had to agree. We stayed on Maui, then went to Honolulu for a few days and I flew back home alone. Tony stayed with his sister. It was really hard getting on that plane by myself, but I did it.

Tony came back a week or two later and was in my video, *Burning Desire,* which I shot in Palm Springs. Several months later I was back in Hawai'i and I saw Tony there, too. He was living there again. I was there with my girlfriend, Jill, and with my boyfriend, James Perry. Tony looked great. He was in a scene in my video, *Hawai'ian Vacation*, and I got to hang out with him a little. It was nice that the tension was finally completely gone, and we could just be friends. Time always seems to do that. He moved back to California for a year or so, then back to Hawai'i again. We remain on friendly terms, even though we don't see each other often.

PAOLO CENTORI

    I met Paolo (or Tom, his real name) in Palm Springs on the shoot for *Desert Paradise, Part II* in November of 1997. My assistant, Eddie, had recommended him and had scheduled him without meeting him or even having seen a picture. When he showed up on the set, it was one of those moments where my heart just started melting. I tried to not pay attention to him, but I couldn't help myself. I was already hooked, even though I didn't know it then. He was really cute in a sweet, goofy sort of way. We flirted with each other all day with our eyes.

That night, when the shoot was over, I was hugging everyone before I went to bed. I hugged him and we just started kissing. We kissed, and we kissed, and we kissed. Then we realized everyone else was gone; they had left us alone to do whatever we might do. We decided that he should come back to my room. He did, and we had wonderful, wonderful sex.

I fucked him first. He rolled back with that gorgeous ass up in the air and I grabbed his legs. His thighs were big and muscular and hairy. I looked at his hairy ass with his huge cock standing up over it and plunged in. He loved my dick and he loved getting fucked hard. I pounded him and waves of ecstasy washed over me. Tom was the first guy I had fucked since I had broken up with Tony West. It felt like I was reclaiming myself as I took his ass.

Then he fucked me with his huge dick. Tony had been a total bottom, and I hadn't been with other guys much while we were boyfriends, so I hadn't been fucked in a long, long time—especially not by a horse cock like Tom's. It took a while to get it all inside me, but I was determined. I sat down on it very, very slowly, then when it was finally all the way in, I just sat on him and breathed in and out for a minute. It really was (is) enormous. It actually hurt a lot, but the satisfaction of getting the whole thing up my ass eased the pain, and it started to feel good. I started moving up and down, sliding it all the way up my ass, then almost all the way out. I started moving faster, then would slow down and then suddenly slam down on it again. It was really feeling good now, even though it still hurt a little. I was remembering how much I loved getting fucked. How had I gone so long with a total bottom boyfriend?

I rolled onto my back with Tom still in me and he moved up on top of me, continuing to fuck me. I came while he was fucking me, then he pulled out, pulled the condom off, and shot his load all over my chest. We slept together that night, but he had to get up very early to get back into town, so when I woke up he was gone.

I don't think he thought I was going to call him again, but I did call him a few days later. I didn't expect to see him more than once or twice. But he came by, we got together again, and he just sort of stayed. For six months. He had his own place in Orange County, but he basically lived with me. He would spend the occasional night at his place, but he usually just stayed at my apartment.

Tom is one of the sweetest, most gentle people I know. He was really easy to be with and got along well with everyone. When I guest starred on *Veronica's Closet*, Jasmine Bleeth guest-starred on the same episode. Tom was with me most of the time on the set, and Jasmine seemed to love him. She was nice to everyone, but she seemed to be especially comfortable with him. She hung out with him a lot in the trailer. After Tom and I broke up, my friend, Stacey Q stayed with him for a few weeks. Tom always treated everyone the same; he wasn't impressed by celebrity at all, and that was one of the things I loved about him. I hate being treated like a star, and he never did, ever. I never had to wonder why he was with me. With some people I have wondered. And with others, it has been obvious later that they weren't really interested in me, just in my fame.

Tom and I would often just lie in bed and watch television or videos and just cuddle all night. We did lots of normal things like going to movies, out to eat, or to the beach. He was really easy and comfortable to be around, and I hoped that the relationship would last a long time. It did last over six months, which at the time, was bordering on a long-term relationship for me.

In the time that we were together, I put him in most of the videos I directed. It really turned me on to watch him doing scenes with and fucking other guys. People have asked me before, if I am in a relationship with someone, doesn't it bother me to see them have sex with someone else or see them in a scene. While once or twice it did with Jason Pride, it never did with Tom. It always really turned me on. We went to Hawai'i together, and I shot some gorgeous jack-off footage of him with waves crashing all around him as he cums. I also shot some other scenes of him with other guys which are in the videos *K-Waikiki* and *Back to K-Waikiki* .

Soon after that trip, things stopped working. I had joked before we went to Hawai'i that my relationship was going too well, so I was going to Hawai'i to ruin it. My relationship with Jason Pride had started to disintegrate while we were in Hawai'i, and Tony West and I broke up in Hawai'i. I didn't really expect it to happen with Tom, but it did, or at least soon after we returned from Hawai'i. We broke up and I was really heartbroken for weeks. But I knew that we really loved each other, and we would always be friends. I wouldn't mind it if we still fucked once in a while though.

JEFFREY FELICIANO

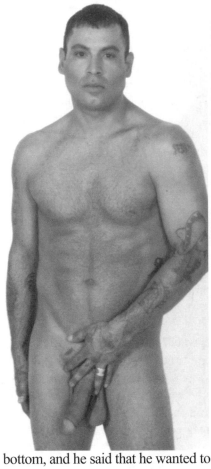

Jeff was referred to me by his friend, Matthew Thomas, in December of 1997. Matthew said,

"I know this big, burly, hot guy that used to be in a gang, and has a huge uncut dick, and who wants to do porn videos. Do you want me to have him call you?"

"Do ya think!?" I asked.

I got hard just hearing the description! A real ex-gang member in a gay porn video. What a coup that would be! Jeff came to meet me for the interview, and I was struck by how sweet and sincere he was. He *was* big and burly, and had tattoos all over him. He looked like he might beat the shit out of you at any minute, but he was a pussycat; a very intelligent, sweet, shy guy. He was incredibly polite and gentle. He also told me that he was the cousin of Jose Feliciano, and that he wanted to use his real name in the videos. I cast him in my very next one.

I asked if he was a top or a bottom, and he said that he wanted to be a top in videos. It is common for guys to actually be versatile in their own lives or be mostly bottoms even, but only want to top on video. I said okay, albeit a bit nervously. I didn't know if he really was a top ever, or was going to try for the first time in the video.

He was actually quite good in the first video he did for me. The other guy was sucking his huge cock and Jeff was slapping it all over his face and shoving it down his throat, dominating the guy like the big, bad, butch he looked like. Then he fucked the guy mercilessly, or at least it seemed on film. In reality every time we would cut, he would ask if the other guy was okay. He always was. He looked better than okay, he looked delirious from the sheer bliss of being fucked silly by Jeff. I couldn't blame him.

When it was time for the come shots, the other guy came and then Jeff tried and tried but just couldn't. I am usually pretty good at figuring out what people need to help them come. The first thing to do is to ask them what they think might help. You would think that this would be obvious, but most directors don't think of it. I had everyone leave the room and I asked Jeff what would help him. Some time alone, a magazine, a blowjob from someone, whatever. He said that he usually comes when he is getting fucked. I asked him if he wanted me to fuck him. His eyes lit up.

"Would you mind?" he asked.

"Are you *kidding*?" I asked. We forbade everyone except the cameraman to enter the room. I started fucking Jeff and he was loving it. I was loving it too, and of course was merely doing my duty as a good director to make sure that the show would go on. The camera was tight on his dick as he shot while I fucked him. Afterwards, I kissed him and he said,

"We have to do that again!"

"Anytime!" I said.

Jeff has been in many of my videos since, like, *Big Deposit*; *In the Shadows*; *Driven By Lust*; *Latin Sex Thing*; and *Inside Men, Part II*. He is an excellent performer. His scenes are always hot and nasty. He never has trouble coming anymore, although we often do find a little time on each set to fool around a bit. Once when I asked him if he would use a dildo in a scene in *All Heated Up* , he perked up and said,

"I love fucking guys with dildos!" He looked like he loved it as much as I do, which is a lot. He continued,

"You have to make sure he can really take it, though, cause once I start, I get out of control, and really fuck the shit out of the guy with the dildo."

He wasn't kidding. When they did their scene, he seemed to love making the other guy scream as he rammed the dildo in farther and farther. He was twisting it around and ramming it all the way in and ripping it all the way out just to shove it back in again. Whenever the guy would say he needed to stop for a while or that he couldn't take it any deeper, Jeff would ram it just a little deeper and twist it before pulling it out for the guy to rest. He was mean with that dildo and I loved it. Now I know I've definitely got to make time to get together with Jeff in private. Anyone that nasty deserves some special attention after class!

DON DAWSON

Don was referred to me by Jamie Hendrix in February of 1998. A few (very few) of the nicer, less competitive directors often refer models to each other. Many do it because they know they will get referrals back. I do it because I was a model and I know what it is like; most of the guys are my friends and I want to help them get work. Anyway, Jamie said that there was this beautiful Belgian boy he wanted me to meet. When Don came in I knew I immediately agreed with Jamie. He was beautiful. We talked.

In the interview, I try to always ask people why they are doing videos. If they say that it is just for money then I tell them that they probably won't have fun and who would want to work with them anyway? I try to talk them out of it if money is their only motivation. Usually it is a combination of wanting to explore their sexuality, being a bit of an exhibitionist, maybe a slight taste for a bit of fame and some extra money. Also, believe it or not, a lot of porn stars are shy. They are these gorgeous guys, who before doing porn almost never got laid because they didn't know how to approach people. Except for the fame part, Don told me basically the above reasons. The extra money was to be for school.

He took off his clothes, and my eyes and dick lit up. A perfect body to match that perfect angel face. He asked me to help him to get hard for the Polaroid. I very happily started sucking his dick. I grabbed his ass from behind, and couldn't help myself—I had to turn him around and stick my tongue up in it. It was the sweetest, smoothest, most delicious asshole. He had told me that he was a bottom so I stuck a finger up his ass. He instantly got hard. We took the picture. He said that he would like to stay and play, but it was late and he had to get up early the next morning. It *was* late. I reluctantly said good-bye to him.

The next week I had cast him in one of my movies. It was *K-Waikiki*, a video that had been shot mostly in Hawai'i the month before, but we needed one more scene to complete the video. We were shooting in a friend's backyard. It looked like a tropical paradise, with all the huge trees and foliage but it was February and it was pretty cold out, even though we were in L.A.

The other guy was very, very sexy too, but this was his first video. He was so nervous that he showed up and had a cold sore on one side of his mouth. Cold sores are brought on by stress. I told him it was okay, we would shoot him from the other side, there would be no kissing in the scene and he wouldn't suck Don's dick. That way the cold sore couldn't be passed on. Still, he was too nervous to get hard. He was supposed to be the top and his dick wouldn't work, he had never been fucked before and obviously couldn't use his mouth for anything sexual. How the hell was I supposed to get a sex scene out of this? Of course you've guessed it by now: I was the stunt dick. I put on his shirt and pants and we filmed close shots of Don sucking on my dick (which made the whole day worthwhile for me) then we would shoot wide angle shots where you couldn't tell that the real model's dick wasn't hard.

It finally got so cold that we decided to move the whole production inside for the fucking scenes. Again, no hard-ons in the room except for mine, so I fucked Don all over the bed, in every position possible with the camera shooting close ups. He is great to fuck, he loves getting pounded and I was pounding him for all I was worth, slamming into those tight, young buns. It's great to fuck someone who really, really loves it, and he obviously does. After the close-ups, we shot the wide angle shots with the two guys mimicking the same positions Don and I had just done. The shoot was saved and I got to fuck Don. Not a bad deal, really.

Don was in several of my other videos and was always a delight to have on the set (or just to have). He was very charming and everyone always liked him. Everyone especially loves fucking that sweet ass of his.

He recently told me that he is going back to school full time and won't be doing any videos for a while. We'll all anxiously await Spring break!

JAMES PERRY

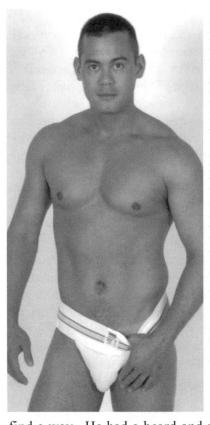

I met James at the International Conference on Bisexuality at Harvard (in Boston) in April of 1998. He came up to me after a lecture and introduced himself and said that he had missed me twice, once a year before when I was supposed to give a lecture, but got sick and couldn't do it, and the night before the lecture, when he had bought a ticket in advance to a show that had sold out. Even many people with tickets for the show didn't get in, as the organizers had way oversold: 2000 tickets for 1000 seats, the rumors went. James had apparently waited outside in the freezing cold for hours and then not gotten in. Boston is fucking cold, even in April; I can't imagine it in January. I felt bad and I thought I should try to make it up to him. The fact that he was hunky and muscular and sexy made me want to find a way. He had a beard and mustache at the time which I didn't really like, but he was still cute. The facial hair went later and I'm sure most will agree with me that such a handsome face ought not to be covered.

I had just met Jill Nagle the night before at a bisexual sex party that was thrown by Carol Queen. My friend, writer Mickey Skee, had practically dragged me to the soirée, nearly against my will. Over the next six months, she would end up being my girlfriend while I dated James as well. They both knew about each other, and didn't mind.

James lived in San Diego, and the weekend after the conference, he came up to visit me. He ended up staying the whole weekend.

It was the weekend of the White Party out in Palm Springs, so a lot of people were out of town. It was quiet and relaxed. We talked about the difficulties and benefits of being bisexual, me fighting AIDS both politically and in my body, his lover who had died of AIDS, my lover, Joey Stefano, who had died from a drug overdose, how we were both writers and found it to be cathartic, how we both feared relationships now after having been burned in the past, and many other personal topics. We went to dinners and movies and even stayed home in bed and watched TV one night. Mostly we fucked, though.

The first night we came home and got in bed, I discovered how wild he was. He yanked down my jeans, pulled my dick out and started sucking like it was the last popsicle on earth. His ass stuck up in the air, and he was sort of wriggling around like a puppy. I could see it in the mirror and it was so gorgeous, I had to fuck him. I turned him around and stuck my tongue up his crack. I pushed it deep inside and he moaned and pushed back. I couldn't wait any more. I had to have him. I started to slide my dick in slowly, but he slammed his ass back on it and started fucking himself on it. Pretty soon I was sticking my fingers up his ass alongside my cock. I was stretching his hole as much as I could and he loved it more and more, the nastier I got.

I pulled some dildos out from under my bed and started fucking him with them. I rammed a huge one all the way up his ass, in and out, slamming it all the way to the rubber balls and then whipping it all the way out of his chute and looking at his pink, quivering, sloppy hole before shoving the rubber cock up it again. James was still begging for more so I pulled it out and put my entire hand up his ass. It went right in, as deep as I had ever been in anyone. I started churning his guts with my fist. James went wild, and so did I. After a good many minutes of this, we both came and I slowly pulled my hand out.

The next night we went to an O Boys orgy. We parked right in front of the Tomcat Theater on Santa Monica Boulevard and walked around the corner to the studio where the party was. We walked in together, but soon were busy with other guys. We ended up on the same bed, side-by-side. We got quite turned on as we watched each other getting fucked by all these different guys. I loved watching him be a slut and letting all those guys ram his bubble butt, each taking their turn at his wet pussy-hole. I loved him watching me too. Then we came home and fucked each other for about three more hours. All around, it was one of the best weekends of my life.

My attraction to him was different than it has been to other people. Actually, almost everyone is different, I guess. It was very delicious. I both liked him and related to his intellect and wanted to stick my fingers, tongue, dick, dildos, my fist, and anything else I could find, up his ass. A lot of guys were only sex. James was more, although boy, the sex was always great. He always turned into an instant sex-pig just like he does on film. Usually, I would fuck him, but sometimes he fucked me and it was just as great.

We started seeing each other every few weekends. Pretty soon I asked him (of course) if he wanted to be in a porn video. He said "Yes". The first one was *Bitanic, the Ship Where Everyone Goes Down* . He was a star waiting to be born into porn. He truly is bisexual; he loves eating pussy and fucking girls as much as he loves getting his ass plowed by a huge dick. The next videos I put him in were *Hawai'ian Vacation Part I* and *II*.

We went to Hawai'i of course, and stayed in my friend Jim's huge mansion for two weeks while filming. It was in March and the weather there was like it always is in Hawai'i, perfect. I was glad to be there with James. Well, actually I *went* with Jill, then she left halfway through my trip and James flew in. Jill could only stay for ten days. James was disappointed to have missed her—he had always hoped we would have a three-way.

Dino Philips also came with us to be in the videos, and the rest of the guys were local Hawai'ian guys, including my ex-boyfriend, Tony West. After I would watch James do a scene, I just had to fuck him. Every time. Sometimes again and again. He never could get enough and never said stop, even though he had just been fucked for three hours by a guy with a huge cock out in the hot sun for the video. You have to love that about a guy, just not being able to say no.

He has since starred in other videos and I think he is going to make a big mark in the porn world for many reasons: He is gorgeous, he loves sex, and the things he can do with that amazing butt haven't even begun to be explored on film. If you see a video with him in it, *buy it*. If you get a chance to fuck him *don't pass it up!*

DEAN SPENCER

I met Dean in 1998 at a party. I was looking for guys for my video, *Inside Men #2*. I didn't recognize Dean from videos, although he had been in several like Falcon's *Code Of Conduct Part I* and *II*. I just noticed that he was gorgeous and had a huge dick running down the leg of his tight pants. I was afraid to even approach him. He was so beautiful in person I thought he would be stuck up. I asked Chad Donovan who he was and whether he did videos. He said "Yeah, but he's just in town for a couple more weeks from England. I'll introduce you." He introduced us and Dean was very sweet and charming, not at all stuck up.

I cast him in the three-way scene in my video with Sam Dixon and newcomer, Joe Austin. The whole video was shot in my bed. Sam and Dean were supposed to fuck Joe, and then Sam and Joe were supposed to fuck Dean, but when it was Joe's turn he said, "I don't think I can do it, I've never been a top before." Dean and I quickly decided that I should be a stunt dick and fuck him. The other guys left the room to take a break.

I took off my clothes and started licking Dean's asshole to help me get hard. His dick was instantly hard as soon as my wet tongue touched his hot wet hole, which made mine hard too, but I was really getting into licking his asshole. I pulled his dick back between his legs and sucked it while I stuck two fingers up his ass. He squirmed around and his rock hard dick leaked some pre-come. I put my cock in his ass and started fucking him. His dick was totally hard the whole time he was getting fucked. Finally, I pulled out and shot all over his ass. He said, "Thanks," and I said "No, thank *you*!"

The other guys came back in and everyone did their come shots. Dean shot a huge load. He called a few days later—he had left his sunglasses at my house. I looked and they were here but Dean was leaving town and didn't make it over to pick them up. I still have them to remember him by. He gave me his number with his boyfriend in England and said to call them the next time I was there. I definitely will.

MICHAEL STEVENS

One day at the beginning of November in 1998, Nancy from Vivid called me and said she had a guy to send to me to do bisexual videos. He came over and met me and I was back on the same old roller coaster. Michael walked in and started charming me immediately. Plus, he was gorgeous. Exactly my type. I like all types, but most of my boyfriends, as I have pointed out, have had dark hair and are either shorter or thinner than me. Michael had brown hair, beautiful sparkling eyes, and was shorter than me, but muscular with beautiful brown baby smooth skin. I found out later he had taken female hormones for a while, which was probably why he had such smooth skin. It also had made his muscular chest a tiny bit breasty.

Before I knew it, we were in my bed with him fucking me. I don't know how it happened so fast. One minute we were in the living room sitting down, and the next he was sliding his cock up my ass and shoving his tongue down my throat, pounding into me while I clawed his back.

His dick wasn't huge, but he knew how to use it to really ravage someone.

"Harder," I begged. "Please, faster, harder!"

"You sure, baby?" he asked.

"Please!" I cried.

He fucked me, pulling my hole in every direction until I was sweating and screaming, and still begging for more. I shot all over us, and told him to keep fucking me. He did for a few more minutes until he came up my ass.

We held each other, kissing passionately with him still inside me. I panted, trying to catch my breath. I knew this was the beginning of one of those relationships. After he left, he called me about thirty minutes later to tell me that he had really liked "meeting me," and I was sure he was hooked as I was. I just didn't know why, yet.

I had so many feelings rushing around through me. I was giddy. I knew it was too much, too fast, too soon, but I didn't care. I had been so hurt for so long over my breakup with Jill, that I was desperate to feel good again, to feel normal. To not wake up in the morning sad and go to bed at night sad. Michael was my new drug that temporarily fixed everything. Having sex with him was incredible—I always ended up screaming, either into a pillow or just right out in the air.

I fucked him sometimes, too, and he always cried out like I was hurting him. I'm pretty sure I was—I don't think he had been fucked much.

"Do you want me to stop?"

"No!"

"Do you want me to slow down?"

"No!"

"What do you want me to do?"

"Fuck me."

"What?"

"Fuck me!"

"How hard?"

"As hard as you can!" he would gasp.

Then I would, as he screamed out.

We went to Chi Chi's birthday party together. There was a curtain of silver streamers hanging behind a stage where the dance floor was. I fucked him behind it while we both looked out at the hundreds of guests dancing away, unable to see us.

Within days, he said he was falling in love with me. I felt like I was falling in love with him. As it turned out, I was falling—falling for his bullshit.

He was so gorgeous, so charming, and so attentive. He opened doors for me. He sat with me all weekend when I was sick, and guarded me furiously. He fussed over me when we were out in public, and when we were alone. Of course within a few days of meeting me, under some sort of mysterious circumstances, he couldn't stay where he was staying anymore and I let him stay with me. Temporarily. At least that's what we agreed.

I wasn't the only one he charmed. A lot of my friends noticed how attentive he was to me, how he said "Ma'am," and "Sir," to people, how he always said "Thank you," all with his Texas accent. He was so cute and charming that when we would go out to eat (I always paid, of course,) by the end of the meal the waiters would love him so much that they would bring us a free dessert. It was as if he cast a spell over everyone he met.

I liked having an instant boyfriend. I always did. I felt secure and loved. But I knew it just wasn't right. I knew he said he loved me too soon. I knew he was working me for what I could do for him. Deep down, I knew. My friends knew, too, though they saw how well he treated me. But they didn't say anything. They couldn't; he had done nothing but shower me with attention—yet. As far as they knew. Michael had come over one night unannounced before he moved in. He was drunk, and the next day he admitted that he was also high on coke. It was one of those early warning signs that I ignored. Well, I didn't totally ignore it, I started a conversation about it. I told him about my drug history. I explained that I was a recovering drug addict, and that I just couldn't be around drugs or people who are high or drunk. He said that he rarely did it, and it was just for fun, and that he would never do it again. He said he could take it or leave it. I felt that that probably wasn't true, but I also wanted to give him a chance.

I also discovered that I had spoken to Michael on the phone two or three years before I had met him, and even had nude pictures of him in my desk drawer. He had been a fan of mine for years. That kind of freaked me out. He and his transsexual girlfriend Page had sent me pictures to do videos. I even knew Page—I had met her when she was in L.A. doing a tranny video. He told me horror stories of the terrible things she supposedly had done to him, but they just didn't totally ring true. If he had said, "and we had both been up all night on coke..." then they might have made sense, but as it was, I will probably never know the whole story.

Michael was in two of my videos, a gay one for All Worlds, in which Stacey Q had a small guest starring role, and a bisexual video called *Both Ways*. Before each of them, he said that he was going to save his pay. To buy a car, to get an apartment, stuff like that. After each one, all his money was gone in a day or two. I don't know exactly how he spent all of it, but he came home with a huge tattoo on his arm, and a new piercing in his nose just after the second video.

Now I was really concerned. Someone—at least a healthy someone—who needs a place to live and really wants to take care of themselves doesn't spend their last few hundred dollars on a tattoo and a nose piercing.

The rest of the story is tedious and not much fun to jack off to, so here it is in a nutshell: He went on a drug binge, stole my money and my car and when he came back, I kicked him out. I was heartbroken for months, once again. He went back to Texas and still calls me, sometimes. I tell more of the particulars in my next book, so if you are curious, you'll just have to buy it, as well.

KURT YOUNG

Kurt Young won more awards at one time than any gay video performer, ever. At the 1996 Gay Video Guide Awards, he won Best Newcomer, Best Sex Scene, with Derek Cameron for *Tradewinds*, and Best Actor for *Flesh and Blood*. Then a month later at the 1996 Adult Video News Awards, he won Best Newcomer, Best Performer of the Year, and Best Actor. You would expect him to have an attitude, right? Wrong. He is one of the sweetest, friendliest, most down-to-earth, attitude-free guys I have ever known.

I met him soon after he started doing videos. He was in *The Showboys*, a group of porn stars that danced, not just stripped and wiggled around, but really danced. At the time it consisted of Kurt, David Thompson, K.C. Hart, and Turbo, a guy who wasn't in porn. We were all going to be doing a benefit show together and I asked them if they would be my backup dancers. They did; in fact, they have many times over the past few years.

One year I was singing at San Diego Gay Pride at their big dance party in front of about four-thousand people. The Showboys were my backup dancers. About half way through the song, these big, burly security guards came on-stage and dragged the boys off. I was confused, but since I was in the middle of my song, I kept singing. The crowd thought that it was part of the act and they loved it. After I finished my song and finally left the stage, I found out what had happened. Apparently, g-strings weren't permitted in San Diego, but no one had bothered to mention this to us. The promoters said, "You're banned from the stage now, you can't go on any more." I said, "Uh... we're done." None of us were invited back to San Diego Gay Pride to perform for a few years, until 1999, when I opened for Berlin and performed *Sex (I'm a...)* with them. Dino Philips was one of my backup dancers both times.

Before I knew it, Kurt was firmly partnered with David Thompson. They were always together. I was disappointed, but happy for them. Whenever I saw them, they would come running up to me and say, "We love you!", hang all over me and publicly molest me. I didn't argue.

When David and Kurt got married they asked me to sing at their wedding. I was very honored. I sang my friend Boy George's *Love Is Love*, and did a pretty good job considering the fact that a car had smashed into mine on the way over and I was a bit shaken. With the wedding, I assumed that any chance of being with Kurt was completely over. Lucky for me, I was wrong.

About a year later, in 1998, Kurt and David broke up. Kurt and his best friend, Dino Phillips, ran into me at a party and said, "We're going to San Francisco this weekend. Want to come with us?" My girlfriend at the time, author Jill Nagle, lived in San Francisco, so I said "Sure." I was often there anyway, or she was here in L.A. with me, so I thought I might as well go with them. I could go up and see Jill, and hang out with the boys.

The first night, Dino and Kurt went out on their own, and Jill and I went to a bisexual sex party. We came home and told the boys all about it. Kurt was especially interested in hearing about a three-way Jill and I had with a guy at the party. The second night I went out with Kurt and Dino. One gorgeous bartender was flirting heavily with me and with Kurt, although he said he was straight. Kurt asked if I wanted anything to drink and I asked for champagne. He came back with a huge bottle. Later the bartender asked if I wanted anything else and I said,

"Yeah, I'm starving, I wish I had some pizza or something." He picked up the phone and ordered pizza. In about fifteen minutes, two huge pizzas were delivered to me at the bar. Later he asked if I wanted anything else. I said I wished I had brought my clove cigarettes. He jumped over the bar and said,

"There's a store on the corner, I'll walk with you." When we got back he asked if I wanted anything else.

"You," I said. He said,

"I've never been with a guy before, but I'd like to try getting fucked." Kurt and I looked at each other. I supplied the reply.

"Um...we'd be glad to help you out with that. Do you want to come home with us to my girlfriend's house?" I asked.

"Will she mind?" the guy and Kurt both asked.

"Are you kidding?" I practically shrieked. Two cute fags bringing home a brand new one? She'll love it."

When the bar closed we all got in a cab and went to Jill's. She had been asleep, but was glad to wake up and let us in. The guy was so excited and nervous, it was obvious he had, indeed, never been with a guy before. It was also obvious that he had wanted to for a long, long time. Jill was participating some in our play, but mostly just watching. She likes watching me with guys. Pretty soon she decided to leave us to continue playing and go back to bed. It *was* late and she *had* been asleep.

We all took turns sucking each other's dicks. The new guy didn't have a lot of skill, but he made up for it with enthusiasm. Kurt

271

definitely had both skill and enthusiasm. At one point I leaned over and smiled at him and kissed him. We were like two little boys who were partners in crime; eating all the cookies out of the cookie jar. We kept giving each other knowing glances when the guy couldn't see us.

We asked the guy if he was sure he wanted to get fucked. He said "Yes". Kurt put on a condom. (I never realized how long his dick was until that moment. The condom completely unrolled and there was an inch or two of dick left at the base.) The guy sat down slowly on Kurt's dick while Kurt sucked mine. Then he started moving up and down on Kurt's dick, going faster and faster. After a while we switched and I fucked the guy. My dick is shorter than Kurt's but fatter, so it took the guy a couple of minutes to get used to my dick. Pretty soon he did, and I was slamming my cock into him. He was loving it but finally he said, "Okay, I have to stop" I pulled out of him and noticed that Kurt was looking at me and smiling wickedly and putting on another condom.

I sat slowly down on his dick, sliding all the way down to the base. It felt great. Actually better than great. It was perfect. I started riding it up and down, bouncing faster and faster. I was grinding down on it, it felt so good getting fucked by him. I had been waiting for this for two years and now it was better than I could ever have hoped. His dick was hitting that perfect spot way up inside me, and felt incredible sliding all the way in and then almost all the way out again. We kissed, and I rode him faster and harder, faster and harder. When I started coming, I slid up off of his dick, and he pulled off the condom and came just as the other guy came from jacking off watching us.

We all collapsed for a minute, then started to laugh. The guy left. Kurt and I fell asleep on the floor holding each other and then when I woke up in the morning, I went and crawled into bed with my girlfriend, and told her all about it. She wanted to hear all the details, as I relived each delicious moment again for her. Dino had stayed out that night, (Hmmm...now that I think of it, that is probably an interesting story in itself) and came home in the morning. I couldn't tell if he was horrified or titillated that Kurt and I had fucked the night before. Maybe a little of both. Or maybe he didn't care.

Now every time Kurt sees me, he hugs me and kisses me and calls me his husband and we laugh about that night. Dino just sort of raises an eyebrow but doesn't say anything. We are all still very good friends.

COLE TUCKER

In 1998 Cole Tucker did a live show in Toronto at a club on-stage on a Harley where he took a belt, a dildo, and then a whole fist up his ass on stage in front of everyone. Not bad for the guy who had just won Best Top at that year's Probie Awards Show. I wish my story with him was that interesting, but it's not quite as flashy.

I actually met Cole the night before the Probie awards. He was the nude bartender at a pre-awards show party. He was pouring drinks and then stirring them with his hard dick. (How did he keep it hard all night? Viagra?) Anyway, Cole was kind enough to insist that I grope his ass and suck his dick in the bedroom (along with a few others), even though he didn't know (I don't think) at the time who I was. He's just that friendly of a guy. Ya gotta love him!

JEREMY BROOKS

Not too long ago I was preparing to shoot a video called *One Of The Gang*. It was supposed to be a gang-bang video with a bunch of older guys (that is to say, over 30,) all fucking one younger guy. A photographer had given me Jeremy's phone number for another video. I had seen a picture of Jeremy in *Unzipped* magazine, so I knew he was really cute. I wasn't sure if he would want to do the video, but when I called him and asked, "Would you like to do a video and get fucked by 10 or 15 guys?" he nearly jumped through the telephone wire saying "Yes." He was really into the idea, which was exactly what I wanted for the video: someone who really wanted to get gang fucked. The more I thought about it, the hotter it sounded. I decided to be in the video too.

Since appearing on *Xena: Warrior Princess*, I had only been in one other porn video. Once my acting career on television and in movies started, I stopped being in adult videos, but then Vivid offered to pay me $15,000. I wanted to prove that someone could have a real acting career *and* be in porn, and I did. Following that, I got another movie part, a commercial, and a television role, all right after shooting that video.

I also wanted to make a statement about people with HIV still being sexy. Cole Tucker came out as being HIV positive and some people were hiring him but some didn't want to. The industry is divided and I wanted to make it clear where I stood. Being in the Vivid video was a political statement for me, but when people started finding out how much I was paid for it, they said that I just did it for the money, so I wanted to do one for *no money*, to prove that I was doing it to make a point. I was paid for directing *One of the Gang* but not for being in it. Although I must say, duh! Who wouldn't want to fuck Jeremy?

Anyway, the shoot was June 4, 1999. All the guys arrived and we were getting ready to shoot. Jeremy was the last to arrive and I was getting a little nervous that he might not show up and we would have no video. He showed up right on time, though. Jeremy was a little nervous, but excited about getting fucked by everyone. He was even more sexy than the picture I had seen, and he was really nice too. The guys were starting to fool around in the office before we were shooting. I always try to keep people apart so that the magic of the first few minutes is captured on video, but with 11 horny guys, I realized it was impossible. I rushed the crew along in getting the lights set up as the guys were blowing each other in the back. Jeremy asked me what I wanted him to wear. I picked out one of my jockstraps and helped him put it on.

Soon we were ready to start. In the beginning, Jeremy was wearing the jockstrap and a blindfold as the guys started fucking him. He had already warmed up with a dildo before we started rolling (as we all watched it sliding in and out of his hot little ass), so the first guy just shoved his dick in and started pounding him. Jeremy loved it. One by one the guys took turns at his ass, and he serviced each of them. I was especially turned on watching my boyfriend, Babaji, fuck Jeremy. Then a guy with a huge dick started fucking him. Jeremy was really starting to yell as that huge cock slid all the way in and out. Everyone crowded around to watch it going in and out. I got closer too; it was amazing being up close and seeing that huge monster disappear up little Jeremy's hole. I could tell he was really straining to take it.

Next it was my turn. There was no need to be gentle; I was the tenth guy up his ass, so I shoved my cock in and started fucking. I expected him to be a little loose by then, but he wasn't, his ass gripped my cock as I slammed in and out. I started fucking harder and harder, pulling all the way out and slamming back in. After that monster cock he had just had, I wanted to make sure Jeremy remembered my dick too. I'm sure he will, as he started moaning louder and louder. He was getting sore by then, but he was still taking it, even though I could tell my dick was hurting him some.

The whole scene looks really hot on film, and it was, fucking him right to the point of him almost not being able to take it. Almost, I say, because he did take it. When the camera wasn't on my face I kept asking him if he was okay, and he kept saying yes. At one point he made me stop for a minute to catch his breath, but soon we started again with me fucking the shit out of him and all the guys jerking off and watching. One by one they all started to come, shooting all over Jeremy's face and chest. Finally I started to come too, I pulled out, pulled off the condom, and shot my load all over him.

Most of us were done, but Jeremy and Leo DeSilver weren't. The scene faded into just them fucking, Jeremy still getting plowed even more. Finally Jeremy came, but Leo couldn't. He tried and tried, but after fifteen minutes I knew he wasn't going to. Or actually, I knew the pressure was too much by then. If someone (me) were a stunt dick and did his cum shot, then he wouldn't have to. Once the pressure was off, people can usually cum; it's a psychological thing. I went back over and started jerking off. Usually I can come almost on command; I did cum shots for people a lot. Once when I first started in the business I did nine cum shots in one day for Bizarre video. This time though, I couldn't ! I had been having sex every day with my boyfriend and had just cum after fucking Jeremy. I was right on the edge but couldn't quite get there.

I looked at Jeremy's asshole, all red and swollen, and knew that playing with it, especially knowing that it was probably sore by then from servicing all the guys, would get me off. I gently stuck a finger up it. Jeremy knew what was up and was into it. "Yeah play with that hole! Shove another finger up my ass!" He was still into having his ass used and sure enough, it did put me right over the edge. I started shooting again, all the while Jeremy urging me on. Of course as soon as he was off the spot, Leo could come, and he did. I'm not sure which one was used for the video. Apparently the editor didn't notice that it wasn't Leo doing both cum shots. Since we used two cameras for the shoot, he thought it was two different angles of Leo's cum shot.

Jeremy is definitely one hot little boy, with one hot little ass, and I am sure I will cast him in more of my videos. If I hadn't been madly in love with my lover at the time, I would have asked Jeremy out, or at least into my bed, but as it was, there wasn't any room!

ABOUT THE AUTHOR

Geoffrey Karen Dior (formerly known as Karen Dior, Geoff Gann, and Rick Van) has been involved in the porn industry since 1988, starring in over 100 videos, and directing over 100 videos. He has won awards for his videos every year since he started directing, is the most nominated performer/director in gay porn history, and was the youngest person ever inducted into the Adult Video Hall of Fame. Often credited with creating the genre of transsexual porn, he is the only performer to successfully cross over from gay porn to mainstream entertainment. He was the first porn star ever to come out publicly as having AIDS and has worked for years to raise consciousness and money for AIDS causes.

He has guest-starred on many television shows including *Veronica's Closet* and *Xena: Warrior Princess*. He has been profiled on *Access Hollywood, Entertainment Tonight*, and *Inside Edition,* as well as appeared on a number of talk shows. He has starred or co-starred in many feature films, and appeared in numerous controversial commercials, including Bud Light (with Don Rickles), Braun Razor, MAC cosmetics, and Fox Sports West. Geoffrey's appearance on *Xena: Warrior Princess* pushed the show to number one in syndication, its highest Nielsen rating ever, and garnered a GLAAD media nomination. The week he appeared on *Veronica's Closet,* the show went to number two.

As a musician, Geoffrey has performed live solo, as well as with other well-known artists. His last album, with The Johnny Depp Clones, is called *Better Late Than Never.* His song "Little Red Riding Hood" with "Two of Hearts" diva Stacey Q, is now available in stores on the *Porn to Rock* compilation CD. His new album, *SEX*, features Stacey Q, Elisa Fiorillo, Nina Hagen, and Sharon Kane.

Geoffrey has also spent the past decade studying different spiritual paths, including with his guru, Babaji, in India, with many Kahunas in Hawai'i, and *A Course In Miracles.* He is a trained rebirther. In 1998, Geoffrey completed his Ph.D. in religion and became an ordained minister.

Geoffrey has been published in a variety of genres over the last ten years. He has written award-winning scripts, hit songs, a syndicated advice column, as well as had interviews and op-ed pieces published in many periodicals. This is his first book. To learn more, visit **www.karendior.com**.

INDEX OF CHAPTERS BY NAME

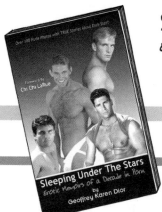

Sleeping Under The Stars

Erotic Memoirs Of a Decade in Porn
by
Geoffrey Karen Dior

item # KD-BK-01
$16.95 each

**13 track compact disc of highly
energetic and spiritually
uplifting music!
Featuring "Sex (I'm a...)" and
"Never Stop" with 80's
pop diva Stacey Q!**
item # KD-CD-01
$14.95 each

The Official
Geoffrey Karen Dior T-Shirt
*100% cotton in sizes
Small, Medium,
Large & Extra Large*
item # KD-TS-01
$8.95 each

Geoffrey Karen Dior

Official Geoffrey Karen Dior Poster
**The official poster of the DIVA
herself - in ALL her naked glory!**

item # KD-PS-01
$8.95 each

Porn To Rock
**featuring
"Little Red Riding Hood"
with Geoffrey Karen Dior
and Stacey Q!**
item # KD-CD-02
$11.95 each

Johnny Depp Clones
**take a glimpse into Dior's
past with his first bands
debut EP!**
item # KD-CD-03
$8.95 each

order online at www.karendior.net

Bedside Press

Order Form

PO Box 461481 Los Angeles, CA 90046-9481 USA
Phone: (323) 969-6927 Fax: (323) 656-3512
Please include your phone number and/or email address (for order inquiries only)

PLEASE PRINT

Name: _____

Address: _____

City: _____ State: _____ Zip: _____

PLEASE PRINT CLEARLY. USE AN ADDITIONAL SHEET OF PAPER IF NECESSARY.

Qty	Title	Item #	Price Each	Total

SHIPPING & HANDLING CHARGES

U.S. SHIPPING AND HANDLING CHARGES (U.S. ONLY)
First Item $4.00 & $1.00 each additional book or CD

CANADA SHIPPING AND HANDLING CHARGES (CANADA)
First Item $5.00 & $1.00 each additional book or CD

OUTSIDE U.S. SHIPPING AND HANDLING CHARGES (OUTSIDE U.S.)
First Item $20.00 & $1.00 each additional book or CD

RUSH FED EX DELIVERY CHARGES (U.S. ONLY)

CHECK ONE AND ADD TO ABOVE CHARGES

Subtotal	$
Discountor Credit (If Applicable)	$
CA Residents Add 7.75% Tax	$
Shipping & Handling (See Left For Rates)	$
Rush Delivery Charges	$
Total	$

__ 2ND DAY, ADD $20.00   __ OVERNIGHT, ADD $25.00   __ SATURDAY DELIVERY, ADD $35.00

Check Payment Method Below

__ VISA   __ MASTERCARD   __ AMEX   __ MONEY ORDER   __ CHECK (U.S. ONLY)

CREDIT CARD # _____   EXP. DATE _____

SIGNATURE _____   DATE _____
I CERTIFY BY SIGNATURE THAT I AM OVER 21 YEARS OLD AND DESIRE TO RECEIVE SEXUALLY ORIENTED
MATERIAL. MY SIGNATURE HERE AUTHORIZES MY CREDIT CARD CHARGE IF I AM PAYING FOR MY ORDER
BY VISA, MASTERCARD OR AMERICAN EXPRESS.

MAKE CHECKS/MONEY ORDERS PAYABLE TO:

Bedside Press
P.O. Box 461481
Los Angeles, CA 90046-9481

NOTE: WE CANNOT SHIP ANY ORDERS WITHOUT A SIGNATURE.

TO EXPEDITE YOUR ORDER - ORDER ONLINE AT
www.karendior.com OR www.sleepingunderthestars.com